DIRE

FEATHERS & FLAMES BOOK ONE

JOHN BAILEY

To Mum, Nan, and Pa, who never stopped believing in me.

Thank you.

1

EURAIYA

Raptorial eyes watched a rat move into the forest clearing. The creature gingerly approached a fallen nut, examining it with tiny hands. It was too early for most predators to be awake, granting a deceptive safety for their prey. The silence in the forest offered a prime hunting opportunity. The brown rodent, engrossed in its find, failed to notice the larger animal obscured by brush on the forest floor. Its form was blended by its camouflage, its scent masked by the strong smell of rain that mixed with the trees and grass. It was waiting.

In a flash of sound and movement, a strong, grey beak punctured the rodent's neck and broke its spine. The bird-like creature raised itself to stand at full height on all fours and dropped the rodent to the ground. Neat feathers covered its rounded eagle-shaped head and flowed down its long neck into the soft plumage of its chest and back and into a rough, short-furred, leonine body.

The opinicus flicked her long tufted tail, tutted, and clicked her beak. "Measly little thing, aren't you?"

She readjusted the large wings on her sides and preened

some leaves out of her feathers. She picked up the carcass in a forepaw, clutching it between four clawed digits. Her amber eyes examined it further, and she decided to consume it for herself.

Behind the brush, the opinicus had accumulated a few kills using the same trap. Rodents didn't learn from the mistakes of their peers, and it remained an effective hunting method. This had been the smallest kill of the morning. The others she had amassed were reserved for her clanmates. Specifically, her kills were for the kits who were too young to hunt.

In the back of her mind, she knew that leaving them the largest pieces of meat would be most beneficial. And besides, she would be reprimanded by her clan if she kept the choicest morsels for herself. She could handle being a little hungry for a while until she was provided her next meal from others who hunted through the forest.

Each carcass was placed on a pile of long leaves, bundled together when the straps were pulled taut. This makeshift bag was a blessing, even if the food smelled like greenery. There was a rustle in the brush across the way. Euraiya's long ears perked and twitched. It was a good time to leave. She wasn't supposed to be hunting alone, and if either the source of the noise or her clan found out about it, she'd be in trouble. She hooked the loop of the strap around her neck and padded out the forest.

Beyond the dense trees and across the grassy plain, an extensive series of shelters formed the clangrounds where gryphs, specifically gryphons and opinici, made their homes. Euraiya moved at her own pace, each paw squelching against the wet grass that covered the distance between the forest and the arrangement of three-walled stick shelters she called her home. Energy preservation was important, and she had no pressing matters, so she took her time.

The small rays of sunshine that managed to poke through the overcast sky were warm and refreshing against the colder air. Light reflected on her feathers, eliciting hints of autumnal oranges from her tree-brown colours with each movement.

Euraiya was proud of her colouration for its ability to allow her camouflage in and around the forested areas. By contrast, aside from the advantage her feathers' iridescence offered to hunting, they made her feel attractive, allowing her to stand out against the muted colours of most other gryphs that inhabited the lands. Without it, she would only have the light barring across her head.

She heard the flapping of wings and sighed.

"There you are." Another opinicus lighted in front of her, sounding as worried as she was angry. "You were supposed to see Sarren before heading off. You need to report in before hunting!"

Euraiya stopped and eyed the green opinicus. The words coming from her beak were the opening statements to the *You Could Have Died* lecture that nobody was fond of. Euraiya shifted her weight to her haunches and balanced on her rear paws. She gestured towards the sky with her forepaws and flattened her ears to her skull. "I have returned to the clangrounds from the dangerous task of hunting ground rats at the edge of the forest. Should I have died let it be known, that it was there!"

"I swear to the spirits, Euraiya. You're going to get yourself killed." The green opinicus, slightly smaller than

Euraiya, had a habit of acting like every opinici's mother. While some considered endearing, Euraiya found it exasperating.

Euraiya rolled her eyes, her feathers flattening against her body in annoyance. "Yes, the deer are going to skin me alive, and use me to carry their grass." She fell back to all fours and raised her own bag for emphasis. The opposable digit on an opinicus' paws allowed them to grip objects, but a lack of dexterity prevented them from doing much else.

Euraiya's not-mother narrowed her eyes in protest at the thought.

"Calm down, Lillia," Euraiya said, setting the bag around her neck again. "I bet you a deer's rump that Sarren isn't even awake yet."

Lillia was suddenly silent. She glanced away, interested in the grass under her.

"I knew it," Euraiya declared proudly. "And guess who's already finished her quota for the day." She trotted around her friend, her feathers fluffing with smug pride.

Lillia sighed and shook her head. "We have designated hunting times for a *reason*. It's-"

"So we don't die, yes. I know. I don't need a guard, Lillia," Euraiya said. "They scare the game away. And besides, I'm hunting rats, not bears. Come on, I need to drop these off and then report to Sarren." Having successfully passed Lillia, Euraiya walked into the clangrounds. To her dismay, Lillia was determined to continue the lecture as she walked beside her.

Euraiya prayed the nursery would be open as they made their way through the haphazard arrangement of homes. They'd heard that other clans had organised their developments more strategically, although it seemed far-fetched. During the clan's founding, gryphs had settled as they arrived and paid little attention to how large or complex the grounds would become in the future. No effort had been made on their direlord's part to clear up, organise, or plan the clangrounds' future development. Today, it was only a matter of remembering the locations in relation to certain landmarks. It was easy to navigate when one knew how.

One such landmark was the nursery. Like other shelters, it was constructed from sticks, stones, feathers, and other natural materials the clan could scrounge up, yet unlike most other shelters, it was enclosed, providing the kits an escape from the light. It housed newly-born kits while their parents were tending to their assigned duties. It was cleaner, stronger, and larger than most other places, rivalled only by the medicine hut and their direlord's shelter. The kitcarers made sure their building served the kits as much as it did their parents by providing them space and security, ensured by a long line of strong and almost terrifying kitcarers. The importance of their assignment gave them sway over many gryphs within the clan, allowing them to report issues directly to the clan's coordinators. A displeased kitcarer was often the cause for a gryph missing their next meal.

Euraiya entered through the hanging leaves that covered the entrance. Lillia followed closely behind. Before they made even two steps inside, a large gryphon blocked them, towering over and staring down with a disgruntled glare. Where opinici had forepaws, gryphons had anisodactyl, taloned forefeet. While gryphons were generally larger than opinici, Jana's parentage had left her larger still. Her head nearly touched the top of the entrance.

"Kitcarer Jana, good morning," Euraiya said politely, keeping her expressions in check and her feathers smooth.

"Euraiya." Jana loomed like a tree. "The kits are sleeping,

and I will not have a clawfoot ruining their much needed sleep." She sneered.

Euraiya ignored the archaic and expected insult. She motioned to the bag around her neck. "I'm not here to see the kits. I'm here to deliver as per my duties, Kitcarer Jana."

"And?"

"And? Kitcarer Jana," the name tasted bad having had so many run-ins with the gryphon, "I was assigned to provide for the nursery today. Whether you're pleased with my being here or not, the food is here." With that, Euraiya pulled at the strings of her bag allowing each rodent to fall to the ground in front of her. One of the carcasses rolled to Jana's forefeet. The gryphon picked it up and examined it carefully.

She pinned the rodent's tail between two talons and inspected the hanging carcass. "Acceptable. Expect Sarren to hear from me about your barging in."

Euraiya's long ears flattened to her skull. "What? I was assigned!" This was a typical response from a kitcarer, and a gryphon at that. It was little surprise, but no less unfair. There was a stirring in the nursery, and Euraiya's stomach dropped.

"And you're about to wake the children. Shoo, both of you. Out!" Jana motioned with a wing towards the two opinici, threatening to buffet both of them. She gathered the rodents and took them further into the nursery. A kit whimpered, causing another to join in.

That was their cue to leave.

Euraiya and Lillia could hear the kits crying in the distance. The underlying threat of a rations cut still sat in

Euraiya's mind. She hoped that Sarren would ignore the request again. In a short time, they found themselves deeper in the clangrounds, in one of the few multipurpose areas. The dried blood mixed with dirt told of its recent usage. Its high traffic had reduced the ground to mud, unlike the grass of much of the rest of the grounds. During the early hours of the morning, however, it was quiet.

Jana hadn't pursued them, likely tied up with hushing the children. They were safe from her wrath for the moment. Jana had a reputation for being overprotective, and by Euraiya's experience, it was true. Angering her was a fun pastime, but it wasn't recommended if one enjoyed eating regularly.

"Don't say a word," Euraiya said quickly as Lillia opened her beak. She paused before asking, "Why are you awake now, anyway? Tenders don't work until after midmark." Euraiya's feathers rose slightly, and she pointed a digit at her friend. "You were working early, too. Weren't you?"

Lillia's own feathers stood up, the skin under them flushed. "I happen to enjoy working as part of a team, thank you! The same can't be said for you. I was awake early."

Euraiya withdrew her digits and chuckled. Lillia was betrayed by a flick of her ears. "Rada woke you, didn't he?"

"Yes," Lillia conceded. Her shelter was near the direlord's den, and she often heard his outbursts. "It was something about wilders."

"That's why you were looking for me." Euraiya had to remind herself that Lillia's mothering wasn't condescending. She was over-protective of the ones she loved. It was annoying, but it was well-intentioned. "I didn't see a single wilder. Didn't even smell one."

"He yelled about Caranel refusing our trade, as well." Lillia was a trustworthy source of news from the direlord's den. There was a lot of hearsay, but she had often proven herself correct. Caranel, a direlord south of Rada's borders, was well known for being brutish and stubborn. It was no wonder why he didn't get along with Rada.

Euraiya clicked her beak. "Caranel's too picky. With a clan the size of his, he should be happy Rada is trading with him at all. I feel for the trade, though."

"And whoever Caranel had promised would join our clan," Lillia countered.

Clans kept within their own borders. Outside of the trading of clanmembers and goods, cooperation was near nonexistent. Members were usually traded if requested. Particularly if their colouration or skill-set would suit them better elsewhere. This ensured each clan would remain functional for their general survival. The trade was always equivalent whether it was with another gryph, or material goods. But for the likes of Rada or Caranel, broken trades were common.

"I heard Sarren hoping for more warriors or hunters. He says he wants to replace the three that we lost after that run-in with the bear." Euraiya grimaced. This was why she hunted rats and alone.

Lillia sighed. "Maybe it's an opinicus. Strong, handsome and-"

"Rejected." A male voice sounded behind them.

Euraiya's hackles raised. The voice sent a shock of anger through her body. She whipped around and glared. She'd half expected him to be skulking around at this time of morning.

A gryphon leaned casually against a boulder. His red feathers shimmered in the breaking light, mixing with oranges and yellows appearing like fire, a signature of his family. His yellow beak opened slightly in a smirk. "The opinicus is probably crying before the fight even starts." He pushed off the rock and strutted towards them. "Enjoying your little gossip, girls?"

Euraiya pushed air from her nares. "Get lost, Ter. Don't you have hippogryphs to chase?" She squared her wings in challenge, instinctively holding her ground against him.

"I don't see wilders around, so I'm clearly doing a good job of it, aren't I? And what about you, *hunter?*" He approached Euraiya specifically as per usual. "I'm seeing hungry kits. Hungry gryphs. And we all know who's to blame for that." Fairly average for a gryphon, he still stood a head taller than any opinicus. He measured himself against Euraiya with confidence.

Euraiya looked up at him, letting out a sharp, derisive laugh. "I'm not the only hunter. Take it up with Sarren if you need to stuff your gut."

The smug look on Ter's face turned as his feathers snapped flat. He rose up to full height and struck Euraiya's cheek with a talon. "Don't speak like that to your betters, clawfoot." Euraiya squawked and held a paw to her cheek, feeling the drips of blood against it. His gaze turned to Lillia. "You lot don't learn, do you?"

"N-no, sir," Lillia whimpered, taking a step back. She had been in the path of Ter's ire before, particularly when he had been in one of his moods.

"What was that?" Ter brought his talons to his ear and leaned forward.

"No, Guardian Ter!" Lillia shouted, clearly forcing herself to enunciate.

Euraiya tested the cut on her face. She slowly looked up to Ter, heat rushing to her cheeks. Her forelegs twitched, itching to strike out, and her tail lashed from side-to-side.

Her opponent mirrored her display with a flick of his own. They stared each other down.

Ter accosted opinici on a daily basis and seemed to delight in Euraiya's reactions particularly. His attitude towards non-gryphons was typical for those raised with more traditional values. Those like Ter went out of their way to antagonise anything lesser than a full blooded gryphon.

"Bastard," Euraiya snapped. Two paws pulled at Euraiya's midsection, away from the gryphon.

"Euraiya, no. Don't get into another fight with him," Lillia said. "It's not worth it."

Euraiya struggled against Lillia's grip. Ter laughed, taunting her just out of her range.

"We're leaving," Lillia said, dragging her backwards.

Euraiya stopped. She wanted more than anything to strike him back. "Fine."

After another snort of air, she turned and followed Lillia's direction. They rounded the corner, leaving Ter to laugh to himself.

He jeered behind them. "I was looking forward to a tussle. Come to the arena later, I'll show you how it would've turned out!"

"Calm down. He's just getting under your feathers," Lillia said.

"And he's damned well succeeded!" Euraiya snapped. "How can someone like that be a guard?"

The sting of the cut throbbed along her cheek. Visions of her raking at Ter's face filled her mind, placating her the moment. He needed to be taught a lesson. Neither of them spoke. Lillia knew to let Euraiya simmer before trying anything else.

Ahead of them, the direlord's den stood proudly in the centre of the grounds. Being the largest structure, it housed their direlord and his coordinators. Designed to allow Dire Rada to lead his clan from his nest, it contained everything he could need. All assignments funnelled through it at some point, whether they were reporting hunts or wilder sightings. Assignments outside the clangrounds tended to be auxiliary to each other. The coordinators, Sarren and Karrik, cooperated where needed to ensure the gryphs, and their direlord, were happy.

As Euraiya fumed, Ter's last words caught her. "Is it really an induction day?"

"Yeah. Proving rites and promotions within the guard," Lillia said, more interested in greeting gryphs as they passed. The clan was beginning to wake. The open-fronted shelters provided views of gryphs waking and preening before organising their day. Some had already left while others tried to sleep through the rising din.

"I need to see this. If anything, I need to see Ter have his tail handed to him by someone stronger. And maybe we can see Yarril fight again!" Euraiya's excitement boiled, melting away the memories of the previous ten minutes.

Lillia thought for a moment. "Yarrin, preferably." A whimsical sigh escaped her beak.

Euraiya scoffed. "More Yarrin fantasies. They're twins! Yarril will be fine, thank you. He's far stronger."

"You don't pay enough attention," Lillia said.

"And you're out of your league..." Euraiya countered.

A row of sharpened logs loomed over them as they approached the den. Guards stood at attention in front of the entrance, already observing as the two opinici approached. Each gryphon had a leather cover across their body, reinforced by bits of metal. These had clearly been traded to the clan, as no clanmember was capable of the craft. Only Rada's personal guards were granted with such protections. However, the ripped leather straps and frayed bindings spoke of what the gryphons thought of their gifts. One of the guards voiced a warning as they arrived.

"Business?" he enquired stiffly.

"Hunter Euraiya, reporting to Hunter Sarren. Daily rations complete and delivered." The words were well-rehearsed and spoken so often that neither truly heard them.

The guard looked to Lillia with a grunt.

"Tender Lillia is accompanying me. She'll wait here," Euraiya said.

"You, in," the guard gestured between Euraiya and the large shelter. "You, stay," then pointed to a specific area at the side of the path.

Euraiya pushed through the hanging leaves over the entrance, accidentally brushing the side of the frame. It didn't budge. The foundation of the building was stronger than the general shelters around the clangrounds. Inside, it was split into three distinct areas for the hunters, guards, and their direlord. On either side of her, there was a similar setup of pelt adornments, armour, and jewels. Maps littered the floors, each with symbols and scribbles that Euraiya couldn't understand. The main difference between the two sides were the trophies. Where one room had a kirin's head mounted on its wall, the other had a piece of leather armour.

Across from the entrance, at the other end of the building, sat a large nest. It was rounded out by wolf pelts and punctuated by various jewels, framed by the red cloth draped on the wall behind it. It could have easily fit Euraiya three times, with room to spare. This was the throne of Dire Rada. Various sized and shaped gems scattered the ground around it, where they had likely been kicked and knocked around during his outburst this morning. It was otherwise as impressive as it had always been. Euraiya liked to imagine herself ruling the pride, ordering the gryphs to gather her food for her, and lounging around until something happened. This was an impossible dream, however, one that was determined even before she was born.

A voice muttered over the silence. She turned left and entered the hunter's room. Respectfully, she stood at the edge until the sound of a grunt granted her entrance. Coordinator Sarren raised himself, surrounded by a mess of maps that barely gave him room to move. He regarded her irritably as she approached.

"Early. Alone. Stirring. Kitcarer Jana has already sent someone to complain about you." The measure in his voice didn't mask his annoyance.

"With all due respect-"

"Lack of." He enunciated both words, slowly, as if lancing her with them.

Euraiya paused, taking a breath and repeating herself. "With all due respect, Kitcarer Jana didn't allow me to pass the food quietly. I didn't want to be there as much as she didn't want me."

Sarren's ear twitched. His eyes narrowed. "You're pushing your luck, Euraiya. It can be appreciated that you complete your tasks early, but the other hunters can't depend on you if they need you to assist them in a hunt." He tapped the floor in front of him, indicating for Euraiya to sit with him. "Even still, you barely cover your quotas with these vermin that you bring in."

Euraiya looked at the floor's disarray. She located a pelt that wasn't covered in Sarren's mess and lay down. The hairs of the soft pelt rubbed against her stomach. Sarren sat in front of her, one taloned foot resting over the other. The rhythmic tapping of his talon made her feathers prickle.

"Dire Rada needs reports. What times did you hunt, where, and what did you see?" Sarren asked. The questions were odd and specific. He usually only cared to know that assignments were completed and not anything surrounding it.

"I was hunting from changemark to the first sunmark" Euraiya said. "The forest to the south of here has been providing a lot of rodents. I can find at least fifteen during my hunt."

Sarren eyed her suspiciously. "What did you see?"

"Nothing unusual," she admitted. "Ter said he's chased all the hippogryphs away." A loud, gruff cough sounded from the room behind them. "*Guardian* Ter," she corrected.

Sarren made a staccatoed hum and looked to the map beside him. Multiple landmarks made it clear that it was of Rada's territory. He located her grounds with a talon and traced them back to the nearest hippogryph camp on the clan's borders. Curiously, they were in the forest when they were supposed to be on the edges.

"What are they doing there?" Euraiya asked.

Sarren shook his head. "See to it you listen for them."

The request took Euraiya by surprise. While it wasn't uncommon for hunters to report wilders, they weren't required to do so. The idea struck Euraiya as obtrusive to their assignments. "Do I have to? Hunters aren't scouts."

"Yes," Sarren said.

"Hunter Sarren, with all due resp—"

"Quiet!" Sarren stood quickly and towered over the

opinicus. His thin frame seemed a lot larger. "Euraiya, you've been given an additional order. It's about time you did something more for the clan than simply laze about after hunting. Should you hear any wilders, you will relay *everything* to me or Guardian Karrik. Do I make myself clear?"

Euraiya sank into the pelt, responding with some form of an affirmative noise. Sarren was often in a poor mood, his feathers permanently sleeked across his body. However, outbursts weren't part of that demeanour. Something clearly troubled him.

Behind them, another gryphon, Karrik emerged from his area. His feathers contained bits of reds and oranges, faded with age. What was once a fiery coat was now an ember. His eyes were firmly planted on Sarren. "You cannot expect an effective scout if you don't encourage them. Hunter Sarren, I will explain the situation, if you are too preoccupied with Dire Rada's scolding to do so."

Awkward silence hung in the area, a result of the many arguments between the two gryphons over how each should lead their assigned cohort. Euraiya had seen many.

Sarren made no movement, other than to sit back down. Euraiya shifted herself to face between the two coordinators. She looked at each of them, waiting for an answer.

With no indication to stop, Karrik continued. "We had an envoy coming to trade. Kristel's clan. That envoy was found dead near the edge of the forest, and we're at a loss as to who killed them. No other clan has reason to attack us, and none would dare stand against Kristel. That leads us to believe it was the wilders, likely thinking they would scare us. We were hoping the hunters had heard something, since they cover ground more consistently. We are beginning to brief hunters as they come through. As it so happens,

Hunter Sarren wanted to speak with you first." Sarren scoffed under his breath. "Per your penchant for organising your own schedule."

Karrik was more level-headed than his colleague. With his training and experience, he was better at organising teams and conveying his plans. Euraiya was disappointed that he wasn't the hunting coordinator.

"That's enough. You don't need to know the specifics," Karrik finished.

Euraiya sighed and forced the words from her beak. "Should I hear anything, I'll be sure to report. I haven't heard anything from the hippogryphs. I assumed they were hunting."

"Indeed," Sarren muttered. "You may leave, Euraiya. I expect to see you at the arena. Dire Rada will be making an official announcement after the proving."

Euraiya made her polite farewells to the two coordinators, particularly Karrik, and left the shelter. Her departure came at a good time. There was a loud growl from the back room, followed by an equally loud curse. The foundations of the shelter quaked from the force of the growl. Rada's foul mood had remained.

She let the new information settle in her head. Something bothered her. Wilders were thieves. Nothing about them was worthy of an announcement. No, what concerned her most was Rada. Euraiya only knew of a few other times when Rada had addressed the clan in any sort of official capacity. The clan always changed for the worst. Whatever he had to say now would not be for the clan's benefit, Euraiya was sure of it.

2

PROOF OF WORTH

Induction. Simultaneously an entrance trial for applicants to join the clan and entertainment for established clanmembers. Surrounded by a stone fence, the perimeter of the dirt-ridden arena was large enough for most of the clan to have prime viewing of the fight. However, some gryphs preferred to watch it from the sky and hovered impatiently above. In the midst of the crowd, Euraiya had found a spot at the fencing, wedged between an opinicus and gryphon. They shoved her from side to side until she pushed back with her wings. She returned their dirty looks.

Amongst the dirt, pebbles, and dried blood stood four gryphs—two gryphons and two opinici. They faced the empty space in the fencing that housed a similar nest to the Dire's Den. The applicants stared intently, trying not to glance around at the various voices shouting and hollering at them. One failed to do so. A yellow opinicus cowered, while the orange one comforted her. It was a disappointing sight. Euraiya had hoped for something more substantive.

Through the din of hollering and betting, the loudest voices were directed at the two gryphons: an exile and a wilder. Overwhelming support sounded for the red gryphon in the middle of the group, a clear favourite judging by the cries and swoons. He stood tall and disciplined, waiting for his chance.

The exile was likely the grey gryphon to the red's left. Ribs protruded from his thin frame and his sunken eyes barely focussed ahead, his gaze trailing away to the ground. His dull feathers had likely lost their sheen an age ago. The fractures hadn't been kind to him. The fact that he stood on those frail legs at all was surprising. This was likely to be his last chance at life, and he had little to lose from trying. Much of the yelling came from older gryphons who seemed to have known him before his exile. Calls of *traitor* filled the air, mixing with cheers for the wilder.

Deep, rhythmic flapping silenced the crowd, louder and slower than the wings of most gryphs. This was the first indication that their direlord approached. Each cast of his wings brought him closer, carrying him faster than anyone in the clan could manage. From a distance, he appeared the size of a normal gryphon. He straightened his wings and glided towards them. As he descended, it was clear that he was not an ordinary gryph. He landed with a heavy thud on the nest and looked over the crowd. A gryphon by all means, yet he dwarfed even the largest gryphons in the clan, standing two heads above them. Each limb was filled with strong, large muscles that led to talons that could crush a gryph's skull. His rigid, pointed feathers glistened in the sunlight, offsetting his spiked appearance and near-permanent scowl.

Direlord Rada. The leader of their clan and monstrous beast of a gryphon. His title was an ancient term rooted in his blessing of dirism. Dire creatures were a rare sight. Euraiya had only ever seen Rada and other pride leaders and their retinue. They were all terrifying. Larger and stronger than any undired gryph and prone to extreme anger and bloodlust. Rada's clan contained only himself. Not a single heir or clanmember had been blessed with dirism, and he had no intention of passing the rule of the clan to the undired.

Quietly, slowly, Rada's piercing eyes found the four applicants. He raised a large, taloned forefoot and gestured toward them.

"Today," his deep voice echoed across the arena, "provides another opportunity. A glorious day to induct new members into our clan, and grant them a better life." The brute gestured around the arena, "It is also a day for our deserving guardians to receive their promotions, so they may serve us in greatest capacity. Today, we will see new peers," his talons stopped over the group of guards standing to the side of his nest, "and new leaders."

The crowd chattered excitedly. These were key events for the clan, and to witness two on the same day was unusual. Euraiya kept quiet. She wanted to enjoy the entertainment ahead, but what waited for them at the end gripped at her stomach.

"Four current members of equal measure will test our new applicants. The applicants shall fight until they are downed, are deemed out, or retreat. Do not forget: kills will result in exile. This applies to everyone. Death will not be tolerated." His gaze returned to the applicants, "Neither will weakness or cowardice. Flee now, if you're so inclined."

None of the applicants faltered. Even the two opinici were quiet. The yellow shivered but remained.

Rada's feathers rose. "Promising. Then let the fighters enter the arena."

Mirroring the applicants, two gryphons and two opinici

approached the arena. Euraiya had seen them around and recognised the opinici as fellow hunters. A flash of anger hit her as Ter measured the red gryphon in front of him. Euraiya wanted Ter to fall. The combatants stood opposite their opponents at a fair distance, allowing for either side to have enough reaction time at the beginning of the fight. Ter saw Euraiya. With a sinister look on his face, he gestured to her. He wanted her to watch what would happen when they squared off. If she were lucky, he would kill his wilder opponent and be cast out.

Karrik stood up, raising his voice. "The applicants consist of: Ralin and Fenri, of Kristel's clan. Aurok, the wilder. And Tharreen, exile of the Rada clan."

At the final announcement the crowd burst in to a series of squawking and jeers. To his credit, Tharreen stood straight and ignored the calls for his death. Not a single gryph cheered for him. They didn't want an exile to rejoin the clan.

Euraiya groused. Most of the clan wouldn't know what it was that he'd done, although in truth, neither did she.

Rada raised his talons, and the arena went silent once more. He relaxed, letting the air settle. "Begin."

WITHOUT A MOMENT'S HESITATION, THE FIGHTERS CLASHED.

Tharreen's dishevelled body belied his speed. His thin limbs carried him quickly, and he flicked his opponent with a wing, catching her eye. She screeched and covered it with a talon, as if testing that it was still there. Tharreen launched, only to be caught by one of the opinici in his side. The crowd cheered as Ralin and Tharreen crumpled across the ground. Rocks flicked and pinged against the stone fencing.

The opportunity wasn't lost on Tharreen's opponent. She pounced and dug her talons into his wings and clamped her beak to his neck.

Ralin rolled around the fallen exile. His opponent barrelled over the two. Ralin caught his opponent's leg and pulled him with a loud thud. Dust obscured the group of scuffling gryphons. Glimpses of the fight could be seen as two of the bodies stopped thrashing. Ralin was on top of his opponent's back, pulling at a wing. The victim's high pitched scream rang through the air. Euraiya shuddered, the same pain throbbed at the base of her wings. She tensed and shivered.

"Out! Ralin succeeds," Karrik declared. Euraiya cheered. It was good that at least one opinicus proved useful.

Applicants were desperate to gain entrance into a clan. Induction wasn't for traded gryphs; it was for volunteers. One couldn't apply for a clan without leaving another. Failure meant they had no home to return to.

Tharreen twisted his body and dislodged his opponent's footing. Rolling to the side, he managed to get up. Blood dripped from his wing and neck. He eyed his opponent, heaving. His opponent moved in quickly and attacked again.

Euraiya watched Fenri skitter away. Outmatched at every turn, she was clearly not a fighter. Fenri's wings twitched, ready to fly. She ran to where Euraiya stood, her eyes pleading for help. The gryphs jeered, some swiping at her. Euraiya watched her, disappointed and disgusted. This was not the sort of behaviour a gryph should display. If Euraiya were fighting, she would stand against her opponent and fight until she fell.

"Don't fly. Fight," her opponent snapped. "Fight!"

Fenri tried to stand her ground. Her opponent charged and she was sent sprawling. The opinicus screeched as Ralin pulled his tail and yanked him backwards. Fenri's voice shook as she called for her friend. Still, she glanced to the air.

Ralin slashed at the opinicus' rump, managing to tear into it. He scratched again until the opinicus managed to get away. Fenri found courage and pounced on the opponent, knocking him over. Ralin swiped at the opinicus' eyes, cutting through. Jeers filled the arena. Many calling for Ralin to leave the grounds. There was no rule stopping him. In response, as if to spite the crowd, Ralin swiped again, this time catching the opinicus' brow. The opinicus crawled away, trying for the edge of the arena.

"Fenri succeeds!" Karrik called out. Euraiya cried foul. Fenri hadn't claimed the victory!

Euraiya looked over to Rada, who impatiently tapped his talons. He leaned forwards, talking to Karrik. Karrik nodded.

"Tharreen fails!" he called.

Euraiya had forgotten about the emaciated gryphon. Fenri's whining distracted her. Looking over, Tharreen was on the ground, unmoving.

Ralin and Fenri moved to the side of the arena. This left only the favourite, Aurok. In his current state, he had the advantage. Blood dripped from under Ter's beak. He limped to the side as Aurok circled him. A tingle of pleasure ran down Euraiya's neck, and she cheered.

"Break his beak!" Euraiya screamed. There wasn't a single gryph in the clan she wanted downed more than Ter. Watching him, she imagined it was her, not Aurok, fighting him. Winning. Putting him in his place. He deserved every cut and bruise.

Aurok spoke, his voice lost in the din of chants and cheers. He continued circling and talking. He seemed calm. He was enjoying this. Ter was his inverse. His feathers stood on end. He snapped and jerked from one side to the next as Aurok moved around him.

Aurok lunged and the two collided, shoulders crashing. Bone against bone echoed through the air. Aurok pushed harder against Ter and shoved him off balance, using his weight to bring him to the ground. Aurok swivelled, grasped Ter's neck in his talon and dug in hard. Ter struggled and writhed, screeched and swore. Blood seeped through his feathers.

"Aurok...succeeds." Karrik shouted. There was a reluctance in his voice. He glared at Ter.

A loud cheer sang through the arena. Aurok, their favourite, had won his place in the clan. Females, and some males, swooned over him, offering a place for him in their own shelters. Euraiya rolled her eyes. Nobody knew anything about him, aside from what he looked like and his now previous status as a wilder.

Now that he was no longer flanked by gryphs, Euraiya saw him properly. His feathers gleamed, reflecting a sheen of reds in the sunlight. They were clean and sleek. The only hint of a struggle was the blood on his talons.

Ter crawled back to whatever hole he had been in before the fight.

Tharreen lay still on the ground. A couple of the carer gryphs made their way to him. They looked over him quickly and crudely, acting only out of expectation. Previous applicants had received much more attention.

Tharreen didn't move. His chest didn't rise with breath. As the gryphs worked, nothing roused him. Euraiya watched, dread slowly crawling over her. But it wasn't for herself or Tharreen.

An opinicus raised her paw into the air and declared, "He's dead."

The cheering stopped. Gryphs parted from Tharreen's combatant as if she were diseased. The gryphon's feathers and ears sat flat, her eyes wide. She babbled something to those around her, then to Rada. She repeated it. Her innocence. How it was an accident. How he was already dying. She fell to the ground, pleading faster and louder. Begging.

Rada stared down at her. Not a muscle or feather moved. The grounds were silent in anticipation of Rada's ire. Not a single gryphon or opinicus twitched. No one would dare help, lest they joined her.

"Out." Rada's voice travelled across the arena, cutting through the silence like talons. "Five fractures exile. Survive, and you may attempt application. Pray that your opponent does not grant you the same fate."

The gryphon stared wide-eyed at Rada. She looked around frantically. She called for gryphs and pleaded with those around her. Each gryph she approached backed away, refusing to touch her. Rada was already paranoid about who lived within his clan. Gryphs were removed at a single sign of disloyalty.

Guards appeared from within the crowd. The gryphon screeched and howled. She swiped with her talons. The guards tackled her, wrestling her down. One grabbed the feathers on the back of her head and slammed it against the ground. She was out cold. The only audible sound was of a gryphon being dragged away.

Euraiya held her breath and glanced at the gryphs around her. An edge had set within the crowd. They knew Rada was serious about his threats of exile, yet could never prepare for their eventuation. Euraiya had seen many exiles during her lifetime, and they were never easy to experience, especially as Rada's paranoia had increased over the years.

"Now," Rada's voice broke the silence once more. His voice calm, as if the exile was forgotten. "We shall continue."

"LET THIS BE A JOYOUS DAY," RADA DECLARED LOUDLY. "AND let us welcome our new clanmembers: Aurok, Ralin and Fenri."

There was a slow, uneasy growth of voices and sound. Even at its height, many gryphs chose to keep to themselves. The three survivors stood stiffly in the middle of the arena. Fenri looked ready to bolt at the slightest hint of trouble. It was disappointing that a gryph could pass the trial with such a poor display. If her presentation in the fight was anything to go by, Fenri would amount to nothing but a tender, maintaining the condition of clangrounds for the rest of her life.

"We welcome all of you to our clan. In seven nights, we will hold a Welcoming ceremony, where you will be officially brought in as one of our own. Until that time, one of our carers will find you shelters and provide rations." Rada held his chest out proudly as he addressed the crowd instead of the applicants themselves. He was always pleased to strengthen his clan and revelled in making a show of it. The three newest clanmembers were directed to the side by one of the carers.

Rada relaxed, shifting on his pelts until he was comfortable and ready. "We have six gryphs ready for promotion, based on their ethics and achievements."

Out of the six gryphons presented by Karrik, none of

them were Ter. A sadistic glee filled her, as if all her dreams had come true in a single day. After this, she tuned out quickly. The presented gryphons were of no importance, barely distinguishable from each other and the rest of the guard. They were muscular and wore the same disciplined scowl as they stood rigidly in the centre of the arena. Opinici were never assigned as guards, despite Karrik's objections. She had no reason to support any of them.

Her gaze cast towards the newcomers. Fenri's reliance on Ralin would cause strife to whomever they were assigned. Neither of them were particularly large, nor were they quick. For all his combat prowess, Ralin was remarkably average, and Fenri, entirely useless.

The red gryphon, however, was far more interesting. He stood tall and disciplined. It was easy to see why he was the favourite. He didn't hold himself the way wilders were known to. They were mostly exiles and hippogryphs, scrounging for food or stealing it from clans. They were nothing but unkempt feathers, foul mouths, and a stench that could down a wyvern. Aurok's clean feathers and quiet demeanour spoke volumes of his heritage, which piqued Euraiya's interest. Whether he smelled like a wilder would have to wait. Still, he was a gryphon. His assignment would likely be to the guard, and he would be taught to treat opinici the same way as others did. Second rate.

The sound of applause snapped her from her thoughts. She found herself staring at Aurok. Gryphs welcomed new leaders within the guard's ranks, applauding and hollering as the exile was quickly forgotten. Euraiya gave them a half-hearted chirp. Her thoughts remained on the newcomers.

"And our final announcement," Rada announced. The gryphs ceased, listening. Euraiya's heart sunk. "I warn all gryphs within my clangrounds: wilders are attempting to

steal from us once again. But they have committed worse."
Murmurs filled the crowd. The gryphs around her
muttered about the safety of their children and loved
ones.

"Some of our gryphs are dead, killed by the wilders who
terrorise our clan. These unwanted blights will not be
allowed to operate within or near my lands. If anybody
hears or sees wilders in my territory, you must alert a
guardian immediately. Hunters will be given the additional
task of reporting any and all non-clan movements to
Guardian Karrik, Hunter Sarren, or myself."

Euraiya balked. There was no reason to warn the entire
clan. In most other cases, the order would be relayed to the
guards, and they would deal with the problem quietly. She
couldn't understand Rada's intentions. Whatever they were,
they worked. Gryphs chattered amongst themselves, yelling
out various reports of unidentified creatures. The din of
voices crescendoed into a cacophony of scared and angry
gryphs.

In the midst of the crowd, Euraiya saw the now ex-
wilder. His beak visibly ground against itself. His hackles
rose, and his eyes pinned. But he remained silent.

"The Guardians are capable," Rada bellowed, silencing
the crowd. "Leave them to their job and report your sightings. I expect us to work together to prevent such disgusting
creatures taking over our harmonious living."

The dire stood and looked over his clan. "Your attendance is pleasing. We will reconvene together during the
Welcoming." With that, he extended his wings. The gryphs
on either side ducked their heads as the feathers clipped
them. With one strong downward push, he was in the air.
The force threw some gryphs off their feet and pushed them
into others. The direlord disappeared as quickly as he'd

arrived. He was not one for ceremoniously parading around, especially when his clan was riled.

Gryphs dispersed, still panicking amongst themselves. Mothers corralled their kits away with looks of panic on their faces. Others frightened themselves with stories of sightings and fights with wilders, each one becoming grander and more terrifying than the last. Gryphs screamed and wailed. Wilders turned into fire-breathing wyverns attacking the clangrounds. Rada's intent was to create an enemy that needed to be destroyed, and he had succeeded.

EURAIYA RETURNED TO HER SHELTER. IT WAS A FAIRLY AVERAGE and small structure, held together with fraying leather and torn leaves. She kept forgetting to request replacement materials to repair the hole in the side wall. Pelts were placed neatly on the floor, creating a soft bed for her to lie on. There were no gold or jewels. She had no desire to gain trophies or recommendations to display like a peacock. She wanted an easy life, one where she could live on the fringes of the community and be left alone. She was comfortable.

She'd been allocated this shelter after receiving her first assignment when she'd come of age. Her brother had lived with her before he transferred to another clan. Only a grey-brown feather remained, wedged between the leather and sticks that held the shelter together. It was as creative as she could be, but it reminded her of better times.

Eural had been a quiet and lonely kit, with his only source of friendship being his sister, just as he was to her. He wasn't a fighter by any measure, more akin to a kitcarer: caring, warm, and passive. Despite having their father's colouration, he didn't have his father's strength. No matter how hard Euraiya had tried to teach him to fight, she always won their roughhousing. Eventually, she took on the role of his protector. He idolised her for much of their kithood, following her like a shadow wherever he could. She couldn't remember where he had transferred to, only that it was in the mountains. He had left within a few days of making his decision. They hadn't been allowed to communicate after that. Envoys gave no news and refused to take any home with them.

She watched the feather, his warmth comforting her. "Doing well, Eural?" she asked for the thousandth time.

"Actually, his name is Aurok, Hunter Euraiya. But we should hope you'll become better acquainted over the next few moons," said a voice behind her.

Euraiya whirled around to see one of the carers. The red gryphon stood uneasily behind her. He offered Euraiya a quick puff of his cheeks, raising his head ever so slightly, in a friendly but awkward gesture. He was tall for an undired. About a head taller than most gryphons and two above her.

"What's this?" Euraiya croaked, trying to understand the sudden change. "Since when was my shelter open to another?"

"Since Guardian Karrik decided as such. Aurok will be with you until an assignment is decided after the Welcoming. If you have any issue with this arrangement"—Euraiya sighed as the carer rattled off the usual script—"you can sod off."

Euraiya lost the words in her beak and managed only to stare at the opinicus carer. That last bit was new.

"Guardian Karrik's words, specifically. You understand, Hunter. So," the carer slapped the side of the shelter, "you two get acquainted. Hunters will increase your rations to

accommodate your guest. I will be along tomorrow." Before
Euraiya could voice opposition, the carer was gone.

Aurok moved past the opinicus and into the shelter. The
space immediately cramped as his mass touched two of the
three walls. His ducked head removed half the height
between them. "I-I'm sorry for this. It wasn't my
intention—"

"Forget it," Euraiya cut the gryphon off with a wave of
her paw. "They put you here because of your wilder status,
and I know why *my* name came on the list." It would have
been either Jana or Ter that allowed Euraiya's name to
miraculously appear on the list of available shelters.

She didn't want to share shelters. She was content with
having the entire area to herself. Other gryphs were a pain
and took up more space than they were entitled to. This
removed her control. She may have been interested in the
gryphon, but she wanted to be interested from a distance.
Now she could see the small black feathers framing his
jawline, and the markings around his cere and eyes. She
could smell him.

Aurok tried to settle, lying on one of Euraiya's wolf pelts.
He tried to keep to one side of the shelter, avoiding Euraiya's
belongings in the confined space. His head and paws hung
outside the shelter. Rain was going to be a problem.

"Trying to be polite?" she quipped.

"Karrik warned me that you liked your privacy." Aurok
shuffled his body around in short spurts, trying to get
comfortable without making too much movement.

"Karrik isn't wrong. You're the first guest I've had in fractures." Euraiya rearranged some of the pelts on the floor,
reluctantly offering another to her new guest. She arranged
her own into a square, big enough for her to curl on. "Wasn't
my intention to ever have another."

Aurok slid the pelt under his leonine body. "It's clear. I'll be out of your feathers when I can."

Euraiya clicked her beak, averting her gaze. It couldn't have been easy, joining a pride and being shoved around for sunmarks by various coordinators and workers, only to receive a poor reception at your new home. "You're not what I expected, for a wilder."

"Your clanmembers don't meet my expectations, either," Aurok countered.

Euraiya regarded him. She didn't know what expectations other clans had of hers. "I suppose." Having settled temporary pelt and space arrangements, she lay down. "Tell me about yourself, then."

He looked at her. "I am Aurok S'Arinach." Euraiya tilted her head. He had two names, something she had never heard of before. Within Rada's clan, you had a one name and a title. "Ex-wilder, and previously of Clan Kristel. If that answers your other questions, too."

She cleared her throat, deflecting her curiosity with a preening of her feathers. Either he had been asked those questions multiple times, or they had been evident in her expression. "It explains a lot. You're clean, you smell..." she trailed off, realising the implications of her words.

Aurok chuckled. "Go on. What do I smell like?"

Nice. "Not awful," Euraiya conceded. "You skipped Kristel's clan for the wilders? Gems weren't enough for you?"

"Gems, jewels, gold..." he waved his paw, "glamour. Doesn't fit with me. Plus, it's even more hierarchical. It wasn't worth the hassle."

She'd take his word for that. Kristel's clan was not well known to most of Rada's. Tales told of its riches and condescension and that no gryph was welcome except for those who could prove their wealth or accomplishment.

Although, she wondered why a gryph would leave such an easy life.

The two spoke for a time. He kept his history quiet, deflecting questions about his family or where he'd learned to fight. He joined Rada's clan out of a need for safety, preferring the security of a clan over a nomadic lifestyle. Living under a direlord was worth sleeping soundly at night. He knew Rada's lands and his hunting grounds, and admitted to seeing Euraiya during her morning hunts. The wilders, he claimed, were good gryphs, but the looming threat of retaliation concerned him.

In return, Euraiya opened up a little more. Perhaps this wouldn't be a bad few moons, if Aurok was making efforts to be friendly.

Wilders were mixed-race groups, and often worked together in packs. In their world, all gryphs were equal. They had to be for survival. But gryphons talking to opinici wasn't a normal occurrence in Rada's clan. This was exampled by the murmurs of passers-by commenting on Euraiya and Aurok's conversations.

The two talked through the day, discussing the differences between their communities. There were many contrasts, and they were mostly against Rada's clan. Aurok claimed that some clans fashioned metal into weapons to make their claws sharper or constructed shelters out of stronger materials by dedicated crafters. Some were crafted into mountainsides or crags, providing neat and efficient housing for entire clans. It sounded fantastical.

Having an ex-wilder inducted into the clan was unprecedented. Yet with the surrounding events, it wasn't surprising. Rada was too paranoid to have allowed this out of his goodwill. Aurok was inducted for a reason.

3

WILD HUNT

The sun had yet to rise, and Euraiya prepared for her morning routine. Karrik arrived at their shelter and cleared his throat. Aurok remained asleep in his corner, his head still hanging out the entrance.

"Guardian Karrik. You should be asleep," Euraiya said. Her feathers fluffed in a smirk.

Karrik's expression broke her quip, and her feathers returned to their neutral position. His feathers were dishevelled, and there was sleep in his eyes. It was likely he was not here willingly.

"Hunter Euraiya." His tone settled the questions. "Your task for today has been changed. Aurok will be assisting you."

Euraiya regarded Karrik quietly. He could have approached them yesterday. She flicked Aurok's wing with her back paw, and he grunted. "Wake up. We've got stuff to do."

Aurok shifted and groaned. "We talked long enough. Wait until morning."

Karrik cleared his throat again. Aurok shot up and

bowed deeply to the gryphon. Euraiya had never seen that much bulk move that quickly. She giggled quietly.

"Deepest apologies, Guardian Karrik," Aurok said.

Karrik snorted, watching them with half-lidded eyes. He seemed ready to retire again and likely would. "It's fine. Aurok, as a member of this clan, we expect your utmost loyalty from the first day. Do you understand?"

"Of course," he said.

"Good. As an ex-wilder, we will be expecting you to show Hunter Euraiya the location of the wilder camps within Rada's borders." Karrik regarded Aurok harshly. His look held an unmistakable warning. If he didn't abide, he would be exiled or worse.

Aurok stiffened. His beak hung open as he tried to form a response. No discernible words escaped him except for a few quiet grunts. His feathers raised and lowered, unsure of how to present themselves.

"Loyalty to the clan is foremost, Aurok. Dire Rada makes his thoughts very clear," Karrik said.

There were enough exiles to prove that, and before Aurok was officially inducted, he was expendable.

"Y-yes, Guardian Karrik. I'll show Hunter Euraiya where the wilder camps are." Aurok struggled to hold himself still. His display may have been enough for exile had Karrik the energy to process it. To Euraiya, Aurok's challenge was clear.

"Both of you are to head out immediately. Understood?" Karrik said.

"Yes, Guardian Karrik," both responded simultaneously.

Karrik turned and left. Aurok visibly shook, his hackles raised. This was unfair, but she couldn't offer much without risking her own status. She could only imagine what was going through his mind.

She clicked her beak. "We can say the camp moved or disbanded. They're just a bunch of nomads, right?"

"No," the firmness in his words took her by surprise. He eyed her, as if challenging her. "They're not."

AUROK PUSHED THROUGH THE BRUSH, SILENTLY LEADING Euraiya through the forest. His larger strides forced her to trot behind him. His body provided a shield for her as they made their way through snapping branches and bushes. Keeping up with him was difficult. He fumed, pushing faster than normal and giving no thought to Euraiya behind him. Moonlight bled through the gaps in the leaves but didn't provide much of a blessing. It was as quiet as it was dark, and Aurok's silence made it sickly and awkward.

Some deep part of her wanted to reassure him or offer some sort of solution. She also didn't want to be on the receiving end of an outburst. His hackles were still raised, and a single glance of his face told her not to try anything. She sympathised with him, truly, but barely knew him. Any words she could offer would be half-cooked and hollow. If he were leading her to the wilders, then he had clearly made his choice. She hoped he would calm down eventually and even forget he was ever a wilder.

Her stomach growled. Her body had accustomed to eating early and now rebelled for being deprived of food. She would have to wait until their task was completed or until Aurok calmed down.

"There," Aurok whispered, stopping behind one of the bushes. He gestured towards a group of sleeping gryphs huddle around a fireplace in the clearing. Three shelters of a fair size sat together, each possibly housing three or five gryphs each. The crude constructions were covered in leaves and scraps of filthy and torn hide, not unlike what adorned Rada's den. She hadn't seen it utilised for shelters before.

Euraiya's feathers rose as she took in the group of creatures sleeping around a cold campfire. They resembled gryphons except for their back half. While their front feet were taloned, the slender bodies and hind paws of gryphons and opinici were replaced by stout frames and hooves. Hippogryphs. Ancient tales resonated in her head of hippogryphs attacking prides of gryphs. They had hunted the gryphs to near-extinction until the dires had retaliated. It was over one thousand fractures later and that anger remained. And while they were once as large as the dired, now they were barely as tall as an opinicus.

Aurok shoved her with his shoulder and glared. "Calm down, for the spirits' sake," he snapped. He gestured at the sleeping wilders. "You know where the camp is, we can report it to Karrik."

"Hippogryphs," Euraiya spat. "Why are they attacking the envoys?"

Aurok balked. "They're not! That's suicide."

A crow cawed. Euraiya's ear twitched, listening for its direction. It was behind her. She ignored it and focussed more on the gryphon that was defending these wilders. She knew Rada's warning had been extreme but wouldn't put it past them to attack smaller groups.

"Is it? From what I've heard, they don't really care about consequence," she said.

"Wilders know far more about the world than any of your clan! They know how to survive, and damn it, the prides attack them for it," Aurok snapped. Another crow sounded, this time behind Aurok. His feathers prickled and he whirled around. "Watch out!"

Euraiya's heart sank as bushes and trees rustled around them. She glimpsed shadows. Three. They dashed between the trees. She snapped her head, following the silhouettes in the darkness. She grounded herself. Aurok made an eagle sound, shifting his tone as he watched the shapes.

Something charged and caught his shoulder. Another shape launched at Euraiya. She ducked and clawed at its underside. A hippogryph tackled her to the ground.

Euraiya's claws scratched and raked. They caught on something. She couldn't see. The creature's talons pushed her head to the ground. It bit at her neck, staved off by her swipes. It screeched loudly in her ear and headbutted. Her world exploded into a mess of white noise. She pulled in her legs and kicked. The creature wheezed and fell backwards. She lay on the ground, recovering from the sudden headache.

They'd fallen into the wilders' trap. Or, she had fallen into Aurok's. She had to get back to the clan and warn them. Her world spun. She couldn't shake the headache.

Weight pressed her down, followed by two sets of talons. They forced her to the ground. She struggled. Whatever held her was far stronger.

Beside her, Aurok lay on the ground, surrendered. A hippogryph stood with him. They looked over to Euraiya. The hippogryph's words were lost in the ringing in her ears.

A hoof collided with her head, and her world turned black.

EURAIYA WOKE TO THE PAIN OF HER LEATHER RUBBING AGAINST

her carpals. She was tied up. Aurok sat beside her, head
hung low. Unlike her, he was not tied up. Around them,
wilders lay about, chatting between each other or watching
their new prisoners. Most were hippogryphs, but there were
a couple of gryphons. She gagged as her nares registered the
stench of rotting meat and unwashed feathers.

"There she is," a snarky voice said at the other end of
the camp. It was an older hippogryph, his blue feathers
matching the short hairs of his horse-like body. Scraps of
blue and red cloth were wrapped around his talons. It was
the same one that had been talking to Aurok. "Welcome
back." He strode across the camp and stood before Aurok.
The smell of horsehair mixed with the stench of the
wilders.

Euraiya snapped at him. She had no patience for his
kind.

"Feisty! Aurok, you sure make interesting friends." He
paused, and looked down at her. "Interesting enemies." As
Euraiya clamped her beak on the leather, he added, "Don't
bite your bonds. Be thankful. There are worse things than
being tied up."

Aurok looked between the two. His tail waved behind
him, fanning the dirt. "I told you, I didn't come voluntarily.
Rada blindsided me." He spoke impatiently, as if he had
been repeating the same thing for hours.

"You say that." The hippogryph trotted up to Euraiya
and looked her over. "And you. Who are you?"

"I'm what's going to lead Rada's clan right here if you
don't let me go." She steeled herself. The wilders would get
nothing.

He clicked his beak. "Really?" He looked to Aurok for
confirmation. Aurok shrugged. "Rada's a paranoid mess.
He'd sooner declare you a wilder than save you."

"*Dire* Rada. You're in his lands. Respect him," Euraiya spat.

"Rada is no direlord of mine. He's an angry, bloody dire, just like the rest of them." The hippogryph's feathers twitched. There was an affirmative cheer around the camp. "Look, little clawfoot. You're not in a position to be giving attitude, so talk to me. Who are you?"

Euraiya turned away. She looked at Aurok expectantly, gesturing to her bonds with her beak.

"Can't help," Aurok responded. He was quiet for a moment, and then spoke. "Her name is Euraiya. She's a hunter. We were assigned a shelter together. The coordinator ordered us to be here. I had no choice, Trein."

"Is it a coincidence that soon after you're accepted into the clan, you're out here, trying to rat us out." The gryphs around them chuckled. One of the hippogryphs and the gryphon that attacked them whispered to each other, laughing at some in-joke. "And what a day for you, little clawfoot! You're assigned with your new best friend, and he gets you caught by wilders." He leaned down to her, raised his crest feathers and narrowed his eyes. "Get acquainted. You'll be here for a while."

The stench that overcame her was indescribable. Her stomach threatened to bring up food that wasn't there. She pulled backward and gagged.

"Oh, you're funny," Trein quipped. He brought himself up to full height and turned. "Aurok, I'm disappointed. You could have gone anywhere, and yet you brought them right to our camp. Are you really that flippant?"

"Come on, Trein. I've been loyal enough for you to know I wouldn't do it willingly." Aurok half-stood. A gryphon next to him forced him down.

"Right. If that's the case, then how about letting us in on

a couple secrets?" Trein returned to Aurok. His stench wafted over her again. "Why have they killed three of our people? And why is it suddenly more dangerous to hunt?"

Euraiya couldn't help but notice something against her lessons on wilders. Trein hadn't struck either of them. His cronies, too, didn't try to kill them.

Aurok glanced to Euraiya. She met him with a warning glare. He returned to Trein. He sighed. "They're blaming you for the recent deaths of *their* people. Rada has declared you enemies. The guard are looking for you."

"We've done no such thing!" Trein snapped. His feather stood on end. His eyes pinned. "We're barely surviving on our own, let alone attacking the clan members of an over-sized pig!"

Another round of laughter, quickly cut off by their leader's glare.

"I know that!" Aurok snapped back. "For the spirit's sake, Trein. I'm trying."

Trein's ears flattened. "Then why are they blaming us?"

"I don't know. They seem to think you're capable of mauling gryphs," Aurok said.

Trein gave a derisive scoff. He turned to Euraiya, anger overtaking him. He crossed the distance, head lowered as if stalking his prey. "Do you think we're wyverns? Kirin? Wolves? Bears?"

Euraiya raised her bound forelegs, and gave Trein a sarcastic look. "I think you're pretty capable of a lot of things." The leather was beginning to cut into her skin. The short fur of her body provided far less protection than her feathers. She shifted her legs as best should could, trying to readjust the bindings to sit somewhere less painful. Whoever had tied them was intent on making sure they'd stay. Welts had formed under her fur where the binds rubbed against her legs.

"We can't trust you to stay still." Trein narrowed his eyes at Euraiya, "We trust you as much as the wyverns over yonder."

"Wyverns?" A small shiver ran down Euraiya's spine at the mention of them. They were rumoured to be as big as a dire, and just as powerful.

"Again?" Aurok interrupted Trein as he was about to answer.

"Both the wyverns and Rada's clan reflect each other in the water. Of course, *again*." Trein turned away from his prisoners, gesturing to a couple of hippogryphs lounging near the deadened fireplace. "Feed them. Keep them quiet. There's more to be answered."

THE CORPSE OF A RAT BOUNCED OFF EURAIYA'S FACE. SHE eyed the thrower, greeted by a quiet snicker. Aurok held her food steady with a talon, allowing her to eat. Eating with her legs tied proved difficult but manageable. It was a fresh kill, but small. It would have to satisfy her for the time being.

The sun had risen far above them. Disoriented, Euraiya couldn't tell if it was first-mark, or third-mark. She wondered if they'd notice her absence or assume that she and Aurok were hunting. The latter was quite likely. She clicked her beak as she lay there, waiting for anything to happen. The wilders barely glanced at her, let alone talked to her. Aurok was silent and pensive, muttering monosyllabic responses to Euraiya's questions. She gave up trying for answers and lay her head on the ground. For having so many gryphs around, it was as if she were isolated. Ignored and avoided like an exile.

Trein had yet to emerge from his tent. Wilders came and went, likely on their own hunting assignments. She saw a small number of gryphons and opinici arriving to the camp, replacing hippogryphs as they left. The camp worked autonomously. When one gryph arrived, another would leave. The stream of food and materials were constant.

Each wilder wore some form of cloth. It was mostly a dirty, brown, ragged piece of material worn in a different fashions on each gryph. Some wore it around their legs, while others had it draped across their back or neck. It wasn't clear if this designated their roles or if it was decorative.

Aurok's feathers rustled as he leaned over. "You okay?"

She continued to stare forwards. "The binds are cutting into me, and I'm bored out of my mind. What do you think?"

Aurok inhaled. "Yeah, they'll do that. If they let you go, they'll give you some ointment. We've all been tied up at some point."

Euraiya choked. She refused to comment.

"I mean," he said quickly, "this is often how gryphs enter the wilder camps. Taken prisoner until it can be deemed you're safe. It's not that different to the clans."

Euraiya gave him a sidelong look. "What are you talking about?"

He focussed on an invisible point in the distance. He was quiet for a moment. "I was held prisoner before they let me fight. It would have been longer if I'd arrived moons earlier."

Euraiya raised her head, regarding him curiously. "We don't keep prisoners. I know Rada is a brute, but...we don't do that." The accusation was surprising. No one in Rada's clan knew of prisoners. Trades and applicants never spoke of it and usually arrived in good health. It didn't make sense.

"They're kept off clangrounds. Tharreen had been there for fourteen nights. Ralin and Fenri for three. There was another who didn't make it." He paused. "Did you think we were traded here?" He regarded her.

Euraiya's brow furrowed, a small vertical line appearing beneath her feathers. "I've never heard of anything like that. Rada may act weird and controlling, but he's not some tyrant."

"No, he's not. But he's not the most forward dire in the land." His head tilted in the same direction his own brow raised. "You...really don't have any idea where you stand, do you?"

"Rada's clan don't got nothing other clans do," a blue gryphon called out from across the campsite. He used a piece of meat in his claw to point at them. He was an unseemly thing. A notable hole in his beak whistled on certain consonants. "'Think they're strong. But they ain't. Ain't nothing compared to even Caranel!"

The gryphs around him laughed, banging on the ground and seats.

Euraiya turned, eyes pinned and ears flat. "Shut your beak! My clan has survived on its own for hundreds of fractures!"

"Sure. But look at the state o' the place. Undeveloped remnants of an old world. Yer lucky anything still stands. Shouldn't've put yer faith in the old guard." The gryph didn't move from his perch, smugly responding to the fiery opinicus. The bone of meat swayed from side to side as he gestured with it.

"Come and say that to my face, rotbreath!" Euraiya lurched forwards as best she could. In her head, she would fly across the camp and attack him. In reality, she fell face first into the dirt. Another round of laughs sounded across the camps.

"Yer not standing, so my point's there," the gryph said.

Chuckles turned into raucous laughter. Even Aurok giggled to himself. Euraiya's face flushed and she pushed herself back up. Blood boiled under her skin. She pulled into her shoulders and looked away.

Aurok placed a talon on her shoulder. "Rada doesn't tell his clan about the outside world. He wants to keep you 'protected.'"

"Protected?" Euraiya said.

He looked to his left and cleared his throat. The words that were spoken were slow, and considered. "Rada believes that if his clan knew about the land outside of his borders, they'd abandon him. His claim is so small that it could be easily overthrown. He allows trades and applicants because it brings in fresh blood and supply. But he forces them to keep quiet, under penalty of exile. It's better to be quiet."

It was true, new clanmembers never spoke of their time outside. They declared full fealty to Rada, and shed their past. She assumed it was basic loyalty. Were she ever to transfer, as unlikely as it would be, she would never dream of talking of her previous clan.

The laughter died down. Euraiya thought of what Aurok said. Rada's clan was the only one she knew. She had assumed it was fairly large, considering the amount of gryphons it contained. Aurok had spoken of fantastical things that existed outside their clan; stronger armour for every guard, regular gryphs who could read and write, and jewellery. He told her of Dire Kristel's gem mines, which were legendary to a clan that rarely saw gems. He spoke so freely about it, as if he'd seen it all.

Euraiya twitched her ear. "Everything you've told me. You're not afraid of exile, are you?"

Aurok chuckled. "What's exile to a wilder? What's Rada going to do, send me to a wilder camp?"

She gestured with her bonded paws. The place was in disrepair, filthy and stunk. She still hadn't gotten used to it. "This place is disgusting. There's no way anyone would voluntarily live like this."

"Everyone present has been in the camp for at least two fractures. I think we're doing pretty well." Aurok glanced around at the camp, a fond look crossing his features. "I advise you to let go about wilders. You'll find they can be more organised, and more pleasant, than Rada has led you to believe."

Euraiya scoffed. Unlikely.

THE DAY PASSED BY. SHE SPOKE WITH NO ONE AND ATE whatever she was given. That gryphon from earlier didn't seem to represent the entire camp. Others bantered and laughed like prided gryphs. The stories that Euraiya had been told didn't manifest in front of her. Her worlds conflicted. She knew wilders to be disgusting, vile thieves. They were still filthy—and smelled as if they slept inside a rotting carcass—but what she saw in front of her were no different to those in her clangrounds.

Then, Trein emerged from his tent. A hippogryph followed after him.

"Still here? Good," he said.

Euraiya regarded him with a cold glare. She was hungry again, and the inability to move was driving her insane.

Each limb begged to be stretched, to return the blood in their veins.

He sat on his haunches in front of her. By the stench that assaulted Euraiya's nares, his tent lacked any form of bathing water. "Let's talk now, shall we?" He was different. What ever mask he had tried to uphold before was gone. She now saw his age showing in his missing feathers and tired eyes. His shoulders were slumped and he held her with a serious gaze.

"You don't need to—"

"Shut it, Aurok. You've got nothing to offer." Trein's gaze remained on her. "Euraiya. Tell me why Rada's clan is killing my people."

Euraiya raised her bonds again in a limited, but forced, gesture. Beads of red surrounded the tight binds. Pain lanced as it rubbed against raw flesh. "Let me go, and I'll tell you."

Trein sighed. He brought his talon to the bonds and pulled. The frayed rope put up little resistance and snapped. He did the same to her back legs and wings.

She stretched each limb individually. Each stretch was euphoric as her muscles relaxed. She stood up and groaned, arching her back in a long, drawn out motion. Aurok huffed and looked away, disgusted as her joints popped and cracked.

"Thank the spirits." She looked down at her forelegs, seeing a long, red mark around the now matted fur. It throbbed and pulsed.

Euraiya continued stretching her limbs. She ignored Trein and forced him to wait. Now standing, she realised that he was a similar size to her. The gryphons around the camp were all larger, if only by at least a head. She realised she had never seen a hippogryph this close before, not that she wanted to. Truthfully, she wanted to get away and leave them to their fate. That deep-seated anger remained.

"We'll fix your legs later. Now, tell me," Trein said.

Some deep part of her revolted against herself, obliging her to keep her deal, something that was etched to her very being. She made a deal, and she had to honour it. "What I've been told is that some escort was found dead. Wilders were seen in those same areas. So Rada figured you did it. Rada told the clan to keep an eye out, and to report any of you within our borders. He only announced it yesterday, but it's likely his guard knew already."

Trein swore under his breath. "That bastard."

"What were wilders doing near the bodies?" Euraiya asked.

"We heard wyverns," a grey hippogryph said, sitting beside Trein. "We went to see what it was, so we could warn the camp."

Trein nodded. "Wyverns live in burrows a little ways away. We've had couple run-ins with them."

Aurok shuddered. Euraiya did, too. A shiver ran down her spine. Gryphs had tales of wyverns. They were always violent and always ended in the death of the protagonist.

"They've never come near Rada's clangrounds," Euraiya said.

"No, they shouldn't. But they have." Trein looked to the hippogryph beside him and nuzzled her cheek. Euraiya hadn't realised they were mates.

Euraiya looked around the campsite. The jostling gryphs quieted, their gazes cast to the floor. The camp dulled and greyed as its energy sapped. In the dimming light, they suddenly seemed a lot less wild and more like a family. The thought frustrated her. She didn't want to sympathise with them, to know they were in as much danger as the clan.

They were still wilders, outcast and unwanted. Thieves and murderers. The two parallels clashed together, and she couldn't work out where she stood. She breathed deeply and thought. She was born and raised in Rada's clan. That was where her loyalties lay. Surely.

"How many have you lost?" Euraiya asked, against her better judgement.

"Enough to consider moving. These are good lands, but if the wyverns are here, then it's not safe. For anyone." His tone was laced with warning.

Aurok pushed past the gryph watching over him and moved in front of Euraiya, cutting her off from Trein. "Then go. Please. Let me tell Karrik that the camp was empty. If they want to exile me, then I'll come and find you." He turned to the hippogryph beside Trein. "Silver, please."

Silver gave Trein a concerned look.

"You've been with the clan for a day, and you're ready to be exiled?" Euraiya said. She huffed. "Some loyalty."

The red gryphon whirled around and snapped his beak at her. "My loyalty lies with those who deserve it. Rada's clan isn't the only means of survival. It's the easiest one. I'm not even a clanmember yet, and they're already turning me against my family." He flared his wings, appearing even larger than before. The disparity between them grew. He stood two heads higher than her, and just as long. Now, he seemed as large as a dire. "Tell your direlord what I've said. It means nothing to me."

Euraiya backed away as his shadow cast over her. She was small. His wings remained flared in a challenge. She lowered her head to him and forced her tail still.

Aurok pulled his wings back and nodded. His scowl didn't soften. "Good." He turned as Trein stood. "Go. Please."

A silence hung in the air, as if unseen eyes watched

them, waiting for a chance to strike. Feeling that if they didn't leave now, they wouldn't leave at all.

Trein nodded and turned to his camp. "Listen up. We're relocating to another border. We're moving out as soon as everyone has checked in. Make sure every single one of you reports directly to me. No one is being left behind. Understand?"

Mass affirmation came across the camp site. Euraiya had never seen such unity. Dissention and laziness were common in Rada's clan. It was difficult to move the clan as a unit. The wilders respected Trein. They were ready to follow him where ever he went. It was admirable to a point.

They were wilders. Hippogryphs. They had killed her ancestors and were stealing Rada's food, Euraiya forcibly reminded herself. This camp was an outlier. They didn't represent wilders as a whole.

The pulsing around her legs reminded her that she needed something for her bind marks. Trein interrupted her before she began.

"You're free to go," Trein said. She hadn't realised that he was watching her. "Do whatever. You won't see us again. But for the sake of the spirits, be safe."

"I..." she glanced to Aurok, and then around the camp. All eyes were on her, waiting. "...will see." She goaded herself for hesitating. She knew better.

Aurok flicked his head towards the forest. "You've got your answers. Let's go."

She did have her answers, and Rada wasn't going to be happy with them. She looked forward to getting back to the camp and putting this behind her. Figuring out where her sympathies lay was too much trouble. She'd tell Rada what happened, and she'd be done with it. Aurok would be exiled, and her life would go back to normal.

Pressure filled her at Aurok's command. She dropped her request for ointment and obeyed his direction. He followed after her quietly. As she left the boundary of the camp, pressure was replaced by crushing weight. The realisation of their actions hit her, and her stomach tightened. A threat of exile hung over her head like the gigantic form of Dire Rada. She had consorted with the enemy.

4

WARNING

"What do you mean the wilders are gone?!" Rada bellowed from his throne. He jolted up from the nest, his eyes like fire. "Why did you not report that they were gone?"

The two gryphs kneeled in front of him, their heads bowed between their forelegs, tails and hind legs pulled under their bodies. They needed to appear small, unchallenging. Euraiya shook as his voice reverberated through her. She was partly relieved that Rada's attention was directed at Aurok.

"We tried to find where they'd moved to, Dire Rada. W-we figured there had to be some trace," Aurok said. His bravado had vanished the moment Rada spoke.

"And not a thought was spared to alert the clan that the wilders had *moved* from their last known campsite? How long ago was this?" Rada's gaze directed itself entirely at the newest addition to the clan. "What did you tell them?"

"I told them nothing, Dire. I've been in your confines for so many days, anything that I'd have known is irrelevant," Aurok said.

"Irrelevant?" Rada looked between his two coordinators, who stood posted outside their respective areas. He let out a bemused chuckle. "Our wilder friend seems to be under the impression that he knows what is and is not relevant to our clan."

"I'm sorry, Dire. I'm still—"

"Everything in my clan is relevant to me," Rada roared. "Your time in this clan is going to be extremely short if you do not learn your place." The large beast dismounted from the throne of wolf pelts, each foot thumping against the ground as he paced between the two gryphs. "Euraiya, Aurok will be your entire responsibility. Make sure he knows everything by the Welcoming. I will not have wilders infiltrating the peace of my clan and using it as a means to steal what is ours."

Euraiya held her breath. She was unsure if she should respond. Even if she was supposed to, she couldn't. The threat of exile held her voice. He only had to say those words.

"Euraiya." The heavy footfalls ceased in front of her and the bottom of his long chest feathers touched the back of her head.

"Yes, Dire Rada?" she squeaked. Her breaths were deep and uncontrolled. Her head throbbed.

Rada leaned in and examined her forelegs, then stood tall once more. "Tell me everything *you* saw." His voice was even again. It was practiced and unsettling. "I expect your loyalty to this clan has yet to waver."

Euraiya's stomach knotted again. Her heart beat in her ears, her chest, her everything. Multiple outcomes rushed through her. Exile, punishment, imprisonment. Anything was possible. If she told him the truth, she'd be announcing her disloyalty. Words caught in her throat. She couldn't find the ones that would help her clan and save herself.

"We found..."

Duties and sympathies clashed. Her clan was her life, and she needed to protect it. The glimpse into the wilders' lives had opened her eyes. They weren't too different. The wilders held the same loyalties to their own, as the clan did to theirs. They lived as a family, a unit of survival. Outing them would be destroying them, but her loyalties would remain intact.

Their entire journey home had been fraught with the dread of this very moment. She had tried to prepare a statement. Something that she could stand by. Yet, each time she had thought of siding with one, she knew she was hurting another. Then, another thought crawled into her mind. She needed to tell Rada of the wyverns. But doing so would tell him where the wilders had been. He would know they lied.

"There was..."

There was nothing. There was a camp. There were hippogryphs. There was a family.

She swallowed. She took a single, deep breath, and spoke.

"They weren't there," she said. "The camp had moved within the last day or so. We tried to look for them, but found nothing. The day got away from us, and I apologise, Dire Rada. We didn't want to waste time." The words came like a torrent of water, unyielding and uncontrolled. Each word another strand in a web of lies and disloyalty. Surprise and disappointment filled her. She had never lied to Rada's face.

The silence weighed heavily on Euraiya's back. It crushed her into the ground.

Rada turned away, returning to his throne. He was silent for a moment. "If this happens again, I will ask more than your whereabouts. Guardian Karrik, Hunter Sarren, organise scouts to scour the borders. If these wilders are still there, remove them."

"Dire?" Karrik asked. It was an unspoken question, one that had been asked many times.

Rada's eyes narrowed. "Move them or destroy them. As long as they are not within my borders. Let Caranel deal with them for all I care. Dismissed. All of you."

Aurok and Euraiya stood, their heads still bowed. Aurok kept an eye on Euraiya and mirrored her body language.

"Before you two go," Rada said.

They halted. Euraiya dared to look at the large mass of black feathers and fur that made their leader. His face was stern, feathers sleek against his body, and his ears pinned to his skull. His eyes haunted her. They were filled with anger. He was close to exiling them, she could sense the words in him.

"Euraiya. Those burns," he said.

Her breath caught in her chest as she thought for an answer. "Ter," she said quickly. "He said he was training."

Rada looked skeptical, his brows creasing further. He huffed. "If you two are going to be troublesome," each word was calculated and precise. "I will personally get rid of you both. Do I make myself clear?"

Euraiya breathed deeply and managed a nod. Both turned and trotted from the den, fleeing Rada's impending explosion.

Euraiya and Aurok promptly returned to their shelter. The night was cold, and their day was long. They kept to their respective sides, split between the invisible line marked by the greyish feather that was strung against the wall. Their feathers opened, trapping warmer air between them. It had the unintended effect of making them appear content. This was far from the case.

The silence between them was as frigid as the air. Euraiya was lost in her own thoughts, shocked to her core. She had saved herself at the cost of lying to her Dire. She wanted to return and tell him everything, but the thought of exile held her firmly in place. Her anger turned to Aurok. She wanted to kill him. It was his fault for putting her in this situation. If he'd stayed a wilder, she'd be safe. It was his fault they'd helped the wilders. His fault Rada was watching them.

He stared at the ground with the intensity of a hunter. His feathers stood rigid.

She wondered if this was his plan. If he was infiltrating her clan to send information back to the wilders so they could attack. Perhaps she was an unfortunate part of it. He caught her eye and looked away. Her anger must have manifested more than she realised. She needed to calm down before she did something stupid.

She breathed and reached up to touch Eural's feather. She closed her eyes and sighed, pretending that her brother's warmth surrounded her. He had always been warm, wanted her to be happy and comforted her whenever Ter and his cronies had attacked her. She focussed on the memories of Eural dressing her wounds and holding her. It filled her with a familiar sense of comfort, swaying her anger. She held it closely.

"Who's is that?" Aurok asked, breaking Euraiya from her memory.

"My brother." The remnant of the memory whisked in her mind before disappearing, taking her warmth with it. "He's in another clan now."

"A transfer," he said. "Is he doing well?"

"I'm not sure," she said.

Aurok's ears flattened and he averted his gaze again. She didn't know whether it was because he regretted the question or realised his intrusion.

"Envoys don't take messages," Euraiya said. "I know he's out there, but I don't know what he's doing."

"Where?" Aurok asked.

It escaped her. She knew the general direction, but its name was nowhere to be found. "North. Somewhere."

"The mountains. Interesting. Perhaps Naralin's, or Haynil's...Kristel's." Aurok shuffled on the spot and turned around to face her. His talons crossed the line. "Tell me about him." His voice was forcibly calm. He was trying to be friendly, she could tell. She didn't want it. She wanted to rake his face. But she knew it would make things worse for both of them if she ignored him. She had to live with him now.

"Eural is his name. He was...a force of good, as best he could be. We only had each other, once our mother had passed. We were inseparable. He was a carer, but he'd always wanted to be a warrior." It wasn't the cold air that caused the feathers along her cheeks and forehead to raise. "To put it bluntly, he was weak. He'd never be a warrior, no matter how hard he tried. But he kept trying. I don't think he ever won a fight against me, but damn did he try."

Calm welled inside her again. The memory comforted and disappointed. She hadn't seen him in fractures. She only had his memory to keep her company, and she was going to hold onto it as long as she could.

Aurok let out a hum. "Admirable. Why did he leave?"

She drew a claw along the grey-brown feather, each little barb flicking upward to the next. It sheened with colour, similar to her own. "He told me he wanted to join a clan where he would be a better fit for hunting. His colouring is more suited to the mountain areas." She lowered her paw and looked at the gryphon. His eyes shone in the moonlight. "You?"

"I've been a wilder for many fractures. I don't know if my family are alive, or dead, well or poor." He shrugged. "They were average. Nothing particularly much to say about them, outside of my father's hoarding of gems and gold. He was obsessive." He paused. "You've met those I consider a family."

Euraiya regarded him then looked away. It wasn't unusual for gryph families to be split across multiple clans. Her father and brother lived in two different clans. Family was a complex matter. It mattered strongly to those within the same clan, but a gryph's desires to live elsewhere was held above all. The moment Eural announced he was leaving, Euraiya was expected to let him. They were still a family, but if they never saw each other again, that was life. However, Aurok's case was more unique. He left his family and clan to join the wilders. She couldn't imagine their reaction.

"Speaking of fractures..." he changed the subject quickly, perking up again. "Spirits have been expelled in the sky for the past two moons, so that means the Fracture should be the night after the Welcoming ceremony. Does Rada's clan do anything to celebrate the new cycles?"

The Fracture was a special event. The land opened into

the sky and displayed its beauty to the world. Some clans celebrated it as an event, while others mostly observed its happening. Rada's clan was the latter. Euraiya was indifferent but held to the general belief of what it signified.

"No." She huffed. "It's just something to watch."

Aurok leaned closer, his eyes filled with excitement. "Wilders choose a gryph in the camp to go to the cliffs." He gripped her foreleg lightly, and her feathers rose. He reciprocated. "We spend the entire night under the fracture and watch it from beginning to end."

Euraiya's face turned hot as Aurok filled her vision. The eagle-like face that stared at her blocked his non-opinicus features. For a moment, she forgot he was a gryphon. If it weren't for his talons gripping her foreleg, she would think he were a remarkably large opinicus.

"One?" she asked.

"The closest gryph we know. The Fracture is supposed to be shared. It's my favourite time in a fracture," he said.

"That's..." she couldn't finish her sentence. Aurok released her, and the unfamiliar sensation faded. She hadn't had a friendly touch in fractures.

"It's soon. I can't wait to see it." He puffed his feathers at her again. He seemed genuinely excited. She had never considered it. Rada's culture held no significance to the event. It was simply something beautiful that gryphs would watch. Watching it with another gryph would be more enjoyable.

She looked at the red gryphon, a warmth encompassing her. Aurok seemed intent on calming them both, and it was working. Her mood improved, despite the lingering desire to kill him. Her thoughts still weighed heavily on her. Her mood dipped again, worry setting in once more. Aurok, perceptive, spoke.

"We'll be okay, you know," he said

She looked at him sidelong. "Hm?"

"Dire Rada. He's not going to exile you. Or me. The clan needs gryphs to survive. He doesn't have enough power to take land, so he'll keep us," he said.

Euraiya's silence spoke for itself.

"Trust me," Aurok said. "And if he does, I'll make sure you have somewhere to go. I may be a wilder, but I won't see a fellow gryph be punished for my actions."

Euraiya forced a chuckle. "You don't act like a gryphon, you know that?"

She knew that wilders held different values, particularly in regard to gryphs. A gryphon had never given her the time of day before. The pure blooded gryphons stood above opinici. They were often stronger and always larger than the half-blooded subspecies. Euraiya had been bullied more times than she could count. Now, a gryphon offered her friendship.

"Your clan don't act like gryphs," he said. "Other prides don't actively segregate their members."

She didn't correct him on his mistake. *Pride* wasn't what they were called.

"And hippogryphs?" she asked.

"No, unfortunately." He sighed. "They're wilders to everyone. But, you've seen them." He chuckled lightly. "Hippogryphs don't generally like clans. They're not fond of such large groups..." he trailed off, watching her.

Euraiya lowered her head and closed her eyes. The day's events caught up with her, draining her of energy quicker than she could imagine. She yawned, the cold air barely keeping her awake. Something warm brushed her feathers. She opened an eye, to see Aurok's back pressed against her, the short hairs prickling against hers. She hadn't felt this in

fractures. Perhaps this relationship could work, if they kept
out of trouble. She wanted to like him. He was an anomaly
of a gryph that treated her like an equal, something that no
other gryphon had ever tried. They would be close, if he
didn't uproot her life and let her stay exactly as she was.

5

THE FOOL AND THE FLAME

A few days passed. The two scarcely spoke about what happened in the Direlord's Den and never of the wilders. Though something niggled on her mind about it. She should have mentioned the wyverns. She tried to keep those thoughts at bay. It was unlikely the wyverns would attack a clan of gryphs.

Only one event of note occurred during the week. Rada received a visit from another dire gryphon. She didn't recognise him, but the stranger carried himself with an arrogance reserved only for direlords of other lands. The two gryphons following after him backed that claim. As quickly as he had arrived, the unknown direlord had left. The shouting from within the den indicated another failed agreement. This was normal, by Rada's standards.

Euraiya set to doing what Rada had ordered: teaching Aurok the ways of the clan in preparation for the Welcoming. Aurok's openness to learning new customs made the matter simple. He understood the generic similarities well, but the specifics to Rada's clan took longer to grasp or even accept.

"I'm not giving up my second name, Euraiya," Aurok said with a forced laugh. "You won't find a gryph outside this clan who has less than that. Whether it's a secondary title, a family name, or something else. This is just Rada being—"

"Yes, yes. 'Remnant,' I know. You keep saying that." Euraiya clicked her beak. She dug her claws into the ground and flicked dirt at him. "Likewise, we don't care what you think. Your name, after the Welcoming, is Aurok." To Euraiya, a second name was pompous. It was a superfluity that gryphs didn't need and only served to separate Aurok from the rest of the clan.

Aurok raised his wing and shielded against the dirt. "For the intent of this clan, yes. But I'm not forgetting it."

The two sat together near the edge of the clangrounds, away from the majority of gryphs who were preparing for the upcoming night. The silence was needed while they went over everything. Euraiya made sure Aurok knew exactly what Rada wanted him to know.

Euraiya nudged his foreleg with her wing. "You ready?"

"I've memorised the speech too many times to forget it, thanks to your incessant nagging," he said.

Euraiya chuckled. She had mimicked Lillia to motivate him over the past week. Part of her enjoyed it. "I've seen gryphs make absolute fools of themselves in the Welcoming, and they never live it down. Besides, I have a reputation to keep."

Aurok eyed her curiously.

"I spoke to Guardian Karrik, requesting that your shelter remains where it is," she said. "You're a good gryph repellent."

Aurok's feathers puffed and nudged her with his side. "Look at you, making friends."

"Yeah, well, you're the type of friend I could do with making. As much of a fringe-walker as I try to be," she said.

Aurok rolled his eyes. "Tell me about it."

Since their first night, Aurok had spent a lot of time with Euraiya. Without knowing their orders, clanmembers watched them both curiously. Some with varying levels of disdain. The favourite who had fought and won in the arena had quickly lost that status when he was seen treating Euraiya as an equal amongst the clan. It was an undesirable position for a gryphon, but Aurok didn't have a choice. Nor did he seem to want it. It appeared to be his mission to be friendly with her after their first day together.

Euraiya, however, had little ground to lose. She was an opinicus, and by her own nature, she was solitary. Her main source of socialising had been with Lillia, who could only be taken in small doses. Euraiya hadn't chosen to be like she was, she just was. As such, she had a reputation for being lonesome and avoidant, a fringe-walker. This was aside what her fellow hunters thought of her early morning hunting schedules.

Aurok and Euraiya's friendship bloomed from a mutual status. Part of Euraiya was still conflicted about being friends with a gryphon. She had been raised to avoid them, and defer to them in their natural hierarchy. Aurok was determined to prove her wrong. So far, he was succeeding.

Two opinici came out of the clangrounds talking to each other. One preened the other's ear before he noticed Aurok and Euraiya. Euraiya inwardly sighed.

"Euraiya, Aurok!" Ralin exclaimed, approaching them. Fenri followed suit, standing slightly behind the other. "We're going to be fully fledged clanmembers tonight. Can you believe it?"

If those two had found them, it was time to move.

Euraiya gestured to Aurok, and the two walked towards the clangrounds. The two opinici followed beside them.

"I certainly can." Euraiya forced an audible sigh. "I've seen enough of them to know what happens." She stiffened her posture to stand taller than the other two. It wasn't difficult, as they were both small by opinicus standards. Many clanmembers mistook them for kits.

"Oh, right. We haven't had the chance to ask you about it. We never see you around." Ralin sounded disappointed, but it was likely because he wanted to talk her ears off.

Euraiya glanced sidelong at Fenri, who hung back couple of steps. "That's fine."

Euraiya remained unimpressed by Fenri's display in the arena. It was Ralin's success that brought her to the clan, and it was undeserved. She was too weak and quiet to be of use to anyone. Ralin didn't get a pass, either. Bouncy, excitable, and overly annoying, the clash of personalities was impressive. And, as life would have it, Ralin still hadn't gotten the hint.

"You two have gotten *pretty* friendly. Are you..." Ralin leaned in, his eyes mischievous.

"No!" Euraiya snapped. "For the spirits sake, that's not how things work here."

Aurok chuckled beside her. She pushed at him lightly. The insinuation made her uneasy. Gryphons and opinici were never paired.

"Euraiya's been good to me, since Rada ordered her to be so," Aurok said.

"Oh, I see. So is it true, are you a fringe-walker?" Ralin said, pulling back to walk with Fenri. Fenri kept her beak shut and her head lowered. The group rounded one of the shelters, which was full of gryphs. They eyed the group warily as they passed. Euraiya was being consumed by the outcasts. Her status within the clan would be forever changed.

"Sure," Euraiya responded. "I've been making sure Aurok is ready for the Welcoming. Wilders need that extra bit of understanding."

"I heard! I've met wilders. They smell. We didn't stick around," Ralin said.

Or they didn't stick around Ralin, Euraiya thought bitterly. She breathed in deeply, forcing herself to remain friendly to the other two. Once their assignments were given, they would be too busy to bother her. She glanced up towards the sky, noting the sun's position. It was beginning to set. "It's changemark."

"It's sunset," Aurok corrected. "Are you two joining us for the Welcoming? We should talk."

Euraiya groaned in her head. She couldn't tell if Aurok was trying to make her life difficult.

Ralin's eyes shone. "Sure! Fenri, you don't mind? We should make friends."

"No." Fenri's voice was overly quiet, reaching Euraiya's ears as a whisper.

Euraiya tried to catch Aurok's eye, but it was too late. Euraiya shook her head and sighed, briefly watching them. She was hoping to have spent more time with Aurok before the ceremony began, to make sure that he was fully prepared. There was no telling what Rada had planned after their little escapade. For now, they could only look forward. The smell of fire filled the clangrounds. It was time for the Welcoming.

THE COMMUNAL GATHERING AREA WAS THE LARGEST OPEN

space in the clangrounds. Mostly used as a lounging area, tonight it had been cleared out for the Welcoming ceremony. Rada's nest had been relocated to the middle of it. It was still surrounded by gems, pelts and gold. In four equidistant locations at each edge of the grounds was a bonfire, roaring with flames. Each shone brilliantly in the moonlit night, providing warmth and vision for the celebration. The grounds appeared to be on fire in the light of the flames. Around them, gryphs roasted their meat, shared meals, danced, and played throughout the area.

Dire Rada sat in his nest, flanked by his coordinators and two guards behind him. Rada laughed with a couple of gryphons. It was one of the rare times that Rada acted like he belonged within the clan as opposed to ruling it. This was likely for the benefit of the ceremony, not to enjoy the company of his subjects. He needed to appear approachable in order for his newest clan members to pledge their loyalty. By this point, however, most applicants saw through this facade.

Despite the importance of the event, the grounds weren't adorned any further than Rada's nest and the bonfires. In most cases, the event ended as soon as the induction finished. But it was a chance for gryphs to get together, eat, and enjoy the clan's company. It was relaxing to see the clan act like a community rather than as factions.

"This is the entire clan?" Ralin asked.

"Yep," Euraiya said. She looked over the gathering, found Lillia and waved to her. Lillia returned the gesture and returned to her conversations.

"It's so..." Ralin started.

"Small," Aurok finished, disappointed.

"Can we please stop criticising my home? *Your* new home." Euraiya sucked in a breath and let it out sharply.

The two males apologised.

"If you have problems with the clan, you should have applied elsewhere," she snapped.

The group made their way around the ceremony. Ralin greeted a few opinici he'd met over the past few days. At one point, to Euraiya's pleasure, he was lost in the crowd. He appeared again shortly and reassured the panicking Fenri. A few gryphs took the time from their activities to eye Aurok and Euraiya as they made their way around. While unfazed, it was enough for them to avert their gazes.

The noise was inescapable. Gryphons and opinici alike, the gryphs sang and laughed throughout the grounds, filling the sky with chirps and chirrups on an otherwise quiet night. Euraiya and Aurok shouted over the din, the atmosphere smothering their words. Eventually, they found a spot near a store of meat, lay down, and roasted it over the flame. Ralin and Fenri followed like flies.

Euraiya ripped a piece of red meat from the bone and swallowed. The barely cooked juices filled her beak and washed over her tongue. Aurok sounded impressed. Ralin attempted to emulate her and only succeeded in choking and coughing it back up.

"This is fun," Aurok managed between bites. "Rustic."

A familiar red gryphon approached them. A mess of leaves and pelts wrapped around his jaw. He limped slightly. Aurok raised his head and puffed his feathers.

"Ter! Good evening!" His words were too pleasant and forced. Euraiya glanced at him, surprised.

Ter started. He stiffened before focussing his attention on Euraiya and approached nonchalantly, as if Aurok wasn't present.

"Who let you here?" Ter said. There was a lack of coordination to his words as the bindings held his jaw together.

"Shut it, beakbreath. This meat's for the clan," Euraiya said. To punctuate her point, she ripped another piece off and swallowed. It was as much a threat as it was eating.

"Make way, then. Gryphon's got priority." Ter reached over, shoving Euraiya to the side.

Aurok's talons suddenly grasped Ter's foreleg. He narrowed his eyes and thrashed his tail. "If that's the case, then Euraiya has priority over you."

The chewed piece of meat fell out of Euraiya's open beak. She stared at Aurok. They all did.

"You should've stayed in your shelter, Ter. Parading yourself around like you're top of the crags. I fixed your jaw for good reason." There was an unusual sternness in Aurok's voice that took Euraiya by surprise. Aurok stood up and pulled Ter closer to him. He was larger, giving him the advantage. Aurok's grip twisted, bending Ter's elbow at an angle and pulling him in closer. "If the stunts you pulled in my captivity are anything to go by, your presence around the opinici is nothing but a nuisance. You're not a gryphon. You're barely a gryph. Take yourself away before I do it myself."

Ter pulled back, trying to escape Aurok's grip. Aurok let go, Ter stumbled backwards and examined the puncture marks on his leg. Aurok's hard stare kept Ter's head low. The two stood there, silence filling the area between them despite the noise from the other side of the grounds. Aurok's glare was fierce and as strong as the grip that had held the other gryphon. Eventually, Ter skulked away. Aurok sat down and chewed into the meat in front of him. The gryphs around them were silent while the confrontation set in. They then returned to their activities as if it had never happened.

"What was that?" Euraiya asked.

"I'll tell you some other time," Aurok said.

Euraiya looked over to Ralin and Fenri. They shook their heads. What did Ter do to them?

A loud, hawkish call cut through the noise. Rada spoke loudly and clearly, "It is time!"

"LET THE APPLICANTS STAND FORTH," KARRIK CALLED OUT. IT was his responsibility to direct gryphs, something which he took great delight in doing. Everyone fell silent and turned to the centre.

Aurok, Ralin, and Fenri came forwards and stood in front of the ring of gold and gems that surrounded Rada's throne. They bowed and spread their wings in a mantle to their new direlord. Aurok stood in between Ralin and Fenri, squarely in front of Rada.

Rada sat tall in his nest. The orange light made him seem larger and more intimidating than usual. He looked down at the three gryphs in front of him and nodded in approval.

"Rise," he commanded, and they did. "Aurok, Ralin, and Fenri. You have proven yourselves worthy of acceptance within my clan, by order of combat." He paused, letting his words carry to every gryph. "From this moment forward, your past will be unquestioned. Your previous clans," Rada glanced to Aurok, "or lack thereof, will be forgotten. For you are to be considered once, and always, a member of the clan Rada."

Only the sound of crackling fire filled the air as he paused once more.

"Let it be known that this will be your last chance to leave. Once you have been accepted within the clan, your loyalty will be full and unwavering. Your clanmates will treat you with respect, and you to them." Rada's gaze lingered further on Aurok, punctuating his previous threat from earlier in the week.

Aurok faced forward, his limbs held still like ice. He knew better than to look a Dire in the eye. Euraiya had taught him that Rada, in particular, took offence in the challenge.

"You may now pledge yourself to the clan," Karrik said.

Aurok raised his head. He spoke loudly from his chest, his voice reaching Euraiya's ears clearly. "I pledge myself to this clan, and to you, the esteemed Dire Rada. I renounce my previous association," a word Euraiya had allowed him to use as a substitute to his pride, "and pledge myself completely to this clan for my life. I renounce my previous loyalties that do not abide by the clan's tenet, and I renounce..." he faltered. He swallowed, noting that Rada was looking at him expectantly. "I renounce my full name, Aurok S'Arinach, to fall in line with the customs of my clan and its clanmates."

Despite the rising applause through the clan, Euraiya could see that Aurok deflated. She saw regret fill his features as the realisation of his decision caught him. It was too late for him now. If Rada noticed, he didn't make it known.

Beside him, Ralin and Fenri recited the same script. It registered as vague, dull noise. She focussed on her new friend and tried to see his thoughts. Rada's clan was a better life than as a wilder. The idea that he would regret it was incomprehensible.

"I welcome you all, wholeheartedly, to my clan. May your time here be fruitful, and beneficial for us all. As the final part of our celebration, Guardian Karrik will designate our newest clanmembers to their own shelters and assignments."

Karrik checked the parchment in front of him and cleared his throat. Aurok's eyes fell onto it, as if trying to read it. Could he? Literacy wasn't taught to gryphs that didn't need it.

"The opinici Ralin and Fenri will be assigned to their own shelter, amongst the opinici. Ralin is to be assigned Hunter. Fenri is to be assigned as tender." The crowd around them cheered. Euraiya had expected this based off their performance in the arena. Fenri's eyes widened and she turned to Ralin. Her words were drowned out by the applause. It seemed her entire existence revolved around Ralin, and now they would be separated. A small part of Euraiya felt for her, another chastised her for relying so heavily on her mate.

"The gryphon Aurok will remain where he is currently situated, amongst the opinici and with Hunter Euraiya." The crowd murmured amongst each other. "He will be assigned as a hunter."

A group of gryphs cackled around her. They shoved each other, whispering loud enough so that she could hear.

"I'll bet you a week of meat that they're exiled with their future children," one said.

"Hey, you can't bet on certainties!" another replied.

Euraiya turned and snapped, "Shut it! There's nothing going on between us. He's there because Rada put him there!"

"Sure he is, clawfoot. We'll be listening," a gryphon said. "The moment you two get friendly, you're exiled."

"I hope your spirits are sent to oblivion." Euraiya turned back to Aurok, trying to drown out the remarks around her. She hadn't thought the clan would turn on her this quickly.

She had hoped that, as a fringe-walker, they would ignore her new friendship. She would need to put them in their place as time went on in whatever way she had to.

Sarren whispered something in Aurok's ear and chuckled. Aurok's feathers fluffed and he reciprocated.

"With that, I declare our ceremony completed. Thank you all for your attendance." Without missing a beat, Rada turned and left. The crowd dispersed, with some choosing to stay and continue feasting, while others retired to their shelters.

Aurok, Ralin and Fenri returned to Euraiya.

Euraiya snapped her beak at the gryphons walking around her. "Groundlings. Thinking I'm going the wilder way."

Aurok eyed her disapprovingly, a darkness in that look added to his visible regret. Something clearly whirled in his mind.

"They did!" Euraiya's feathers prickled. She huffed. She didn't have the energy to deal with this, and Aurok's misunderstanding. "I'm going back to the shelter."

Aurok nodded. "Sure."

"You don't seem pleased," Euraiya said.

"It's nothing. Don't worry," Aurok replied.

Euraiya regarded him before shrugging her wings. "Suit yourself." She turned towards home. Aurok's issues could wait until morning, after he had cooled. He had offered her help, and she would return it. If he was having second thoughts, she needed to help him through them. She couldn't afford to lose the only friend she could manage.

Ralin clapped his paws together excitedly and bounded after her. "Neighbours! You have to show us where we're staying. We're going to have so much fun."

"Oh, goodie," Euraiya muttered.

As Euraiya prepared the next morning, Aurok awoke. He hadn't said a word since he had returned from the ceremony and had slept as soon as he lay down. By his flattened feathers and ears, something was still bothering him. She flattened her ears as curious worry crossed her.

"There's still something wrong," she said. "You're not very good at hiding your emotions."

He sighed. "I don't know if I've made a mistake."

Euraiya furrowed her brow. "You've been accepted into a clan. What's there to mistake?"

His feathers ruffled and his tail twitched. "You don't understand what we've had to give up to be here. He expects me to lose my name and my past? I can't do that."

She held his gaze for a moment. It was true, she didn't understand. She'd never had to lose her past or give up her name. They weren't important things to hold on to. Perhaps in the wider world, those things did matter, but here, they were superfluous.

She settled down near him. "There's a lot for you here. You shouldn't worry about what you're losing. Look at what you're gaining."

He prickled but didn't say anything.

"I'll help you where I can," Euraiya said.

Joining a clan meant unwavering loyalty, and Rada demanded it. His expectations were that outsiders would shed their past identities and pledge themselves to him. As part of a clan, that was all that mattered. She had never experienced another clan and was all the better for it. She didn't have to shed more than her own feathers.

For Aurok, it was something he would learn to live with as long as he was a member of the clan. He wouldn't be allowed to meet with his wilder friends or visit his family in Kristel's lands. They were no longer relevant. Like Euraiya's brother, they would be remembered, but would have no bearing on his life.

Aurok turned and looked her in the eyes. The excitement and strength that she knew had disappeared. "The Fracture is tonight. You'll come with me?"

She wasn't convinced she would enjoy the event. The idea of spending an entire night watching the sky didn't strike her as thrilling, but Aurok needed it. "I guess. Where do we go?"

Aurok's plumage fluffed. "It's the cliffs to the west, overlooking Caranel's borders. There's an amazing spot where you can see *everything*."

She hadn't been to that part of the borders in fractures, she wondered if it had changed. "Sure," she said. There was an element of noncommittal. Not because she didn't want to spend time with him, but because the night seemed long.

"Great," he said. "Meet me here at sunset, and we'll make our way there!"

They continued talking until firstmark. The rest of her day prevented her from hunting in the morning. Lillia needed help, Karrik needed a report, Sarren scolded her for missing more hunts, and to make matters worse, Ralin demanded her undivided attention to tell her things about the clan she already knew. By the time Euraiya was able to hunt, it was thirdmark. One mark until she met with Aurok.

EURAIYA SIGHED. HER ROUTINE WAS BROKEN, TIME WAS LOST, and she still had to fill her quota. Hunting was harder now. The forest was now full of life as animals chittered and played, birds sang in the trees and all were on vigil for predators such as herself. Her usual nut trap didn't work, so she hunted deeper in the forest. As she moved through it, the sounds of creatures quietened until the only the rustle of leaves remained. Something was off.

She crawled low across the ground, hugging trees and moving through bushes until she found a grazing deer. It would suffice to start with. She brought herself into position and waited. The deer's ears flicked, and it raised its head. Its attention was away from Euraiya, but it was still alert. She had to wait.

She thought herself a good hunter, capable of bringing down almost anything within the forest. Her brown feathers kept her hidden where she waited. The wind blew against her, drifting her scent away from the deer. As long as she remained quiet, she could get her kill without trouble.

The deer lowered its head and grazed. It only realised it was being attacked when it hit the ground. Euraiya pounced. With a well-practiced stab of the point of her beak and a ripping motion, the creature was dead. She licked the blood from her beak and examined her kill. It was plump and would provide the clan with some good cuts.

She looked around for another potential kill. Her ears angled, trying to pinpoint something that might lead her. They twitched at a scuffle and she trailed it. It sounded small, busy, and close. The scent of an acorn and fur caught her nares, followed by squirrel skittering into the clearing. She pounced. Her body met the ground, with no creature under her. It dodged and kept running. Euraiya picked herself up and cursed.

Something rumbled in the distance. Her eyes lit and excitement bubbled in her. The deepness of the sound meant it would be large. She hadn't had a challenging hunt in a long time. A larger carcass would certainly keep Jana off her wings. She kept low as she pursued it further into the forest, closing in on the edge of Rada's territory. She hadn't hunted a boar or a bear in many moons. This was a perfect opportunity to do so.

Birds flapped and scurried away as she reached the edge. The rumble was accented by a snort and a crackle. The forest turned silent. The noise ahead became clearer, filled with the same deepness as Rada's voice but sharp and jarring. A shiver ran down her spine. These were not the growls of a bear or a boar. Her excitement was replaced by curiosity. Something deep within her needed to see what it was, but also feared it.

The forest broke before a cavern at the very edge of Rada's borders. Ahead was Caranel's territory. Euraiya stopped in the trees, hearing a sapient language. It was sibilate and glottal, filled with inflections and rasps no gryph would want to imitate. Noises stopped and turned into long hisses mixed with staccatoed words and short vowels. One gravelly voice spoke in short bursts, then another responded in the same manner. It was nothing like the musical notations of the gryph's language. Not a single attractive word reached her ears. It grated, like claws on stone. But it was a recognisable language unlike the howl of a wolf or roar of a bear.

She followed the sounds across the flat, stony ground outside of the trees. Ahead of her, next to the opening, four large, dire-sized beasts argued amongst themselves. Thick hides covered powerful forms. Spikes jutted down their backs, and horns crowned their heads. Their front limbs were long, leathery wings, topped by bone-coloured talons. They stood on two legs, their wings touching the ground for stability.

Vicious, guttural sounds sputtered between sharp, pointed teeth.

Her heart skipped. She shot into the cover of trees and bushes faster than she knew she ever could. She held her breath, her eyes wide. She froze. She knew what they were. She knew to keep as far away from them as possible.

Wyverns.

Euraiya opened a space in a bush to watch the group. Her entire body seized, paralysed, helpless. She stared at the gigantic creatures ahead of her as they continued to argue. One snapped its powerful jaws at another, who swiped it in the face with the spike of its wing. Another slammed its long tail against the ground, cracking the dirt under it.

A mauled corpse lay between them. A gryph. Euraiya's body seized again. Her mind raced and screamed for her to run, to tell the clan. Another part held her in place, forcing her to be small and insignificant. Her breaths came in quick bursts. Her head was light. A rhythmic thumping sounded in her ears. The stories of wyverns were nothing compared to what she saw. They could burn the earth with their breath, kill dires, and destroy clans. They were supposed to keep to their borders, away from the gryphs. Aged treaties forbade them from coming here.

One single thought stabbed her like a beak. She'd failed to tell Rada of the wilders' warnings.

The wyverns continued bickering. One of the wyverns roared. The other three lowered their heads, deferring to what appeared to be their leader. It spoke strongly, in the same manner as Rada or Karrik. It gestured towards the forest, and Euraiya's stomach gripped. Her heart pounded, the beating growing louder in her ears. Her breaths became deeper, quicker, and uncontrolled. Air rushed through her nares. She still couldn't move.

The group roared together. They broke. Two raised their huge, leathery wings and lifted into the air. The other two lumbered towards the forest in different directions, using the edges of their wings to steady themselves as they walked.

Euraiya hugged the tree, making herself as small as possible. She held her breath as the massive creature walked past her, each step vibrating the ground under it. The mixed scent of fire, burning wood, leather, and dirt filled her nares. The creature stopped and looked around with a grunt. It sniffed the air, following the scent towards Euraiya's hiding spot. It took a step forwards.

Euraiya pulled closer to the tree, as if trying to become part of it. The wind carried her scent. The wyvern could sense her. It moved closer, its massive head sniffing across the edge of the forest. The pounding in Euraiya's ears was unbearable.

A short, sharp growl sounded from the air. The wyvern looked up and grunted. It lifted and followed the edge of the forest.

Euraiya chanced a look. Her gaze followed them as they left over the canopy.

Something clicked. She started.

The clan.

SHE BOLTED, RUNNING AS FAST AS SHE COULD, HER LEGS running independently of her mind. She flapped her wings, trying to gain air. They clipped trees and bushes. She couldn't open them wide enough. With each attempt, another gash appeared along her skin. She tripped, hitting the ground with a loud thud, and skidded. Twigs and rocks cut her. She pushed and ran again. She couldn't waste time. Quick breaths fuelled her, endless bouts of energy flooded her body as she charged. But no matter how fast she ran, it wasn't enough.

Thoughts rushed through her. Burning shelters. Screaming gryphons. Dead opinici. She kept running, chanting under her breath.

"They're four wyverns," she panted. "Four wyverns against an entire clan. The guard are trained. They're trained. Trained guards against four wyverns." She could only reassure herself that it wasn't as bad as it seemed.

She jumped around trees, ran through foliage, pushed through a herd of deer. The deer ignored her, running deeper into the forest and away from the clangrounds. She pulled manoeuvres she never thought possible. They still weren't enough. Nothing was.

Sounds cut through the thumping in her head: the screeches of gryphs and the loud, fierce roars of the wyverns. The smell of fire and ash filled the air. Thick, black smoke smothered the forest around her. She could barely see through it. She coughed the soot from her lungs. Animals rushed away from her, fleeing the disaster ahead. Gryphs screeched. Wyverns roared. A loud, fiery sound filled the air. Heat and smoke buffeted her. The clangrounds were close. So were the screams. So was the fighting. Fire spread through the trees, catching from one to the other. She jumped over burning debris, ducked under hanging branches. Fire singed her feathers and her body.

She cursed and screamed. She had been too deep in the forest. She should have kept to her usual hunting spots. She was getting closer, but she was still too far away. She would always be too far away. She swallowed and hurried. Her limbs burned like the fire around her.

She could reach the clan. They were still there. She could fight alongside them. Dire Rada would be fighting a wyvern, and he'd be winning. Surely. She heard a gryphic roar in the distance, loud and fearsome. It was him. It was met by a guttural retort that echoed through the forest.

Shapes moved out of the corner of her eyes. Animals, maybe gryphs. She looked, but saw nothing. They were gone. Her head pounded harder. She coughed smoke from her lungs. She continued running. It was all she could do. The edge of the forest approached. Fire cut her off. She moved to another opening and into the clearing.

The smoke that filled the air was suffocating. It billowed from across the clangrounds and high into the sky. Fires stretched towards the sky; others smouldered under the wreckage of rocks and ash. Embers showered around her. She couldn't see a remaining shelter. The clashes of fighting stopped. The only sound was fire. The wyverns' wings flapped in the distance, disappearing into the din of burning wood. She pumped her wings and flew towards the burning clangrounds, screaming as many names as she could.

"Lillia, Aurok!" she screamed desperately.

There was no answer.

"Karrik! Sarren!" She clawed for names in her head. "Ter!"

None responded. She screamed louder, trying to find any sign of life. Someone.

She landed at the edge of the grounds. What once had been residential shelters were now indistinguishable from the rest of the wreckage. She screamed and pushed through wreckage and ash. Her paw brushed feathers, and she dug.

"Hey!" She pulled the gryphon towards her. "Hey!" she repeated, shaking him.

His head lulled. Slick, wet blood covered her paws. She

stumbled backwards. She looked down at the fresh red stains on her forelegs. Her voice caught in her throat, and she lifted backwards, instinctively. The dead gryph was motionless.

She rounded the clan again and again, calling out for any one she could think of. She flew over the shelters, the kitcarers den, and the Dire's throne. Everything below her was black and burning. Charred bodies covered the grounds. One wyvern was dead. Next to it, a corpse of unmistakable size. Her direlord. There was no sign of movement. She called again. Nothing. She coughed and screamed again. Her throat burned. Her voice croaked.

Her lungs were heavy. The smoke choked her. The smell overpowered everything. A hoarse cough brought the taste of blood. She called again, this time managing only a broken, raspy squawk. Her body weakened as the adrenaline that drove her drained away. Exhausted, it took control.

Her muscles banked from the carnage. Her mind screamed to go back. Her body ignored her. She couldn't tell which way it took her as it flew away. It told her she needed to escape the smoke and flames. She fell and coughed again, blood spitting under her. Realisation grasped her. She screamed. Her throat burned.

Her home, the clan of Dire Rada, was no more.

6

FRACTURED

Euraiya lighted on the grass. Her body was covered in soot and ash, and the edges of her beak were coated with coughed blood. The black, starless sky was the only sign that time had past. She had lost track as she flew as far from the clan as her wings would carry. The area was featureless except for an array of mountains in the distance. She blinked, trying to adjust to the darkness. A rumbling filled the world around her, growing louder. The earth itself shook. And the sky exploded into colour.

Streaks of multicoloured light burst across sky. Every perceptible hue on display for the world. They twisted and turned, merging into patterned splashes. Colours faded, replaced by other, more vibrant tones. Warmth emanated from the spectacle, smothering the cold air in the breeze. This was the Fracture. When the world opened and burst across the sky.

Stories differed from gryph to gryph. Some claimed it was the world's way of declaring that it was in control. Some saw it as a gift from nature. Others saw it as signs of peace or signs of war. There was no unified meaning as to what it signified, though many agreed on one thing.

"A symbol of the end, indeed," Euraiya spat, snapping the words as if they, themselves, were her enemy.

She stopped and glared at the sky, at the world. Something deep and dark welled inside of her, and she screamed into the colourful void. Her voice echoed across the plains. It echoed back, angry and lost.

She staggered, her body intent on getting far away from the burning wreckage. The fire still burned in her nares. The screams still attacked her ears. She kept returning there, and each time it changed.

The first time, everything was aflame. A wyvern hulked over her, rearing with fire in its maw. The next, it was peaceful. Aurok and Lillia walked beside her, laughing. Then, she could see the wyverns in the distance. By the time anyone had noticed, it was already too late. The memories lingered before she jolted back into reality. When she returned, she was always somewhere else.

She didn't know who owned the mountains around her or the river that winded beside her. Without the moon, she could be going anywhere. She knew that to the west, there were Kristel's mountains and to the north were Naralin's. Now, there were no landmarks within the ranges to say who owned the ones she wandered inside.

A thought crossed her mind. Direlords would fight over Rada's territory like vultures, each vying to extend their lands. Would any of them even think about what once stood there before laying claim to it?

The lights in the sky turned red and pink as the fracture continued. She tried to ignore them and focussed on moving. Her body refused to let her stop. She stumbled left and right, following a direction until she lost her bearing once again. The lights continued to change around her, growing brighter, and dimmer, and brighter again.

Memories rolled in her head, crushing her with their weight. Her eye twitched. A prickle spiked from her tail to the base of her skull. Another memory whisked around her. The wilder leader, Trein, called behind her, warning her to be careful. Pain struck through her chest, filled with all the words she should have said. There were hundreds of things in hundreds of ways and any of them could have saved the clan, yet she'd uttered none.

The thought was cyclical. She thought of yet another thing she could have done to save the clan. She could have told him after their report. Rada would have made her suffer, but at least they would be alive. They were not, and she suffered still.

Out of another delirium, Euraiya's body dragged behind her. Something burned under her gut. Her wings sagged off her body, pulling heavily behind her. She didn't realise the heat of the sun on her back. She couldn't remember when it had risen. The last of her energy drained. She fell forward and the world came with her.

Everything whirled like a repeating dream, spinning and restarting. She saw figures around her. Four, then eight, each phasing in to the other. Two spoke to the other six. Their voices were dull, indistinguishable noises muted against the pounding in her head. She tried to speak, only managing a quiet garble. Her world reset around her and moved once more.

It turned to flashes. The only constant was the thumping in her head.

The gryphs talked over her and it went dark.

She was carried over the mountains and it went dark.

She was surrounded by the blurry forms of gryphs, and it went dark.

Euraiya lay on the ground, unable to comprehend anything. Angry voices cried around her. Whites and greys were prominent amongst them. Something dragged her. A voice sounded above the rest; she was dropped. Something approached her and looked her over. It rose, stomped, and yelled at the shapes around it. They grabbed her again.

Finally, everything went dark.

EURAIYA JOLTED AWAKE. SHE LOST COUNT HOW MANY TIMES she had, only to fall back to sleep. She still didn't know where she was, but with each minute she could stay awake, she pieced more of her surroundings together. The nest she lay in was unkempt and messy, pressed hard against the stony cave walls. Outside, mountain spires stood proudly against the sky and blocked the view of the setting sun. A musty scent that sat in the air made clear the cave's owner was a male gryph and an active one at that. It lacked the greenery smell of a gardener, or the medicinal scent of a carer. Her vision was blurry. The items that lay around the cave were barely visible.

Refilled bowls of food and water were the only sign of outside life. A dirty piece of material lay draped over the deer pelts lining the nest, covered in specks of blood and black soot. She looked down, noting the red stains that now marred her feathers and paws. The faint, reddish rings around her limbs reminded her of days before. Whoever had been trying to clean her had soothed them.

She managed to stay awake. Perhaps she had slept long enough to regain her energy. She couldn't move. Each limb, while seemingly unscathed, was like stone. She laid her head on her forepaws and sighed, her thoughts washing over her. Emotions fought for dominance. None of them were pleasant. They made her slow and cumbersome. Each movement was considered before giving up and staring at some invisible point. Even the fresh food beside her was uninteresting and bland.

Gryphs muttered from the cave's entrance, and Euraiya looked over. The silhouette of a gryph stood in front of the sun, talking to another out of view.

It hopped on three legs, carrying a jug and fresh materials in a talon, unable to fly within the confines of the cave. She scented as a female. Euraiya watched, her eyes adjusting toward the gryph. It was an older, grey gryphon. A large, long, feathery mane covered her neck and breast, flowing down between her forelegs. Euraiya raised her head, curious.

The gryphon jumped and gasped, juggling the contents between her talons and beak, eyes wide. "You're awake!"

Euraiya stared at her indifferently. She had so many questions but little desire to ask them.

The gryphon moved in close, placing a taloned forefoot on Euraiya's back and chest. "It's okay. My name is Inilrin. You're in Naralin's pridelands." She reached over and picked up the cloth, wiping at Euraiya's beak. There must have been more blood. "You've coughed your throat raw. It's nothing to worry about, but it'll hurt for a bit."

Inilrin called out to the entrance. Another gryphon poked his head from around the wall.

"She's awake," Inilrin said.

Without a word, the gryph lifted from the ground and left. Inilrin turned back to Euraiya. She held a calm presence, similar to the carers in Rada's clan. Perhaps that was the case.

"Can you speak? What's your name?" Inilrin asked.

Euraiya swallowed hard and forced herself, "Eurai—" she coughed, the consonant catching in her throat. It was so sore and dry. Inilrin brought the cloth to her beak again. Euraiya tried to pronounce the letter and failed. She skipped it. "—a."

"Good. What's your pride?" Inilrin asked.

"Rada. No." The memories rushed back; her ears flattened. "It's gone."

Inilrin inhaled sharply and removed her talons from Euraiya, going quiet.

"I am...very sorry for what happened to your clan. I just need to make sure you're thinking straight," she said.

Euraiya let out a soft snort from her nares. Her hackles rose. Thinking straight was not how she would describe it. She gave her a sidelong look. "You're a carer, then?"

"Y-yes. That's what you call them?" Inilrin said.

Inilrin didn't deserve such a harsh tone, and Euraiya knew that. She couldn't help it, her emotions were uncontrollable. It was difficult to calm herself, to stop from screaming. Inilrin was trying to help, and she deserved some respect for it. "How'd I get in here, Carer Inilrin?" She raised herself to meet the gryphon's eyes. The many fractures and losses within them told of what drove Inilrin to tend to the sick and injured.

Inilrin's feathers fluffed and she giggled. "It's just Inilrin. We don't use titles." It was a gentle correction, and Euraiya took note. "A group of scouts brought you here after they were sent to investigate the fire. They say you were exhausted and delirious. Do you know how you got to the base of the mountain?"

Euraiya shook her head. "I don't remember. There was fire, and the wyverns, and...and the screa—" Inilrin massaged the base of Euraiya's neck, hushing quietly. She let out long breath.

"Don't talk about that yet. Let your throat heal, then we can move on to other matters," Inilrin said.

Inilrin leaned over and dipped the material in the old water. She ringed it over the bowl and brought it to Euraiya's head. She gently dabbed it over her feathers. "I've been assigned to look after you while you're here. You were a mess. Luckily for you, you have someone watching over you."

The long, feathery down of Inilrin's warm mane brushed against Euraiya's body. It was an evolutionary trait and indication of the mountain gryphs, used to insulate their bodies from the harsh and cold weather. Instinctively, Euraiya leaned into the plumage. Memories of her mother caressed her.

Euraiya's head cleared, and she looked around the cave.

Metal armour and metal claws rested against the walls, seemingly on display. Others were tossed in a corner, dented and ruined. Animal pelts symmetrically dotted parts of the floor. Two red gems and small bit of silver were purposefully placed where any guest would notice them.

Inilrin fluffed her feathers. "There," she put the rag back down into the water bowl. "You'll probably find more soot in your plumage, but a good bath'll fix that. Now, tell me if it hurts..." She looked over Euraiya's beak and eyes, then inspected her paws. She pressed the sensitive spots at each of her four digits, forcing Euraiya's claws to unsheathe. She did this for each paw before moving on, pressing against Euraiya's sides. Her touch was soft but hard enough for Euraiya to respond the way she wanted.

Euraiya sat quietly, listening as Inilrin asked her questions. She barely paid attention, automatically answering as she tuned out of the world around her, trying to make sense of the disordered and chaotic timeline in her head. Some memories fizzled, others were vivid and loud. She grew frustrated, unable to make sense of anything.

As her mood began to fall, a bright voice echoed through the cave.

"Euraiya!"

Euraiya leapt up, wide-eyed and filled with energy.

An opinicus bounded into the cave and brought her to the ground in a strong embrace. At Inilrin's protests he let her go, and they both stood, staring at each other. Euraiya sucked in a breath as she took in the greyish-brown sight before her. He stood tall, his yellow eyes full of excited glee.

"Eural," Euraiya gasped. "I-I don't believe it."

She saw him entirely. Her brother had changed since she had last seen him. He now stood slightly taller than her and more confidently than she had ever seen him. He was stockier, displaying sets of muscles befitting of a warrior. Despite his larger size, he still retained that familiar sense of warmth and openness, his eyes still bright and lively and his feathers iridesced in the sunlight. It was clear that the many fractures had been good to him, and Euraiya's gut twinged. She pushed the feeling down, refusing to let it surface.

"Neither me. It was lucky the scouts brought you when they did. Any later and I wouldn't have known." Eural embraced again, his strong foreleg forcing Euraiya into his chest. "I'm so glad you're safe."

Euraiya stepped back when Eural released her. His strength was an unimaginable change from the brother she once knew.

"Me too. I think," she said.

"Eural, please, don't break her. She's only started heal-ing." Inilrin came beside Euraiya and giggled. The gryphon was barely half a head taller than her, easily making her one of the smallest gryphons in the land. By the dulling of her eyes and her slowed, deliberate movements, her growing had ceased well before Euraiya was even born. She looked from one sibling to the other. "You weren't kidding about how similar you two are. Your colours aside."

Euraiya looked her brother over. The resemblance was still there, for the most part. Their beaks had the same grey hue and shape, and their eyes were the same colour. Those were where the similarities ended, as far as she was concerned. He outshone her, his feathers practically glowed in the sunlight. The feeling sparked in her again, another in the complex pool of emotion that refused to disperse.

He chuckled and nodded. He turned, speaking directly to Inilrin. "Dire Naralin wanted to speak with Euraiya as soon as she was up to it. What do you think?"

"Give her another three days, and it can be done. Euraiya's memory is intact, but she needs to rest." She lowered her head apologetically. "She's in pretty good health despite the smoke inhalation and a few cuts and bruises. Let's try to keep her that way, shall we?" Her expression to Eural told of a history that Euraiya wasn't sure she wanted to know.

Eural splayed a paw across his breast and scoffed. "Me? Hurt an upcoming pridemember? I should take exception to that." He smirked, winking to his sister.

She regarded Eural incredulously and twitched her ear. They both seemed to forget that she had no clue as to what they were talking about or that she was in the wrong state of mind.

"You should, if you hadn't already done so," Inilrin said. "Your last victim still remembers, and so do I."

"Well that was one time," he protested.

Inilrin's feathers slickened, unimpressed...

"Twice..." Eural said.

Inilrin shook her head and gestured at Euraiya. "Just don't hurt this one. She doesn't need further trauma." She bowed her head to Euraiya, "Stay safe and well. I'll check on you later tonight." With that, Inilrin took her leave, walked to the edge of the cave and flew away.

Euraiya followed Inilrin's path to the edge of the platform and took in the sight before her. Against the clear sky, rows of mountains and crags filled the area around them, each porous with caves likely similar to where she currently stood. Below her, trees and grass filled the gaps between the mountains, and she saw the river had brought her to these lands, winding into the distance. From Rada's clangrounds, these mountains had seemed more numerous and vast but were more spaced out than expected. Naralin's lands were far more diverse than the simple forest and plains that Rada claimed. There wasn't a hint of her home in the distance. Even the plumes of smoke had long since dissipated.

Eural chuckled and followed her to the edge. "Inilrin is our best healer. I requested she look after you." He embraced her again. "It's so good to see you." His contact was getting on her nerves. She was unprepared for how touchy he was going to be. Regardless, she returned the embrace. She was happy to see him.

"I've missed you," Euraiya muttered.

"And I've missed you. I've still got your feather on the wall, see?" He let her go and pointed at the far wall. A brow secondary wing feather was displayed along side three others, a grey secondary and two primaries, brown and grey, organised like a splayed wing. She knew them all. Had she had more than Eural's feather, her own display would have been the same.

"You kept them better than I did." She swallowed, a lump of regret forming in her throat. "When mother passed, I destroyed the feather she gave me." It was a hard time. Her mother passed after an infection claimed her, leaving Euraiya alone in the clan. She'd blamed her for everything.

Eural was quiet. She could feel his gaze at the back of her head.

"I was angry. She left me," she said.

Eural nudged her shoulder with his own. He gestured to their mother's feather on the display, "She's here now. And so are you."

Euraiya turned, realising his implication. "You said I was an 'upcoming pridemember'?"

"Well," Eural listed his head to the side, clicking his beak, "it's not written in the stones, yet. But I have faith in you."

Euraiya furrowed her brow and her tail whipped to one side. "What are you talking about?"

Eural's ears fell flat to their sides, and rotated until they sat upright once again. "I'm sponsoring you for member-ship. If I could have waited, I would have, but I had no choice. They were already arguing about which wilder camp to throw you to."

She took a deep breath. One of the blurred memories revealed itself to show Eural standing over her, shouting at the gryphs around them. "Thank you, I think." In truth, she wasn't entirely sure. She had lost her home, her friends. She didn't know if she'd see Lillia or Aurok again or if they were even alive. The thought stabbed her like a claw. Thinking about her future was the last thing she was prepared for. It was the last thing she wanted.

"I...I don't know what else to say," Eural said. "Rada's clan meant a lot to me as well."

"You haven't step—" she stopped herself too late, the half-spoken words were enough.

Eural look away, his feathers lifting and falling. The silence that filled the space between them also made it larger.

"It was horrible," Euraiya whispered.

"I know," Eural said.

Eural sat on his haunches, regarding Euraiya with a neutral, but friendly expression. It was one she remembered. "Naralin is a good direlord. He'll take care of you. He and his children have worked hard to make sure the pride is strong."

Euraiya mused. She had taught Aurok how to live in a clan, and now it was Eural's turn to teach her. "It feels weird to be on this end of an induction lecture."

Eural laughed. "Well, there aren't as many things to cover. You'll be required to first meet Dire Naralin, which is probably part of the reason he wants to see you. After that, you'll be trialled to make sure you fit in with an assignment." His feathers rose with mischief. "I reckon you're a fighter or a hunter."

"I was a hunter," Euraiya said.

His chest puffed out, clearly proud that he could identify her assignment. This was despite that he had been there when she was assigned to it. "You'll be fine. If you fail, though, you'll be denied entry and sent to the wilders."

"The wilders?" Euraiya said.

Eural nodded, a look of contempt crossing his face. "Yes. Dire Naralin was pressured into it sending exiles to the wilder camps. He hates the wilders as much as Rada, but the upper-tier forces his talons and won't let him destroy them." His tail flicked behind him as he spoke. His thoughts on the wilders were clear. It seemed that some things remained the same despite the leader.

Deep down, she didn't want to prepare for an application. She wanted to return home and continue her life as she always had. Yet, she had no home and nowhere to go. Her next best option would have been wandering the lands in pseudoexile. Regardless of what she had seen, she was intent on avoiding the wilders. This left her with only the option of applying to Naralin's clan and facing his trials. As unprepared as she was for this, she had no choice.

7

THE KINSBANE

Euraiya recovered over the next three days, and Eural accompanied her as she lay in the nest. Their time was interspersed by Eural's duties to the pride, his priorities to it were clear. As soon as he was alerted of a shift, or requested to cover another, he left. When together, they discussed the lives they had created and pursued, and the chasm between them was wider than Euraiya had thought. Compared to his tales of fighting for his direlord and protecting his pride, her routine of hunting and tolerating Lillia was lifeless and boring. Very little in her life seemed worth mentioning. After her mother had passed, Euraiya had settled into her daily routine, and had found contentment—but, she realised, no progression in her status. She was in the same place she had been fractures ago.

She answered every questions Eural had about her life in Rada's clan. She told him of her hunting escapades, leaning on a wealth of stories about trapping rodents. She had been the only gryph in the clan to hunt alone, and considered herself better for it. Eural was impressed, at least, and she felt a small amount of pride until he went into further detail about his life in Naralin's pride.

The time following Eural's transfer had been tumultuous. The weak-willed and -bodied gryph committed to training harder, often to the point of exhaustion. The pride's hard-lined approach had been beneficial. He had grown stronger, learned to fight, and become as capable as any other warrior in the pride. He needed to in order to fit within the culture of dominance centralised within the guard. One had to display their skill for the pride to see if they were to be accepted.

His years were spent on scouting missions and training drills, preparing him for any conflict that might arise. Naralin boasted a powerful force, but there was no guarantee it would survive an attack from a neighbouring pride. Eural's missions had allowed him to see the outside world, one that Euraiya hadn't known existed. He told her of Dire Kristel's ostentatious pride, of priestesses and musicians wearing gems around their necks and studded coverings around their body.

Kristel's pride coveted culture above most things, an extension of the pride's location. She owned the God's Tear, the legendary birthing place of the dires. It served well for her to exert her power through displays of treasure, knowledge, and cultural supremacy. Every gryph knew of the crystalline chamber of the God's Tear and its magic, and Eural had witnessed it.

The stories made her uneasy. They were larger than her own, as he was to her. She was happy that he had attained what he had always desired, but a part of her cringed at his success. An unusual, unexpected emotion pushed to the surface. She tried to crush it, but the strains of jealousy slipped through like water rushing between spaces in the rocks. She wanted to be where Eural stood, to have what he had. There was a whisper in her ear; he didn't deserve it.

Their conversations turned to the pride. Eural explained that *clan* was an archaic term, used when the communities were smaller and more segregated, from a time when the undired served their dired counterparts. A pride was more open and diverse. The idea that the guard be made entirely of gryphons, such as Rada's, was entirely unheard of within Naralin's pride. But the hierarchy between gryphons and opinici still remained in more subtle ways. It was still uncommon for gryphons and opinici to form strong friendships or eat together.

Eural told her that Rada's clan was an anachronism. Even the wilders had access to better crafts and knowledge than Rada had allowed his clanmembers. Most of Naralin's pridemembers, including Eural, could read and write. He demonstrated this to her by reading one of the letters he'd tried to have delivered. He'd even kept a diary of his time in the pride.

"I never understood why Rada wouldn't let us read," Euraiya said after Eural had finished his letter.

"He was as archaic as Caslir," Eural said.

Euraiya scratched her beak with a single claw. "Not a familiar name."

Eural clicked his beak. "Caslir is like Rada, but on a larger scale. He comes from a long line of dires. It's said that his ancestors were dethroned by Blackbeak."

Euraiya perked. "Really?" The story of the Blackbeak rebellion was another that had been ingrained in every gryph, especially the undired. It was an important event that had turned the land into what it was today. The dired once lorded over the undired, ruled by the self-proclaimed true rulers. Blackbeak and an alliance of undired and dired rose and overthrew them in a long battle that ended at the God's Tear on the seventh night. A pawful of dires split the lands between themselves, promising the undired that they would be protected. This remained mostly true.

"So they say." Eural muttered.

Euraiya had a lot to learn. The disparity between Rada's clan and Naralin's pride was astounding. Like Kristel's pride, second names were important to Naralin's society. They were considered honours. Eural had earned one and hoped his sister would too. Euraiya saw little glamour in it. Yet another superfluity that held no bearing on life. Still, if it meant that she could be included in this new world, she would think about it.

ON THE THIRD DAY THAT EURAIYA HAD BEEN IN THE pridelands, she was brought before Naralin. The stone-carved entrance loomed over them. Sculpted deep into the mountainside, it turned into a hall decorated by gems and lined with silver and gold. A path of red cloth led into a chamber far grander and larger. At the end stood a platform with an embellished nest, surrounded various pelts and treasures. Watching them from his throne, the large, white dire gryphon's red eyes pierced through her even from a distance.

Specifically, her.

Inilrin lighted beside them. She inclined her head, raising her crest at Euraiya reassuringly.

"My father is waiting for you." She peered down the hallway, and clicked her beak. "As you can see."

Euraiya's stomach sank at her words, realisation striking

her. Naralin's children were watching her. It was likely that Naralin knew everything she had told Inilrin.

Eural flicked his tail, brushing Euraiya's side with its tuft. "Be calm. He looks intimidating, but he's a big softy. Right, Inilrin?" His tone betrayed his attempt to calm the air, and Inilrin's expression broke it entirely.

"No. He is as he looks." Inilrin shifted her wings. "Be respectful. He doesn't trust you, despite your sponsorship." She gave Eural a troubled look, then returned to Euraiya. "Be honest, be straight, and for the spirits' sake, don't challenge him."

Euraiya shivered as Naralin's gaze bore into her. Impressing a direlord was difficult, especially one who was already untrusting of her. If she were lucky, she might make it out with only minor trauma.

The two gryphs led her down the seemingly endless hallway. The more they walked, the further the watchful direlord appeared. She glanced at the various gems along the wall, full of blues, greens and reds were arranged in order of their size and brilliance and lined perfectly with an alternating silver and gold. The largest framed the opening to the room ahead of them.

The hall opened up into a chamber twice as large as Rada's den. Walls of dired and undired gryphs sat, straight-backed in raised sections on either side of the room, watching her. Each wore an aura of importance, looking down on her with a condescending sneer. It struck her to see such beasts sitting alongside undired gryphs, yet served to make them seem that much larger. She couldn't comprehend the dynamics of the upper tier and had no intention of trying. She felt like a mouse caught between a gryphon's talons.

Ahead of them, raised by a platform of crafted rock that was twice as high as his audience, sat the gigantic form of Dire Naralin framed by pale red cloth, the same that Rada kept in his den. Large, white, pointed feathers covered his face, flowing over his head and down his neck. Unlike his daughter and some of his mountain-faring pride, he did not have a feathery mane. Instead, thick feathers covered his forelegs, making him appear unusually wide despite his slender frame. His eyes were as old as they were intense, their weight holding Euraiya to the ground heavier than any guard.

Eural and Inilrin parted to their own corners of the room, leaving Euraiya standing before the jagged edge leading up to their direlord. She mantled and waited. Naralin held a long silence in the room. A familiar thumping filled Euraiya's ears.

"Euraiya the Prideless. Rise." His voice was as sharp as his talons. It wasn't as deep as Rada's, nor did it carry as well, but it cut through her like the long talons of his forefeet.

She did as she was ordered. Each movement was stiff and uncoordinated.

"Your arrival here is unorthodox." He glanced at Eural, who stood to attention. "But fortuitous. Your brother speaks highly of you, and we can use skilled gryphs."

Eural, who hadn't known her in fractures, had spoken for her. The bitter thought surprised her.

"You have been in the care of my daughter, Inilrin. She, too, speaks well of you." Inilrin stood with a group of similar-looking gryphons, each a form of grey or white. Three undired gryphons stood at the front row and behind them, two female dires. One an older yellowish-white and the other a younger reflection of her father.

He paused. Euraiya held her breath. "Our clan offers its deepest condolences for the remainder of Rada's clan."

She exhaled. "Thank you, Dire."

"However, do not think that sympathy is acceptance. You will answer to my concerns, and then we might move on to the matter of your pridelessness." His voice was steady, diplomatic, and calculated. Each word was enunciated as he weighed their effect on her. He sat so still, staring down at her, as he had likely done for so many others. "While I do not deny you have been affected by the destruction of Rada's clan, it is curious as to why you appear to be the sole survivor." His eyes narrowed. "Explain."

Euraiya held her breath. She tried to hold her herself as steadily as Naralin, mentally seizing her shaking limbs. Perhaps if she impressed him, he would grant some form of leniency or acceptance. "My clan was attacked by wyverns. I was hunting when they attacked. By the time I arrived, everything was gone." Despite her intention, her voice faltered. It came out weak, and quiet.

Naralin eyed her. "Convenient."

"With all due respect, it's the truth!" Euraiya snapped.

Naralin let out a short, distrustful hum. He watched her, his expression giving nothing away. Not a single thought or emotion. "If you believe so, then explain."

Euraiya coughed. Her heart pounded in her ears. It was hard to breathe. She hadn't prepared to explain anything more. She didn't want to admit anything in front of him. "I-I saw them. I saw them at the edge of the forest. They were there, and then they flew off and destroyed the clan!" She gasped. "They're coming here next. Y-you have to stop them. We have to do something!"

"Silence," Naralin snapped.

His order clamped her beak shut and echoed in her mind.

"You saw wyverns, and yet here you stand before me," he said incisively.

"Father, what are you saying?" Inilrin asked, breaking away from the two gryphons on either side of her.

Naralin glanced at her. "Euraiya the Prideless appears to be the sole survivor of the Rada clan. She claims to have seen wyverns, yet remains unharmed. I am wondering if it was not her that led the wyverns there." As he spoke, he addressed either side of the room, before ending on Euraiya. His words punctuated to strike her.

Euraiya balked, her hackles rising. She grounded herself and squared her shoulders. "If I worked with the wyverns," she snapped, "I would be dead. I saw them because I was in the forest!"

He let her words sit in the air while he considered them. The constant throbbing in her ears was the only break in the silence within chamber. She realised she'd make a mistake. He lifted his back and wings and stared down his beak at her, challenging her sudden offence. "They did not see you."

The boost in her confidence disappeared as quickly as it came. She was out of her league. Inilrin's instructions resurfaced in her head: be honest, straight, and don't challenge him. Already, she had broken two of those and she was about to break the third.

"No, they didn't."

"Explain."

"I—" Euraiya stuttered. Her challenge shattered.

"*Explain* how they did not see you." His words were forceful and commanding.

"I was..."

"Speak!"

"I hid!" Euraiya snapped. Her voice reverberated around

the walls of the chamber and back, spitting the words back to her, mocking her. The echoes cut through the pulsing sound in her head. The crowd gasped and muttered between themselves.

"Silence." And there was. "Euraiya the Prideless, you are saying you hid from a threat that destroyed your clan. You are saying that, given time, you could have warned them. Instead, you quivered like a kit." He leaned forwards from his seat and studied her. His age appeared on his face, and she realised just how powerless she was. "There is more. Speak."

Euraiya stared at the ground, her tail lashing from side to side. She quivered, as if Naralin had ordered her to.

Naralin pulled himself back and sat tall. "You knew."

Euraiya was silent. Naralin had hunted the one thing she wanted to remain hidden. "I knew."

"Explain," Naralin said.

The words that came from her beak were independent of her defences. She told them of her capture by the wilders and their concerns about the wyverns. She told them of Rada's threats and how she had said nothing. She told them of her fears and of her failure. Murmurs filled the room. The gryphs talked amongst themselves warily. Their voices melded into a cacophony of whispers.

Naralin straightened, silent as he watched her. Her words sat heavily, as he intended. Just as they had since she had woken in Eural's cave. Familiar fears rose to the forefront of her mind and a familiar sense filled her. The threat of exile hung above her head.

Naralin sat as still as his mountains for an eternity. His expression, unmoving and unreadable. Then, "Acceptable."

Euraiya looked up. The room was silent again. The thumping became a quiet annoyance.

"Your story is acceptable," he said.

Euraiya's heart slowed, the sound in her ears drowning away.

"Prideless are exclusively assigned as hunters or warriors. This will be your only chance to impress us. You will be admitted into the trials in order to prove your worth to my pride. Your first will be by combat. Your second, by hunting. You will then hunt until a decision is reached. Pray you pass at least one of these, Euraiya the Prideless. We expect our own to hold themselves, and cowardice and laze will not be tolerated. I expect that is clear."

Her breathing calmed as the words sunk in. Naralin looked larger than when she had arrived, controlling her view with his words. Around her, whispers filled the air. They questioned her, accused her of spinelessness and weakness. Naralin sought to censure her in front of everyone, including her brother, and had succeeded. She shrunk to where he forced her. The smallest, lowest point of the pride. She breathed deeply, caught her breath, and forced the next words from her throat.

"It's clear," she said.

"One further thing: while in our lands, you are advised to focus on passing your trials. Do not scare my pride with talk of wyvern attacks and burning clans. If such stories are brought to my attention, your exile will be swift. Even the wilders will not receive you." He watched her for a moment, assessing the clarity of his warning. "Your first trial will commence in one mark. You are dismissed."

Conversations grew around her as gryphs moved out of the chamber. Naralin turned to the group of gryphs near the base of his throne, talking to them as if the nothing had happened.

Euraiya all but ran from the chamber.

EURAIYA LANDED. SHE DIDN'T KNOW WHERE SHE WAS, AND SHE didn't care. It was away from Naralin, and that was all that mattered. Someone lighted behind her. His wing draped over her and pulled her close, bringing her head to his chest. His scent filled her nares, mixing with the white daisies that surrounded them. Florets drifted around them, catching in their feathers and brushing against their fur. Euraiya looked at the field of white flowers in front of them. In the middle stood a single, lonely tree. Its branches twisted between each other, grasping at the white leaves at its tips.

"I'm sorry. I had no idea," Eural said quietly, unsettled.

"What *was* that?" Euraiya muttered through Eural's feathers.

"He and Rada were always butting heads," Eural said. "I imagine he expected you were similar."

"I'm not anything like Rada!" Euraiya snapped.

Eural was quiet for a moment. "I know."

Euraiya sighed and pushed out of the embrace. She shook feathers, trying to rid herself of the tension. Naralin's words sat in the air around her, echoing in her ears. They were dense, suffocating. "I don't know what to say. Spirits take him."

Eural blew air from his nares. "You won't be seeing much of him. Most who aren't guards or in the upper tiers go about their lives only seeing him once or twice per fracture." He shifted his wings, watching her. There was a hint of disappointment in his eyes, but for what, she couldn't say.

She looked up to him, her wings hanging from her sides. His face betrayed his questions. Her ears lowered backwards against her skull and she sighed. "I told the truth. When I saw the wyverns, I hid. I couldn't move." It was harder to admit it to Eural than it was to Naralin. He had grown so much stronger and accomplished so much more. The rift between them split into a gaping chasm.

The look in his eyes softened and he nodded. "It's natural, and I don't think many will blame you for it." He nudged her beak with his paw. "If you get in to the guard, they'll train that out of you."

Jealousy took hold of her stomach and squeezed. "Train fear out of me?" As they had to him, fractures ago.

He gave her an odd look. Something in her tone slipped. Accepting how much further her younger brother was ahead of her was difficult. It didn't seem right.

"We use our fear to fight." He fluffed his cheeks, clearly proud of himself. "Warriors are expected to be able to fight. So, they make sure you can under any circumstance."

Euraiya nodded. Multiple emotions from multiple events mixed together until they were unrecognisable. The meanings behind each emotion were lost, and they burned together, swirling like the florets around her and impossible to differentiate. This was part of Naralin's plan, she realised. She was expected to perform for the clan after her interrogation and prove she could stand after being beaten. Right now, looking at her brother, she wanted to run. Escape him and his *perfect life.*

She needed to go somewhere and get a hold of herself before she failed the first trial or did something she regretted. Maybe go somewhere quiet and alone, or go back to her nest and sleep. "So, getting into the guard. It's just an arena fight, right?" It was an effort to convince herself of her own naivety.

Eural nodded. "Yes. I'm looking forward to seeing you fight. You were pretty decent when we were young."

Euraiya forced a chuckle. "Right. It should be interesting."

As kits, she was always the victor. While she hadn't fought since then, transferring her hunting skills wouldn't be too difficult. If she did, she should stand a chance against him if they fought. She closed her thoughts to anything else, focussing on that single point. Winning the fight would prove she was still the stronger of the two. Size meant nothing. She looked her brother over, forcing him to appear smaller in her mind's eye. He wouldn't hurt her.

8

THE FIRST TRIAL

S he was not prepared. There was not enough time.

One mark in Naralin's clan was not the same as she knew. It was half a mark, based on Rada's teachings. Eural explained the difference, all too late. What had sounded like plenty of time was in fact, none at all. The pride followed a seven mark cycle, as opposed to Rada's five. The two models were incompatible, and she would need to memorise each sun-position once again. Although, she admitted, it was a more accurate system.

The arena was larger than Rada's. Euraiya had come to terms that most things would be. This included the size of each individual guard. Each were stronger and larger than any guard she had seen in her clan, and even the opinici would likely keep up with the likes of Ter. A group lounged around the edges of the wooden fence that surrounded the dust- and rock-covered fighting ground, laughing and roughhousing with each other. These grounds were not kept to the same clean standard as Rada's, covered in dust and rocks, and Euraiya wondered if this was intentional.

They were approached by an off-white gryphon, one

that had been with Inilrin. Dark grey bars led from the tip of his cere to the base of his neck. Similar to Naralin, he had a thicker set of feathers down his front, ending at the base of his talons. His feathers were not as heavy as his father's, rather a middle-ground between Naralin and any other gryph. A metal plate sat around his chest, hidden by his slight mane, indicating that he was a guard, and by the way he held himself, it was easy to guess his importance.

He was another child of Naralin's. It seemed that each of his children were responsible for something within the pride. Lenrin didn't carry his same age the same way as Inilrin. In fact, he seemed much younger, although still older than Euraiya. Watching him, Euraiya wondered just how old Naralin was.

"Euraiya the Prideless?" he enquired, as if he were unaware.

"Yes," she said.

"Lenrin," he said, not bothering to even gesture. "Your goal here is to prove yourself a trainable fighter. To yield is to lose." By his monotonous tone, he had recited the same words for every prideless gryph that had come through. His half-lidded eyes suggested as much. "Understand?"

Euraiya nodded. There was nothing more she could do other than to try. Damning thoughts rose from under her, and she quashed them before they spread. She could win this.

"My father expects each pridemember to be trained, so you'll see me regardless of where you're assigned." He looked Euraiya up and down and shrugged. His expression spoke clearly of his expectations.

"Joy," Euraiya said.

Lenrin turned to the group of guards off the side and gave a loud, quick shout. Within seconds, Eural joined them and they stood to attention. The casual guffawing that Euraiya had seen earlier was replaced by a discipline she had seen many times before.

He moved up to the group and paced in front of them. It was as much an order as it was a show of power for Euraiya's sake. "I need one volunteer to test the Prideless. Keep in mind, she's untrained and a remnant. Her fighting style is likely to be basic, but don't underestimate her. They can be ruthless."

Remnant. The word caught Euraiya off-guard. She stared at the back of Lenrin's head, unsure as to whether she should be offended. It was the same word that wilders had used. Perhaps there was an understanding of how Rada operated his clan that his own members weren't privy to. It had worked within itself and remained stagnant, unknowing of the developing world around it.

She realised how Rada had held the clan in its own bubble, preventing it from growing. Everything in Naralin's clan was larger and grander. His gryphs were stronger, smarter, and happier. They had materials and metals she'd never seen before, used in ways that were nearly unimaginable. Remnant was beginning to seem like a correct description.

The group was silent. A couple of gryphs glanced between themselves. Lenrin waited expectantly. Not a single gryph moved from their line. Eventually, Eural stepped forwards. "I'll fight her."

Euraiya's gaze snapped to him, eyes wide.

"Very well. Don't break her." Lenrin's eyes narrowed. The group of guards laughed between themselves. What Euraiya had thought was an in-joke between a healer and a guard may have been reality. Lenrin gestured toward the arena with a flick of his head. "Off you go, both of you. Let's get this done."

The guards eased and moved to the fencing. They began cheering for Eural even before the two had reached the centre of the arena.

"Break this one's wing!" called an opinicus.

"No, knock her out!" call a gryphon.

The two then nudged the opinicus between them, who looked concerned.

Euraiya brushed off their jabs with a forced laugh. "What are they talking about?"

"Don't worry about it. Harmless fun." He chuckled, brushing off further questions as they faced each other. A cool wind settled between them.

Dust kicked up easily as Euraiya scuffed her paws on the dirt, kicking a pebble away. This was going to be an issue. She glanced over to their audience. Lenrin watched her closely, and the other guards continued their cheers. She focussed back on Eural. He was calm, even happy. His eyes brimmed with the same excitement as when he first saw her. A breath caught in her chest. His look pierced through her defences, doubt flooding through her.

"It's been so long, hasn't it?" he said.

"Yeah..." Euraiya had trouble keeping her eyes on him. They lowered from his face, down to the powerful limbs that carried him. Her thoughts flashed to when they were kits. They'd stood the same way in Rada's arena. The lack of muscles had made his legs seem like sticks. She'd even broken one of them at one point. He had been such an easy target. But now, things were different.

The two circled each other. Rocks dug into her paws as they moved. The cheers of the audience dulled as her senses focussed on the opinicus before her. She steeled herself, waiting. Still, he seemed relaxed.

"It'll be like when we were kits," Eural said, trying to appear reassuring. She caught the confidence in his voice and couldn't deny it was likely warranted. Nor could she deny it made her all the more uneasy.

It wasn't going to be anything like that.

EURAIYA CHARGED FIRST, SLAMMING HER SHOULDER INTO HIM. Eural stood firm, and she bounced off his chest. He hadn't moved an inch. He looked at her expectantly, waiting for her.

She charged again with the same motion and was deflected again. She tried from another angle. Eural's body twisted, and he kicked her from behind. Her momentum threw her forwards. She careened into the dusty ground. She slid and rolled, rocks grazing across her skin. Dust kicked under her. She picked herself up and eyed him. He paced, still waiting to attack.

She tried again, feigning from side to side like a deer. Eural grounded himself. Pushing hard, she pounced to his left. She turned her body, grabbing the feathers along the side of his neck, pulling him backwards and throwing him off balance. He snapped his wings, ceasing her movement and righting himself. His feathers ripped, and she hit the ground with a thud. He stomped her hind quarter with his rear foot. Pain exploded through her. She cried out.

Their audience cheered.

Euraiya stood and backed away as Eural pursued her. He knew he was winning. She narrowed her eyes. She flapped her wings and lifted. Eural pounced, bringing her down.

They struggled, she pulled out from under him. She pounced, grabbed his wing and pulled. Eural screeched and rolled, crushing her under his weight. She gasped and released, winded.

The crowd cheered again, calling for Eural to finish it. To force Euraiya to yield. Not a single name came in her favour.

Eural rolled to a stand. He charged. She scrambled, narrowly avoiding his swipes.

Hunted by a much larger and stronger creature, she retreated. Cornered. She wasn't a trained warrior and only knew the basic skills she had picked up from play-fighting as a kit. Eural had clearly surpassed her. Her eyes watered. She squinted, trying to see him through the haze of dust. She realised why he had volunteered to fight her. Shame mixed with her boiling anger. She tried to keep calm. His excitement had turned to focus, as if he were following a fleeing deer. Eural had never beaten her in a fight, and she was determined to keep it as such. A flash of anger cut through her, and she thought of something.

She lifted backwards and into the air, pushing dust towards him. Eural covered his eyes. She flew higher. Eural shot through the dust cloud towards her, claws drawn. At her peak, she pulled her wings in and flipped. Eural halted, flapping backwards, a quick look of panic crossing his face. He was too late. She dove at him, claws out. She dug into his shoulders, cutting into his skin. She forced her weight, screaming at him. He grabbed her, twisted her leg, and took control. She snapped her beak at his face, trying to gain any advantage she could.

His grip tightened, he kicked a spot below her stomach, hard. A sharp spike ran through her bones, blossoming into a lance of pain. It flowed through her body, from her organs to the very tips of her wings. Her veins lit like fire, breath left her and her energy drained. Her vision flashed black. Then, as quickly as her strength left her, it returned.

They fell together in a mess of limbs and wings, spinning wildly around each other. The ground rose to meet them, as did the rising cheers of the crowd. Eural's wings snapped opened, and a loud scraping filled the arena as he rode Euraiya's body across the grounds. A plume of dust flew into the air around the two combatants.

It settled, revealing them. Eural pinned her, one paw firmly gripping her throat. Small streaks of blood followed the impact zone to where Euraiya had been dragged across the ground, stinging pain throbbed in her back. She struggled to free herself, unable to find enough power to pull Eural's paw from her throat. Eural glared at her fiercely, intent on ending the fight. Her world was starting to go dark. She couldn't find the strength.

A chant of "choke, choke, choke!" filled the air.

"Yield," he said.

She struggled as hard as she could, her limbs flailing weaker and weaker.

"Yield, Euraiya!" he said.

Her strength gave, and she choked out a sound. Eural released her.

The arena erupted into cheers as Eural stood victorious. Gryphs chanted his name.

His face softened, and he offered Euraiya his paw. "Sorry."

As she gathered her senses, anger further spiked within her and she slapped his paw away. She eyed him, pulling herself up. Eural withdrew and stared at her, his beak open and ears slicked back. The crowd's cheers ceased. A few gryphs laughed amongst themselves.

They stared at each other, Euraiya's glare aimed squarely

at her brother. She knew why he'd volunteered. It hadn't been for her benefit, but his. She turned from him, flapped her wings, and flew. Jeers and sarcastic cries sounded behind her, reminiscent of Ter's quips as she ran from him. She ignored them and kept flying.

EURAIYA'S CLAWS RAKED THE GROUND AS SHE LANDED, KICKING it again for good measure. She paced a circle, cussing and muttering to herself. A familiar heat rose within her. Burning anger.

He'd turned her into a spectacle. The disparity in their skills was as wide as the mountains, and yet he still volunteered. He'd made sure to straighten the record from their kithood and prove that he was stronger. Better. She ripped a clump of grass from under her and threw it with an exasperated shout.

"Bastard," she spat.

Something heavy landed behind her. Her brow furrowed, and she groaned. He cleared his throat and she snapped around, anger controlling her every facet.

"What in oblivion was that?" she snapped.

Eural kept his head level with hers, but stood firm, his shoulders hunched and hackles raised.

"Why would you humiliate me like that? What were you trying to prove?" She knew the answer, but she wanted him to say it, to admit that the fight was entirely for his benefit.

"That wasn't my inten—"

"Then *what*?" She stormed up to him, her wings opened to make herself seem large. He pulled his head back, the difference in height causing Euraiya to lean on her paws to meet him. "Were you trying to impress your friends with how you can snap someone's neck?"

"No! It—"

"You knew I didn't have a chance against you, and yet you volunteered!" She pushed his chest with her paws, his mass pushed back. She pushed her weight into him, and he held firm, grounding himself. She gave up, defeat replacing her fury. "I get it. I knew it from the moment I saw you."

Eural looked confused. He said nothing, which only fuelled her anger once more.

She gestured to him, and then around them. "Everything has worked out for you, while I was stuck in Rada's clan hunting rodents. I'm clearly not the 'big sister' I was back when we were kits, and I'm clearly not retaking that role."

"Euraiya, that wasn—"

"It damned well looked like it."

Eural stomped the ground and snapped his beak. "Let me speak!"

Euraiya huffed and turned away, whipping her tail behind her. She stomped to the lake to drink.

"Spirits be damned, you're fiery," he quipped. "You haven't changed, and that's not my fault. I meant what I said, because I thought that's what it was going to be." He followed her to the lake. "I went too far, and I'm sorry. But," he paused, his voice softening, "I wanted to show you what I could do."

Euraiya choked. Water splashed down her chest, matting her feathers together. She'd wanted him to admit it, yet she still wasn't prepared to hear it. Especially during an apology.

"It wasn't supposed to be like that. I wanted to show you that I'm not the miserable little kit you knew back in Rada's clan." He watched her, keeping her head level with hers as she scooped water in her beak. "You know I'd always wanted to be a guard. I had to work hard for it, and I proved myself here. I thought you'd be proud of me." He looked away, his tail curling around his back leg. His gaze rested on the ground. "I apologise for the fight. But I thought you'd be proud of me."

Euraiya was quiet. Doubt filled her, masking his sincerity and twisting it into something else. She wanted to believe him, but something within her refused to let her. A stubborn, jealous part that needed her to be on top. Eural had always said that he wanted to be a warrior. She'd figured he would never accomplish it.

Euraiya didn't look at him. "I'm trying to be proud of you. But it's hard enough that I've lost the life I've built, only to find out that I could've come with you in the first place and maybe grown up as something worthwhile."

Eural shook his head. "It is how it is. But you're here now."

Euraiya sighed gruffly, her anger flaring once more. "Don't give me that. It's easy for you to say." The shelter she was building around her now encompassed her. She'd said what she'd said, and now she had to stand by it. "You have everything you wanted. Training, assignments, you're well-fed, and even the gryphons treat you with respect. And you still had to humiliate me."

"Spirits, I apologised!" He backed away from her, throwing his paw towards in her a stiff gesture. "You're going to keep coming back to that? Did you want me to throw the fight? Lenrin would know, and we'd both be in trouble."

"You don't get it, do you?" Euraiya snapped. "I've got two chances to prove myself." She pivoted and shoved his chest hard. "And you've just ruined one of them!"

Eural stopped, his eyes widened. His chest moved heavily as he visibly tried to control his breathing. His muscles tensed, and he ground his beak. She'd pushed him too far.

"Alright," he said shakily, clearly trying not to snap. "I've tried to explain myself. Deal with it yourself, and talk to me when you're over whatever this is." He turned away from her and opened his wings before glancing back. "Think about this, Euraiya: I'm here because I made the effort. If you sit idle, then that's how you remain."

With one flap of his wings, he lifted and flew off before she could respond.

Euraiya ground her beak, watching her brother fly away. Her mind raced. She knew, deep down, that her outburst had damaged something between them. She knew she was right, despite what he told her. His volunteering was nothing but braggadocio, showing off for his friends to prove that he was stronger. Perhaps he had told them of all the times she had beaten him and needed this opportunity to show otherwise. Regardless, he *had* forced everything he owned in her face, humiliated her, and ruined one of the only chances she had to be accepted in the pride. She didn't want to admit that she was jealous of everything he had and everything he was. But she couldn't deny it either. The conflicting emotion frustrated her further.

She wondered how much he had changed since she had known him and if she could trust him. If his pride was more important than her life, then she would need to do this on her own. Her new life didn't need to include her brother just as her old one hadn't. That was one air current of many.

His final words struck her. She couldn't deny they were true. If she wanted to build a new life, she would need to do it herself.

9

ADJUSTMENTS

The nexus, named for its large network of chambers and tunnels, was the pride's main hub of activity. Set deep inside a mountain, much of the non-physical assignments took place within various rooms. Crafters created and stored their works, medical gryphs worked tirelessly after their patients, and in the middle of the vast, winding corridors was the mess hall. It was large enough to fit half the pride at a single time. It was the main point of contact for meeting pridemates, and the only place where meat was provided freely upon request. Controlled fires sat in the middle of pitted areas for gryphs to cook and discard waste, which was quickly cleared by the on-duty tenders.

Eural feasted around one such pit with three others who were also part of Naralin's warrior assignment. Wiril, a guard within Naralin's retinue, and Fiir and Tilear, who were strikers. The guard was only a small subset of warriors, making ten percent of the total group. Strikers, quick-fighters versed in causing as much damage as possible, made up the bulk of the pride's force. For those who knew Naralin, this was not at all surprising.

Eural ripped a piece of cooked meat from the bone, savoured the taste, and swallowed. He laughed alongside the other three opinici, followed by elbowing and ribbing over spars during the last week. It had been a while since they had gotten together.

"Speaking of which," the black opinicus, Wiril, said. He pointed his stripped bone at Eural and tapped it lazily on the ground. "Good job with the new kit."

"You fought the applicant?" Fiir, a white opinicus, queried.

"Yeah, shoulda seen him," Wiril said. "Caught that girl in the air, brought her down in a choke. That prideless groundling had no idea what was coming to her."

The third, a stony grey, made a thoughtful noise. "Right, the Prideless. Tell us about it, Eural."

Eural put his food in front of him and shrugged. He took a moment to listen to the rhythmic drumming that filled the hall. Their musicians were talented but didn't offer the variety of instruments that Kristel's halls did. "It was nothing. Just another fight."

He knew it was a lie. After their encounter in the field, Eural had considered his actions. He had been too forceful at the fight, and the words that followed it had been too sharp and callous. He had made a huge mistake. He hadn't considered the consequences of trying to prove himself to her. That winning meant she would fail her first trial. In truth, he wanted her to be proud of him. That was unlikely to happen now.

"You hunted her!" Wiril shouted. "Serves her right for trying to fight like she did. Shoulda seen her, Fiir, she shouldered and pounced him like a play-fighting kit. She got wise near the end, but he fixed her."

Tilear snorted. "So you think she's a dud?"

"I don't know," Eural said, brushing it off. "If she passes, I don't think she'll make it as a guard or a striker." Truthfully, he regretted giving her a hard time. He didn't realise how little training she'd had.

Fiir chuckled. He took a final bite from the bone and casually tossed it into the shallow pit. He leaned forwards. "Something's got your feathers riled."

"That's because the prideless little kit's Eural's sister," Wiril teased.

"I'll stuff that bone down your throat if you keep at it, Wiril," Eural snapped. He punctuated his threat with a stab of the bone in his paw. "She's not used to this, that's all."

"Not used to this," Wiril gestured around the chamber, "or not used to being choked out by her brother? I can help her with that if she'd like."

Eural lunged with a growl and plucked a clump of Wiril's feathers, throwing them in the fire. Wiril squawked and rubbed the hole in his plumage. He smoothed it over and glared. "You don't have to get so defensive."

"That was too far, Wiril," Tilear said with a glare, shaking his head. He leaned over to Fiir and whispered something. Fiir shrugged.

Wiril was one of those annoying gnats who didn't get a hint. His inappropriate and offensive behaviour was constantly rebuked by their group. Yet, despite their reprimands, he never tempered himself. If there was anyone Eural would stop interacting with Euraiya, it would be him.

"That's my sister. And it was only a fight," Eural repeated, righting himself. "She understands."

"Don't look it," Wiril quipped as he pointed through the crowd. A brown opinicus sat at the other end of the chamber, her head lowered and feathers flat. The gryphs next to her ignored her, engrossed in their own conversation. It served to make her that much more alone. "Did Lenrin fail her already?"

Euraiya briefly caught them staring. She flustered and looked away.

"It doesn't help that she was always so fiery." Eural sighed. He'd liked her flame as a kit, but now it was insufferable and embarrassing. Conflict bubbled within him. As much as he wanted to help her, he knew well how this would play out. "As kits, she'd do this for a day or two, and come back. I'm not concerned."

He was concerned and had failed to convince himself otherwise. This time, Euraiya had a reason.

Fiir made a thoughtful hum. He stood up slowly and kicked his scraps into the pit. His eyes were solely on Euraiya. Without a word, he stepped over Eural and made his way over.

"Wait, what're you doing?" Eural shot up. He quickly whirled to Wiril and thrust a digit in his face, "You stay away from her."

Wiril scoffed and picked out another piece of meat from inside the pit. Tilear, not missing the chance, left Wiril to his own devices. Eural turned and chased after Fiir, who had already reached her.

"Good evening, Euraiya," he said and introduced himself. Euraiya turned, huffing. Her hackles rose once more. "A little sore from today? I'm not surprised. Eural's got a reputation for being rough." He puffed his cheeks, trying to convey his friendly intentions. "Mind if we sit?"

"Do as you please," Euraiya said.

"Excellent, I will." Fiir reminded Eural of a friend they knew back in Rada's clan, a green opinicus called Lillia. Like her, he cared for those around him and tried to be inclusive where others weren't. He was likely the reason Wiril hadn't been chased off.

Eural and Fiir lay down opposite Euraiya, with Eural placing himself between the other two. He looked at her. Amongst the myriad of emotions she displayed, she was tired. Exhausted. "You doing alright?" he asked softly.

"Just fine," she said.

Fiir lowered his head, resting it on his paws. "I'm well acquainted with Eural. If he's doing your head in, you're welcome to come and talk to me. Perhaps I can show you the pride outside of a guard's perspective."

Euraiya perked her ears and turned to him. Fiir told her where to find him if she ever needed another ear, and her hard gaze began to soften. She relaxed further as they spoke. Eural remained silent, letting Fiir lead the conversation. Every so often, she glanced at him, if only to reiterate her feelings towards him with scowl or a glare. She was still mad, and he expected that. He had to remind himself that this time, it wasn't for show. He *had* ruined one of her chances. There was a real possibility that she could fail, and she was seething.

At last, she opened her beak and closed it. Something unsaid came between them, a look and a turn of her head. He fluffed his feathers and nodded to her. She mirrored him. This was likely the closest thing he would get to reconciliation for now, and he would take it.

Fiir bowed his head. "Seems like you two need to talk some more. I'll see you, Euraiya. Don't let this brute push you around. Sometimes, his duty outweighs everything else," he said and left to rejoin Wiril. Eural sighed and shook his head.

The silence between him and Euraiya was long and awkward. They knew the words that needed to be said.

Only, they wouldn't be. Her gaze stuck on the meat in front of her. The quiet was beginning to affect him, and he tried to fill it.

"You've still got the hunt. You said you're a great hunter. All you need to do is impress them," he said.

"And if I don't?" Euraiya snapped.

"You will if you try." Her laziness was a trait he knew well and something he had hoped she'd overcome. Clearly, he realised, that hadn't been the case. Euraiya had one chance left at the next trial. She needed to apply herself. If she failed it, she would be rejected from the pride.

Eural suddenly felt ill. If that came to pass, he would be responsible for half of her failure.

She finally looked at him. Anger, frustration, fear, and contempt, all mixed into a single bitter expression. "I *tried* to fight in the arena. And look how that turned out!"

The two gryphs glanced over at them, muttering. Eural assured them with a gesture with his paw. He leaned in and whispered, "I apologised for that. But if that's how you fight, then you would have lost to anyone." The look on her face stuck him as harshly as he had her.

He gave her an apologetic look and tried again, "We can help you ge—"

"No, I get it." She stood up, glaring. "Stick to hunting."

Before he realised what had happened, Euraiya was gone.

Eural was stuck. He clicked his beak. Euraiya would need more help than he could offer. It was unlikely she was going to be accepted into Naralin's forces. She needed to focus on her next trial.

Her performance in the arena was a sure failure, and she now needed to impress Tayrin. Everything he had assumed about her was turning wrong. His memory, he realised, was coloured by idolisation. A lot had changed during the fractures they were separated. The sister he knew had changed with them. Now, she was unknown. An unknown with a lot to lose. He hoped she was as skilled as she'd said. Her confidence in her hunting skills may be as misplaced as they were in the arena.

For her sake, they'd better not be.

10

WILDER

R ock and earth split and cracked underneath the camp. The sound of birds filled the sky as they searched for food. In the distance, Naralin's mountains challenged the sky for control of the horizon. Barely noticeable were the gryphs that inhabited the crests of the mountains.

The border between the mountain direlords' lands sat unguarded, but the environment served as its own divider. A camp of wilders sat near the forest that split the two lands. Those who didn't hunt talked amongst themselves and fought over the unnatural alliance of prided gryphs and wilders.

The attack on Rada's clan had been unexpected, but Trein's decision to move the camp had been the right one. With a lack of true direction, or other wilder camps to communicate with, they had to make use of whatever space they could. While this near-barren land was not ideal, hunting grounds were still accessible. It would just take longer to traverse between them and this poor excuse for a camp.

The blue hippogryph, Trein, stood to the side of the

main gathering of the camp with two others. He stomped his hoof and exclaimed with exasperation. Silver, grey from head-to-hoof, nuzzled him reassuringly.

In front of them stood a tall, red gryphon, feathers singed and filthy. His tone was stern but soft. "I know this is hard. But I'll be damned if I almost died saving them only for them to starve." Especially, a voice told him in the back of his mind, because he had failed to alert them before the attack. Because he was too interested in letting Rada suffer.

Aurok towered over Trein, two heads taller and half one wider. Memories of his escape and subsequent rescue of some of his clanmembers kept flashing in his vision. It was the spirits, or perhaps luck, that had saved them that day. He looked behind at the earth- and forest-coloured gryphs that had followed him, each in their own state of grief or anger. There was distinct split between Rada's survivors and Trein's wilders, both figuratively and physically. They were all scared. Unfortunately, he was the only gryph who could direct them.

There was only one gryph that he recognised: small, frightened Fenri. Aside from her, not a single familiar face was among the group. Not Sarren or Karrik, and not Euraiya.

"Then get your lot out there and hunting," Trein said, gesturing to the gryphs behind Aurok. "If they didn't eat last night, they can eat this morning. Or, do it yourself, if you're that concerned. I'm happy to keep them around for safety, but damn it, I have my own gryphs to look out for." He'd said the same thing, in different ways, for the past few days.

"Silver, please help," Aurok pleaded to the grey hippogryph.

"Sorry, Aurok. I'm with Trein on this one. You've brought enough gryphs to hunt, and they need to be capable of it if they're going to survive. It's an awful position they're in, but life doesn't stop for tragedy." Her soft voice was even and considered. She wanted to help, but Aurok knew she had a duty to prioritise her own camp first.

Aurok sighed, running his talons through his feathers. "Alright. I'll try and organise a hunt. I don't know what they want to do once they've recovered."

"First thing would be to get them to stop attacking my camp," Trein snapped. He thrust a talon towards two gryphs and two hippogryphs. They postured against each other, wings raised. Belligerent shouts rang through the camp, causing gryphs to stop and stare.

Aurok growled and turned. With a flap of his wings, he launched over and between the two, eyeing Rada's gryphs. "What in oblivion are you doing?" he snapped, raising his own wings against them.

"Hippogryphs! That's what." A yellow gryphon snapped. "Those sneaky bastards will kill us in our sleep."

"We'll do it if you keep pushing us around, gryphon!" one of the hippogryphs snapped. "If Trein wasn't making us play nice, you'd be bleeding where you stand."

Aurok whipped his tail at the hippogryphs, and he glanced over. "You're not making this any better." He stood over the two gryphons. He knew when to use his size to his advantage. As much as he didn't like to, it was necessary. "If you can't stand them, then leave. I'll even help you do it. Otherwise, keep your head down and your beak shut. I don't care what you were told the hippogryphs did to your ancestors. Because right now, they're the best hope you've got for survival."

One of the gryphons met Aurok's challenge, mirroring his stance and pushing forwards. They circled each other, glaring. Each threatened the other to make the first move.

Aurok's feathers bristled, and his eyes pinned. The gryphs' audacity to be this ungrateful struck him deeply. If he needed to root it out, he would. He owed it to Trein to control them.

"They're your ancestors, too, if you've forgotten," The yellow gryphon said. "We should be honouring their deaths by spilling the blood of *theirs*."

"A single drop and I will personally deliver you to the wyverns myself," Aurok snapped. He moved in, his chest touching the other's. Now, the disparity in size was laughable, and he saw a glint of regret in the other's eyes.

"Calm down, both of you!" Trein yelled as he approached.

He stopped near them, favouring Aurok's side for the small ounce of protection it might provide against a gryphon with a grudge. Trein placed a taloned forefoot on Aurok's chest, and pushed him back, separating him from the two gryphons. "Challenging your pride isn't going to confer leadership." Trein turned, "And you," he addressed the other gryphons, "no one is holding you here. Take your family and try surviving alone, if you wish. But remember, it's hard out there. If you don't hunt, you don't eat. If you're not watching, you're dead."

One gryphon went quiet, glancing over to his mate and kit. He kept his head low and skulked off, muttering under his breath. Aurok watched the challenger, waiting for a response. A flash of fear opened in his eyes, and he lowered himself. "Fine. But I don't want any of those hoofbacks coming near me."

Aurok opened the feathers on his cheeks. "That can be arranged." He raised his voice, calling the entire camp. "Attention, please, wilders. This is Urugan. You are to avoid him, specifically, until he decides to pull the stick—"

"Okay!" the gryphon snapped, turning and following his friend.

Aurok chuckled and relaxed. As much as he disliked using his size against other gryphs, there was a part of him that enjoyed it. He looked to Trein. "Thank you."

The hippogryph nodded. "You've got a lot of work to do. Keep your head in place and remind them of the alternative." He paused for a moment and clicked his beak. "Don't bully them, otherwise you're no better than a direlord."

Trein was a good leader. He was well-respected, and the wilders followed his orders to the letter. Aurok knew that if he were to manage Rada's clan, he would need to follow Trein's example. A task that was more easily said than done, considering the state of them. Not a single gryph had offered to hunt since they had escaped from the burning wreckage, and with Trein ordering his camp against feeding Aurok's gryphs, their chances of getting food were slim. Trein's action was fair, Aurok admitted, but they were in danger of starving if they didn't commit to hunting.

"So," Aurok broke the silence. "Hunting. I need hunters."

"I'll go," a green opinicus approached them, a somewhat familiar face and someone Aurok remembered seeing around the clangrounds.

"You're Euraiya's friend," he said without thinking.

Lillia craned to meet Aurok's eyes until she stood back to ease her neck. "That's right. Have you heard anything from her?"

He shook his head, the weight returning to him. He missed her. "No. She was hunting, and I can only hope she fled when she could. If she's still out there, I'm hoping she's okay."

Lillia swallowed and nodded. A look of deep concern

crossed her face. "The wyverns attacked so suddenly, I can only hope they didn't catch her."

Aurok's breath caught in his chest. His eyes widened. That voice returned to him: if he had warned the clan, Euraiya would be here with him. Rada would have exile him, and any who stood against him, but those who left would be alive and it would have hopefully been more than he had found now.

"What's wrong?" Lillia asked.

"N-nothing." He couldn't tell her or anyone what he had failed to do. "I didn't think about what might have happened to Euraiya."

She held her breath, and the expression was gone. "We need to get food for the survivors. I counted fifteen adults, including us. Five less than yesterday. I'm not sure about the kits. If we can get a couple more hunters..."

"I'll see what I can do," Aurok said, forcing an air of confidence. There was no guarantee the gryphs would be cooperative, but he needed to try. He looked over the clan and approached the least dejected-looking. Each refused his request for help in one form or another. He sighed deeply. A film of frustration matted in his feathers.

He turned to the group again. "Listen, all of you. We need to eat. That means we need to hunt. Trein's hospitality ends at feeding us, especially when some of us are intent on antagonising him and his camp." He spotted the two gryphons from earlier and eyed them. Both turned away. "I need gryphs to help, otherwise I will hunt with who I have, and we will provide food only for those we can afford to feed. If you don't hunt, you don't eat. Simple as that."

The clan turned to him. Realisation dawned on some faces as the threat was laid out to them. Most gryphs were led by their stomachs, and the threat of hunger was a long forgotten motivator for a well-fed clansgryph. He made a note to remember it for the future. As much as he didn't want to use it, it was a tool that would be available to him.

"This is how it's going to be until we can figure out what we're doing. I was a wilder. Listen to me. I didn't find you only to let you die here. Help me." He stood as tall as he could manage, trying to hide the shaking in his shoulders as a mix of anxiety and adrenaline filled him. He looked over the clan, feeling their pain. They had lost so much. Silver was right, though. They needed to keep living.

Three gryphs offered to help. Between the five of them, they would only need three kills each, then one or two carcasses for the kits. He organised where each gryph would hunt, making sure they were close enough to hear any communications between them. An eagle's screech would signal trouble and a call for help, should it come to that. They broke and prepared for their hunt. While he didn't expect trouble, he had to remember they were unprided within a direlord's borders.

11

THE SECOND TRIAL

E uraiya gasped and sat up. She choked short breaths as her eyes darted around the cave. Another nightmare, the same one as before, in such strong, vivid detail. She could smell the smoke, hear the screams, and feel the sticky, sickly blood on her chest as another gryph was slaughtered.

She brought a paw to her chest. Every feather stood stiffly to warn away her imaginary predators. Heat drained from her face as the realisation of safety returned. The nightmare disappeared from her mind. Her clan was not burning.

A throat cleared, and the nest jerked. She jumped. A white gryphon stared at her from the edge of the nest, eyeing her with disapproval. The gryphon's tail whipped back and forth behind her. Euraiya blinked a few times, clearing the sleep. Before her stood another of Naralin's children. It was clear that they were coordinators of most, if not all of the assignments in the clan.

"Euraiya," she said. "Your second trial will begin today. You're joining us in the morning hunt." She nudged the nest again, impatiently.

Euraiya's world slowly came together as the sleep faded. She looked at Eural, who slept on a pile of pelts. He didn't stir. He'd sleep through anything, she mused bitterly. The nightmare had unsettled her, and she was tired. Her sleeping habits had been forcibly changed after she had spent the last week in her new clan. *Pride.*

"Who're you?" Euraiya's words fell out of her beak. She didn't have the energy to correct herself with a more polite question.

"Tayrin," she responded simply. "Now let's go. I was under the impression that the bear had told you." The gryphon gestured to the snoring, slumbering mess of twisted limbs beside the nest. Euraiya wondered how Eural could feel even remotely comfortable.

Euraiya looked Tayrin over properly, now that she could see. She didn't look much like her father, more similar to the second dire in the group, particularly due to her feathery mane. Perhaps it was her mother. Across the top of her head and down her neck was the slightest hint of grey, pale enough to seem like a trick of the light.

Euraiya moved out of the nest, glancing at Eural again. "Should I tell him?" She didn't want to.

"I made it clear to him yesterday. He knows," Tayrin responded curtly, herding Euraiya out of the cave with her wing. "Let's go, let's go."

Euraiya huffed. She was not prepared to move this quickly.

Tayrin lead Euraiya through the mountains, winding between the ranges, not speaking a word for the half-mark they flew. Euraiya was left to her own thoughts of the previous night. She had pretended to be asleep when Eural returned to the nest. He hadn't said anything but had still taken his spot next to her as usual. When he slept near her, she felt an old comfort and truly slept.

She was beginning to regret her behaviour now that she had calmed down. It would be some time before the uneasiness faded. Figuring things out between them was proving to be difficult, with their differing schedules and Eural rigidly holding to a well-established routine and duty to his pride. She didn't know when she'd see him next, nor did she know if she could. Her mind turned to the test before her. If she didn't pass this, she might never see him again.

The smell of greenery filled Euraiya's nares, and she cast a glance at the dense shrubbery she and Tayrin flew over. Animals were barely waking and beginning their own search for food. She could smell something else mixing within the air, something familiar, yet different. She had scented it on a lot of her food. Salt.

"Where are we going?" she asked, raising her voice above the wind.

"Hunting," Tayrin replied quickly. "Need to see what you can do."

"I was a hunter for fractures. I can *show* you," Euraiya said.

Whatever Tayrin said next was lost to the air.

The ground broke into endless sand and water. The scent of salt was now overpowering, making Euraiya's eyes water. New sounds filled her ears, the calls of unknown birds and the constant, loud washing of water. It was both soothing and exciting.

She sank into white sand as they lighted. She played with it between her digits, letting it run around the edges of her paw.

It was fun for all of a few beats, until the sand stuck in her fur. A shake of her paw did nothing to rid her of the rising itch. She preened at the grains, trying to remove them. The earthy taste of sand filled her tongue, she spat.

Tayrin was unimpressed. "You really are a remnant, aren't you?" Before Euraiya could respond, she continued. "While the group is searching for a big kill, you'll catch fish." She gestured toward the ocean. "I expected you to catch at least five fish within the half-mark, but now I'll be surprised if you manage even one."

Euraiya looked out over the water. She'd never flown over the ocean, let alone tried to hunt in it. She had spent her entire life in the small, landlocked confines of Rada's borders. She had never seen a body of water larger than a lake. Fear flickered within her. The ocean was incredible, and if a lake was anything to go by, dangerous. Tayrin already looked disappointed. Euraiya needed to prove herself quickly. The thought bolstered her. Surely, it wouldn't be too difficult to fish. She was a strong hunter and should be able manage it.

Euraiya rushed over into the water, her paws submerging into the damp sand. The sharp plunge in temperature shocked her body and froze her. A cold tingle spiked up her limbs and through her. She screeched and lifted into the air, hovering. She stared down, her paws soaked and dripping.

"You're not serious," Tayrin's displeased voice came from the beach. "You've never even seen the ocean?"

Euraiya turned, "No. Rada's clan was far enough inland that we didn't need to."

Tayrin sighed and followed after her with laboured and forced pumps of her wings. She looked over Euraiya with flattened ears and half-lidded eyes. "I'm going to have to show you, aren't I? Fishing is a common practice in the pride. We own a good portion of the ocean, so it's expected that you'll catch fish for it." She sighed again at Euraiya's curious look. "Follow me."

Tayrin took Euraiya further out until they hover over a mass of moving black shapes. The fish separated and congealed together, moving around between each other like the lights of the Fracture. Euraiya watched with wide-eyed fascination. Tayrin called for her attention. She hovered higher, watching the shapes and keenly following individual fish. Then, in a swift and solid movement, she swooped over in a long arc. Her foretalons touched the surface, clasped, and pulled something from the water. The fluidity and confidence of her movements made it look easy.

"That's the most basic method. If you can't do that... spirits save you," she said.

The only time Euraiya had seen fish was when it was presented as a gift to the clan. One that was consumed by their direlord. The fish wriggled in Tayrin's grip, trying to escape. Her talons punctured the fish, and it went still. Its pungent odour caught Euraiya by surprise, and she nearly gagged. It reminded her of the wilder leader. Her expression must have been obvious.

"This is a fish. You eat it." Tayrin exampled this by holding the fish above her face and dropping it down her throat.

"I know what a fish is. This one is just...alive." Euraiya shuddered.

Tayrin sighed gruffly. "Do what I did. Below us is a 'school,' it's like a pride. Except it's fish."

As Tayrin had, Euraiya brought herself higher into the air. She looked down at the school. Her eyes followed one fish, then another, and lost them both within the mass. She couldn't focus on a single fish. This wasn't like hunting rodents or pulling frogs from the bank. Tayrin's gaze urged her to move, and she dropped down. She held her claws out.

Her wings touched the surface. The force of her upswing pulled her down, and the ocean rushed to meet her. Water rushed through her nares and beak and burned her eyes. She gasped, and it rushed down her throat. Panic gripped her as the sky drifted away. She kicked and grabbed and thrashed, barely able to bring herself back above the surface. Her lungs became heavy, and fear took over. She screamed, bubbles rushing above her.

She was lightheaded. Everything left her quickly. She kicked again, trying to keep afloat. It did little good. She could only manage just enough air to keep her lungs filled for another few seconds. She was going to die.

Something grabbed her foreleg from above. She pulled at it, trying to claw her way out of her soon-to-be prison. The grabber dug its sharp talons into her wrist and heaved her from the water. She gasped loudly, filling her lungs with air again. She hung limp above the water as Tayrin took her to shore, her tail limply dragging behind her on the surface. She stared below her, shocked. The calming, soothing ocean had turned into a grasping monster, ready to swallow her. Tayrin calmly dragged her back to shore.

Euraiya coughed and spluttered as she lay on the wet sand. She gasped loudly, rolling onto her side. She coughed and spat, freeing her chest from the blockage. Her head pounded and spun. She looked to Tayrin, confused.

"You thought you were a fish," Tayrin mused, her crest feathers rising. She chuckled, the first sign of emotion since she'd met her. She may have joined her, had she not almost drowned. "That's a fail. We've got a while before we're moving on. So, let's see if you can learn to fish."

Euraiya's head rushed as she sat up. She slouched, trying to ease her dizziness. "I'm not doing that again."

"You will if you want to be prided. All hunters can fish." She threw a fish on the ground and pointed at it. "Get up, and do that again. If it helps, pretend the water is the ground. You don't charge at the ground, do you?"

When she didn't move, Tayrin repeated herself more forcefully. "Get up." She watched her. "I can make sure you remain Euraiya the Prideless if you're determined to act like a kit. Don't think I don't know what happened at the arena."

Anger flashed through her, and she found her paws. She wanted to leave that behind her. She should have expected that the coordinators would share her failures. She followed Tayin's direction, her lightheadedness forgotten and replaced by determination. She would not be made a wilder.

She lifted and rose, hovering above the ground, level with the trees. While the fish was unmoving it was the perfect target for training the eye. Now in her element, the movements came to her as easily as breathing. She swooped low, grabbed, and returned to the sky. The tips of her wings had flicked ground.

"Do it again," Tayrin commanded.

She lifted and pulled back. In her mind, the sand melted into an ocean around her. She was back to where she had started. The fish was near the surface, close enough that she could catch it if she tried. She glided down towards the target, her claws outstretched and clutched the fish. She pulled up again, holding her prize. The sand returned.

"Not *that* hard, is it?" Tayrin said. "At least you're not useless as a swooper. Again."

Euraiya dropped the fish and swooped it over and over.

Tayrin didn't let her try the water again. One near-death experience was enough for the day.

"The sea is dangerous, as you learned today. It's always angry, and you need to respect it." Tayrin looked over the calm water. "Even now, you can't trust it." She returned her gaze back to Euraiya, "You need to control your flight. A single clip of your wings and you can crash to your death. If no one is around to help you, you'll drown. I'm not teaching you how to swim. Now, again."

They continued until a jay called in the distance. That was their summon. Prey had been found, and Euraiya, ready to put her honed skills to use, followed Tayrin eagerly.

THE HIGH ALTITUDE AIR CHILLED EURAIYA'S NARES WHEN SHE looked down. The varied ranges of Naralin's pridelands were vast and surprising. Ahead were thin trees at the base of the snow-covered mountains, below them a forest surrounded by rows of mountains and crags, and a half-mark behind them was the vicious ocean that had almost killed Euraiya. Comparatively, Rada's territory consisted of a single grassy plain, a lake, and the forest.

Her simple life of hunting for Rada's clan and watching new applicants fight for entry had seemed almost perfect at a time when she didn't know better. Now that she'd experienced more of the world, seen gryphons and opinici work together, and felt the comforts of civilisation, she could see her old clan for what it truly was: a trap. One designed to ensure that none would tip Rada's balance of power.

And she still experienced new things with the pride. She had fished, been within Naralin's audience chambers, and was soon to see how they hunted. Her enjoyment, however, was only undermined by the fact that everything that was new and exciting to her was mundane to any other gryph within the pride.

It made her past seem bleak and uninteresting. Functional, spacious shelters now seemed crude and cramped, her culture boorish, and their direlord tyrannical. It was a depressing thought, but one that sparked a new flame within her, further driving her to join this new world.

Euraiya and Tayrin tucked their wings and dove through a gap in the trees, landing quietly near three opinici hiding amongst the brush. Tayrin hushed Euraiya and crouched beside them. Euraiya knew not to make a sound but followed Tayrin's instructions regardless.

Ahead of them, a bear slept in the middle of a clearing, basking in the sun between the trees.

"That's all?" Tayrin asked one of the hunters.

"'Fraid so. I'd've looked further, but not much's left," one of the opinici said. "Bears spreadin' out, gettin' harder t' find."

"Damn. Alright. The Prideless will be helping us. Cooperate." The last word was directed to the other hunters with a hint of warning. They nodded. Euraiya wondered what had been said before her arrival.

Euraiya flexed her claws. This was her element. Opinici were naturally stronger ground hunters, as opposed to gryphs, whose talons were better suited to swooping from the air. An opinicus' size, sleeker shape, and claws made them better hunters along the forest floor.

She eyed the bear as it slept. Its torso undulated with each breath. It was of fair size, one that would prove challenging should it be awoken. But asleep, it was a simple target. She considered her approach. She could sneak through the brush and pounce. A strike to its eyes and throat, and it would be dead. She had done it before, and she could do so again. The confidence of one hundred kills pushed her forwards, but she halted when Tayrin made a quick, disapproving chirp.

"It goes for you, too. You're hunting with us, or not at all," she said.

Euraiya eyed her. Any question Euraiya was about to voice was left unanswered as one of the opinici tossed a rock at the bear's head. It stirred and woke. It stood up groggily and looked for its attacker.

"What are you doing?" Euraiya hissed. "We could have killed it in its sleep."

"Yes," Tayrin said. "But you would be untested. Any gryph worth feeding can hunt from the bushes."

"'Sides, s'more fun this way," an opinicus chuckled. Euraiya was beginning to dislike that particular one.

"Now," Tayrin said, "Prideless will take the back. Dig in and keep it distracted." She gestured to the other opinici, "You three take each other side. Once surrounded, I will take the kill. Understand?"

The three opinici called the affirmative. Tayrin eyed Euraiya expectantly.

Euraiya was denied her chance to prove herself. She could have killed that bear.

"Got it," she said bitterly.

The four opinici skulked into the foliage around the bear while Tayrin waited. Euraiya watched the bear, locking her eyes on it in the clearing. She kept her claws out and dug at the ground, waiting for a signal. She heard Tayrin's command and burst out.

The bear whirled around and growled deeply. It stood and hulked over Euraiya, larger than Tayrin.

Euraiya's ears flattened, and she took a step back,

bravado faltering. She swallowed and forced herself forwards, raising her wings in challenge. The bear stalked closer, stopped, and roared. Bits of spittle flew in Euraiya's face.

Adrenaline filled her body. She pushed to the side and away. Excitement rose as she rounded the bear and jumped on its flanks, sinking her claws deep into its flesh along its side. The bear rose on two legs and shook its body, but Euraiya held. The flesh ripped, and Euraiya lost some of her grip. She grasped at a patch of seemingly endless fur.

Euraiya saw one of the hunters run in front of the bear and nip at its leg as she went past. Another did the same, clipping its side with her claws. The bear lunged at them, always failing to catch them. It fell to its fours, almost throwing Euraiya off.

Euraiya crawled up and dug her beak deep into its nape. The taste of flesh and blood filled covered her tongue. The bear roared and tried to shake her again. The three opinici were relentless in their tactic. They screeched at it, trying to draw its attention away from the previous attacker. The bear turned in circles as each opinicus led it in a new direction. Euraiya's biting further distracted it, periodically reminding it she was there.

Tayrin approached from the side. She pounced as the bear rose to its feet again. In one swift motion, her beak was at its neck, her body dragging the bear's head to the ground. Euraiya dug in deeper and tore the flesh away. Tayrin did the same. The bear crashed to the ground.

Euraiya rolled off the kill and admired their work. "Interesting."

Tayrin nodded. The other three opinici approached from their points. "Indeed. You would be surprised at the usefulness of teamwork in a hunt, Prideless. I'd advise you to keep it in mind."

She looked at the group as they began tearing the bear apart. It was a common practice that allowed the group to take the bear back in pieces, rather than trying to coordinate a flight effort. Had she cared to join the hunts in Rada's clan, she would have done this as well. She realised, though, that she didn't know how Rada's teams stalked their prey or the tactics they used to kill it. She had acted so early and alone for so long that she only knew how to work as such. She avoided larger targets for that reason. She had held herself in high esteem for not needing to work with others, but now, she doubted that she had any right to. What would have been a difficult fight was made kitsplay with a team.

Tayrin's shout snapped her out of her thoughts. "Wilders! Secure the kill!"

Euraiya's eyes widened, and she spun around. She saw shapes in the distance, each low to the ground. She watched them, edging forwards with the group. The wilders muttered amongst themselves. She expected a call for backup.

"Leave, both of you!" Tayrin shouted at the wilders. "You're outnumbered and outclassed."

Euraiya narrowed her eyes, squinting at the shapes. She recognised a gryphon and an opinicus, or perhaps it was a hippogryph. She joined her team in raising their wings in a display of unified power, threatening the would-be thieves. It worked, and the wilders retreated.

Euraiya and the group turned to the kill to finish their job. They each grabbed pieces of the bear and left for the pridelands.

As they flew over the forest, Euraiya considered the

wilders. She had seen a side to them that most never saw. In a way, she pitied the wilders. They were surviving in their own way, a way that prided gryphs across the land hated. Her opinion of them had changed, as much as she didn't want to admit it. Although she still resented the hippogryphs, the wilders themselves weren't a threat, unlike the wyverns who had destroyed everything she held close. If there were any creature that gryphs should abhor, it was wyverns. She huffed, suppressing those thoughts. If she empathised with the wilders, she might lose track of her goal.

Her memories drifted to Rada's clan, and her stomach churned as a wave of sickness flushed over her. She hoped that Aurok, by some miracle, had survived the attack, although it was nearly impossible. The attack had been sudden and devastating. She would never see him or anyone from her clan again. Her chest tightened as memories of Lillia and Aurok returned to her. She missed them. Her emotions were becoming a little easier to manage but still overwhelmed her at times. Eural and the pride had distracted her, but now, the hole forming under her was threatening to swallow her. She hated being alone, for those thoughts would return eventually.

"See Eural when we get back." Tayrin flew beside her. "Talk to him. Or anyone, for that matter."

Euraiya sniffed. She looked over at the gryphon.

"Not me," Tayrin said. "Someone who has time for it."

She flushed. It sounded like an insult, despite the look on Tayrin's face that suggested otherwise.

"Look," she said quickly, "it's going to take a bit for the pride to come to a conclusion about you. Take that time to learn some things, make some friends, and try not to think too hard. It'll be difficult, but you'll come out better for it."

"So you're saying to not think about it?" Euraiya snapped.

"My solution is to distract yourself and let everything take its natural course. You have a life to live, for now. You'll still have one if you don't make it." She paused and clicked her beak. "I'm sure Inilrin has given you her sage advice."

Life doesn't stop for tragedy. The words echoed in her head.

"I'll see how it goes." Euraiya meant it. If there was going to be a positive conclusion, she would need to sway them. If her trials weren't going to impress them, then she needed to find something that would.

12

PROGRESS

Aurok paced, waiting for two hunters who had yet to return. If gryphs had died on their first hunting assignment, he would never forgive himself. He made an abortive move to where he had last seen them. But the camp still needed him.

Trein waited, watching him. "Give them time."

"Time?" Aurok snapped. "They've been gone too long! Do we know if we're far enough from the wyve—"

The hunters' shapes appeared in the distance, and Aurok relaxed with an audible sigh, tension leaving his body. Trein padded next to him.

The hunters' wings pumped with an erratic beat, their faces shocked and chests heaving, their landing almost indistinguishable from a crash. Something had happened in the forest.

"We had a run in with another pride," one breathed. "They stole our kill." He was an average-looking, orange-feathered gryphon but deserved credit for stepping up when no other would.

"Four opinici and a gryphon leader," a brown opinicus

added. By his ragged feathers, the encounter had struck him hardest.

Aurok cursed. "Naralin's pride. What are they doing this far out?"

His hunters shrugged.

"Keep away from them. They're never in a group less than five," Aurok said.

Trein nodded. "Keep out of their feathers. I don't want the likes of Naralin coming down on us. Of all the direlords, he's the most protective of his borders."

"That's not a surprise," Aurok scoffed. Naralin had a poor reputation for friendliness. He was a strong leader and well-liked within his pride, but when his power was threatened, he was ruthless in its defence. His reputation left him on uneasy grounds with most other gryphs in the land. Wilders, in particular, both despised and feared him. They were lucky that he left them alone in return for taking every exile that was passed on to them. It was an act of quiet destruction disguised as mutual benefit. While it placated Naralin's critics within his pride, it strained the wilders' resources and left their stomachs empty.

Trein's camp had made contact with other wilders, which had opened an avenue of information but not of trade. Aurok was lucky that Trein passed that information on to him. Aurok, however, had yet to figure out how to use it. He had no direction and a lack of resources. The current hunting grounds were too far away, and the open lands provided them no cover or hiding space. He still relied on Trein's kindness to help him and his gryphs through this.

Aurok looked back to his camp. In truth, he had no idea what to call them. They weren't a pride, nor were they wilders. They were lost. Thanks to the earlier hunt they had some food, but that would only last them today. They would need to hunt again and again. The recurring thought that he would not see them die of starvation after avoiding conflagration weighed on him. He needed to step up and find a way to lead them until he found a more permanent solution.

Direlords were a blight on these lands. Aurok had joined Rada's clan for the security of a large community and the simplicity that a prided lifestyle offered. He had once been optimistic his views on direlords were misled. Only when Rada had imprisoned him and Ter had interrogated, beaten, and starved him, did he realise his mistake. Yet, because of Euraiya, he had tried again. He'd been given a reason to stay.

The way Rada led his clan, if one could call it leading, was exactly what Aurok had expected. From the moment he'd stepped into those grounds, Rada's mission had been to use him as a pawn against the wilders, forcing him to shed his name and past in exchange for the supposed safety his clan offered. The safety that had shattered the moment the flames began burning.

He would never join another pride. But, he wondered almost bitterly, if he was founding one.

Aurok left the group to meet with Lillia and Fenri. Fenri looked over the healing burns of two kits. They cried and squealed, screaming for their parents. Aurok's heart sunk for them both, but more for one in particular. Not all kits were lucky to escape with their parents. Fenri coddled the kit, trying to sooth her cries. It was the best she would be able to do.

"How are they doing?" he asked.

"It's nothing to be worried about," Lillia said. "We just need to make sure the burns don't get infected."

Aurok looked over Lillia's work. She had brought fresh water, washed the wound, and covered it with some clean material and salve that Trein's gryphs had provided her. The same salve that Euraiya had never received.

"You were medicinal?" He asked. At her curious look, he clarified. "Carer."

"Oh, no. My mother was, and she taught me some things. Euraiya kept my skills sharp." She chuckled lightly.

"That doesn't surprise me," Aurok said. Two parents held their kit softly, allowing Lillia to do her work. He offered them a supportive puff of his feathers. "Do we have any other carers?"

"I don't know. The clan refuses to do anything," Lillia said.

"If I need to step in again, I will. Surely we have at least *one* carer around here." Aurok raised his head, looking over the camp. Some gryphs were with their families, while others were alone and quiet. There were no obvious signs as to which gryph was trained in what assignment. Carers didn't identify themselves as easily as guards did. Even then, they were uninterested in assisting. Injured gryphs were ignored by those closest to them. Rada's culture wasn't designed for their situation. Aurok sighed. He needed to fix this.

"You can teach me," Fenri said. A little kit squirmed in her hold, but was beginning to calm. "I can help."

Fenri had proven herself useful in their escape from the wyverns by calling to gryphs lost in the fire, although Aurok had his doubts she had the personality or strength to be a carer. She had grown close to Lillia, likely in an attempt to distract herself from thoughts of her missing mate.

Lillia nodded, "Yes. We can work on things as we go."

"Thank you, both of you. I'll see to it that you receive food for your effort." It was the least he could do. Aurok turned and made for the middle of camp. He sighed, looking over the gryphs as he walked by. He didn't have it in him to make another speech. He wasn't a leader, as much as Trein thought he could be. He didn't know if they would listen to him or if he would make the correct decisions. Yet, he was the only one willing to take charge. He would grow as a leader over time, if he didn't kill them first. He wanted to do so much. He wanted them to have a new home, to work together and grow as a family, and to exist peacefully. In truth, he wanted to teach them to be wilders. But he needed their cooperation and patience while he tried to make things work.

Trein caught Aurok's attention, and he stopped.

Trein's shoulders were squared, and his wings slightly raised. "We have an issue," he said. "A few of my hunters returned from the wilder camp down south. They're saying that wyverns have been seen further within Rada's borders."

Aurok's eyes widened, his stomach sunk, and his hackles rose. An urgency filled him, a sudden panic. If the wyverns descended on them, they wouldn't stand a chance.

"We need to move." He didn't want to force them to leave only days after they had stopped. Part of being a wilder was being prepared to live nomadically. As a wilder, Aurok had followed Trein to six different locations. He had seen how Trein held himself and how he directed his gryphs. Now, it was Aurok's turn to move his own camp. It would be hard, but it needed to be done.

"We're leaving tomorrow," Trein said. "That'll give us more than enough time to find a better spot between Naralin's and Kristel's borders and keep out of their sight."

Aurok growled under his breath. "If it's not one thing, it's another."

Trein chuckled, placing a talon on Aurok's shoulder, the

act requiring him to stand on his hooves. "Welcome to leadership."

Aurok sighed.

Trein pulled himself away and turned. "Untwist your tail from your leg and prepare your camp. We're leaving with or without them."

Aurok turned to his camp. The gryphs needed someone to guide them. These weren't wilders who knew how to survive outside of a pride; they knew a life of safety and control. Telling them to act wasn't going to be enough. He needed to lead them. He swallowed and held himself tall.

"Listen up," he shouted. "We need to move again. Don't grumble. This is an unfortunate part of our lives, but it needs to be done." He stopped and considered his words. They had just survived an attack and would panic. "Naralin and Kristel are about to divide these lands between themselves, and they don't take kindly to gryphs like us." In truth, he didn't know when that would happen, but it would be soon. Direlords descended on emptied lands like vultures on a corpse. "If we don't move, they will kill us. Another day, and we can find a place to truly set up. I promise."

"You promise?" Urugan came from within the small crowd of gryphs, skulking between them. "You promised to save us before, and now half of us are starving!"

"They're starving because only a talonful of you offered to hunt," Aurok said, his hackles rising.

Urugan approached him. "And who's fault is that?"

"If they don't hunt, they don't feed." Aurok knew Urugan was trapping him. He had to watch his words.

Urugan huffed. "We don't know these lands, Aurok. If you don't show us where to go, we can't hunt. I've seen you, laying around with your hippogryph friend. Instead of talking and yelling, perhaps you can do something."

"That's not—"

Urugan pushed in further, his beak inches from Aurok's face. "You're leading us to our death." A few gryphs cried their support. They stood behind Urugan. "We can't trust you and those...beasts," he threw a talon at Trein's camp.

"You can't go by yourselves," Aurok said. "If Naralin and Kristel don't get to you first, the wyverns will. We don't know where their burrows are. You need to come with us or you'll die!"

"We don't need to do anything. We're fine where we are." Urugan turned and faced Rada's clan. "Any of you who want to live, then stay here with me. Let those with a death wish start walking."

The gryphs murmured amongst themselves, uneasiness settling across them. Some stood and began walking with Trein's camp, others stayed where they were. Mates began to squabble, fighting over whether to stay or go, friends cried after each other as they left. Aurok stared, stunned. His ears and feathers flattened as he realised what had happened. The light of his confidence drained, shadowed by the gryphon in front of him.

Urugan snorted air from his nares. "Good luck out there, Aurok. You'll need it."

"You can't do this. Please, think about what you're doing," Aurok said. He knew he was begging.

Urugan scoffed. "Take your tail and go die with the rest of them." He took his gryphs away to the forest, not caring to look at who joined him.

He's a fool, Aurok thought. Prided gryphs living in the wilderness would be lucky to survive to the next fracture.

Lillia nudged Aurok's side. He didn't know how long she had been there. "Come on," she said softly.

"O-okay." He cleared his throat, addressing the

remaining gryphs. "Those of you who are coming, we need to move now. We'll find somewhere better. Trust me." He felt subdued and unsure. What had seemed like an easy script to follow had crumbled in his throat. He followed Trein's camp, words lost. Those who followed him were silent.

A roar echoed behind them.

13

CASLIR

Naralin sat on his nest-throne as still as the platform it stood on. Naralin's tightened beak and stiff back made Eural uneasy and wary. The chamber was sparse of gryphs aside from Naralin's mate and daughter. Eural and Ilir, a white gryphon and Eural's assigned partner, stood at either side of his throne, with one dired guard on each of the side platforms. Unease gripped Eural, heightened by the guards at the entrance of the hallway, who turned away any upper-tier pridesmember demanding to be part of the audience. The chamber was closed, and Naralin only did so when something concerned him.

Whispers of the upcoming meeting with the foreign direlord met Eural's ears as Naralin talked with his advisors. His daughter, Ainlin, was a reflection of her father in many ways. The only noticeable difference was the softness in her feathers and demeanour. She didn't share his intensity nor his penchant for displays of power. Ainlin was his advisor and next in line to lead the pride and during Eural's time guarding their direlord had yet to steer him wrong.

Beside Naralin's nest stood Reniya, a smoky grey dire

gryphon. She was his mate and secondary advisor, voicing her own thoughts to their conversation.

"Father, Caslir's vagueness is a sign of poor conduct. He means to surprise and undermine you," Ainlin said. She always maintained a respectable posture in her father's presence.

"Caslir has been a private dire since he was born. He is young, much as you are," Naralin said.

Eural noted that even to his own family, Naralin's gaze was harsh and his voice strict. However, the edge that Eural often heard in Naralin's voice, the one that had cut through Euraiya, softened.

"I understand," Ainlin said. "But Caslir has been seen with different pride leaders in the last few cycles. No good words have come from them."

"Elaborate," Naralin said.

"There have been multiple claims of broken trades and agreements," Ainlin said.

Naralin scoffed. His posture and stern demeanour broke, and he stared at his daughter incredulously. "You are ill, Ainlin."

Ainlin huffed, letting out a frustrated whine. "Father, listen to me. No other direlord has broken down their trades in as little time as Caslir."

Naralin shuffled his feathers and returned to his usual stiff, high-backed pose. "Because he is a poor leader, you assume he has ill intentions."

If the comment fazed Ainlin, she didn't make it known. She continued, "On top of which, many of his meetings have been private, much like the one he has organised with you."

"My meeting will not be private. All present here will witness it and intervene when necessary. He has been restricted to two guards and no more." In many cases, direlords were permitted to bring a retinue of guards with them. The restriction spoke well of Naralin's concerns.

'All present' only included five gryphs. That was a strange comment to make, Eural thought. He had excluded an audience yet wanted this small group to witness the exchange. Even his other children hadn't been permitted to join them. Had that been one of Caslir's conditions?

"Naralin," Reniya motioned. "Ainlin's concern is not entirely unwarranted. Caslir is a renegade. He causes trouble where he steps. I am still convinced that he has a connection to the death of Rada's clan. He was seen speaking to Rada days before the attack."

"Merely coincidence," Naralin dismissed. "I might say the same about the Prideless, as she was in the forest when the attack commenced." He gave Reniya a sidelong glance, "but that does not make it true." Eural couldn't help but to agree. Just because Caslir had been speaking to direlords before and after the attack didn't make him responsible for it.

"You did say that about her, and it was not true," Reniya huffed. "Perhaps we should listen to the Prideless' warnings. You must be careful."

Naralin often ignored his mate. Eural assumed she was mostly there for show despite her experience within the throne chamber. For as long as Eural was present in the pride, Naralin had cut her down.

"Wyverns attacked Rada's clan, not Caslir," Naralin said. "Lenrin assures me that his strikers have not seen a wyvern since the attack. They have fled their burrows."

"Do you not think that is strange?" Ainlin asked. "We have often seen—" She took an abortive step forwards as a guard called from the entrance.

"Dire, your guests have arrived early. Shall we see them in?" he said.

"Yes, let us. I would like to see Caslir's intentions for myself," Naralin said. He readjusted his position on the nest in preparation for Caslir's arrival.

Ainlin took her place next to Reniya at the side of the throne.

A young dire walked into the chamber, a pale violet gryphon in tow. Both mantled deeply to their host.

Eural's eyes widened as he realised who was before him. Caslir's red feathers were a rare sight to behold, the same colour as the cloth that draped behind Naralin. The top of his head was white, splitting the vermilion colour behind his ears. Long feathers flowed down his neck to a mane more svelte and contained than the mountain gryphs. Patches of black flowed down his back, turning into a strong, leonine body. His eyes were filled with fire as they unflinchingly stared into Naralin's intense gaze. For such a young dire, and despite the little land he claimed for his own, Caslir was as imposing as any other direlord. He was an old world gryphon, one with a lineage that traced back to the creation of the dires. He carried an air of self-importance that declared to the world he was a born ruler despite being forced to the barren edges of the land. It was almost inspiring, were he not so conceited.

"Dire Naralin, thank you for seeing me," he said.

"Dire Caslir." Naralin nodded. "We welcome you to our pridelands." They were the same words as spoken by all direlords, each replaced with a different name. Eural didn't understand why they hid behind pleasantries when it was well known that most direlords were not allies or even friends.

The next words that Caslir spoke were nothing that an

undired could comprehend. They were whimsical and elegant, like a song woven into words. It was a shared language between leaders of all species across the land used only for diplomatic means. It always sounded incredible and beautiful despite the weight those words usually carried. Had it not been used to ignite wars and demand exile and executions, it would be an art form.

Naralin's gaze steeled against Caslir. He raised a talon, cutting the dire off. "You will speak in a way where all present will understand you."

Ainlin made a pleased hum.

Eural's gaze turned to Naralin. This was an unusual request, and a concerning one. Their language was designed to prevent others from understanding discussions, so as not to object or leak the information. Naralin wanted this to be candid.

If Caslir was disappointed, it was well masked. "I come without trade, I must admit. The gryphons I do have are all useful and loyal to my pride. While their colours are not as well-suited as your fine pridemembers," Caslir gestured towards Eural and the other undired guard, "I believe we hunt well. I do, however, have a diplomatic offer for you."

Naralin raised his head, looking down at the dire through his beak. This was a common gesture of curiosity. "Speak."

"The current system of prides has plateaued. While I do admire our current arrangements, I cannot offer you much, and that does not benefit either of us, does it?" Caslir spoke with authority, but something in his voice made Eural tense. A glance to Naralin's family confirmed his agitation was shared.

Naralin narrows his eyes. "I do not appreciate where this is going, Dire Caslir. I have heard this before."

"As you might have!" Caslir said with conviction, his own feathers raising in a jovial, excited expression. "My parents have offered it to you before."

The mention of Caslir's parents slickened Naralin's feathers, and his red eyes pinned. He was old, much older than most of his pride, and had dealt with the old world dires more than once. He made a subtle, restless gesture. The guards on either side of the room tense and crouched. The two dired gryphs growled, the noise resonating through the room.

Caslir raised his head high. It was impossible to misinterpret the smugness on his face. "I, Caslir of the God's Tear, will be reclaiming the land for the dires. We will unite our rule, and the undired will serve us as they did in the time of my ancestors. I will lead us to the same glory we once enjoyed." His wings pulled away from his sides, squaring his body, daring Naralin to approach him.

Naralin held the room's silence. Eural noted subtle movements in Naralin's posture, he fought for a composure his feathers didn't grant him. "You dare bring old rhetoric to my chambers and expect me to relinquish my lands for an unstable rule that was overthrown by the undired." Naralin lost the battle, and his wings squared as Caslir's had. His feathers stood high as he rose to his full height. "Your parents have taught you gryphspittle."

"With all due respect, Dire Naralin, my ancestors' rule was well-proven. It was Blackbeak that destroyed us, not their leadership."

"And she was correct to do so. The Blackbeak Rebellion was of their doing. I will not kill my pride for sport or starve them for food, as did your ancestors. I may keep a tight grasp on my borders, but I am no tyrant. Our numbers require the assistance of the undired to continue our rule.

We rule these lands as our own, not scrambling for control like those before you."

Caslir tilted his head, staggered. He raised his voice to match Naralin's. "You rule as equals to the undired. You allow them to surround you. Your own daughter is lowered to a mere advisor and a diplomat to the gem-scratchers of Kristel's pride." The feathers on his head and neck rose, framing his face like a crown, a calm ember now replaced by a burning flame. His eyes turned on Ainlin. "You arrange for your heirs to mate with dired diluted by generations of poor breeding. You should be promoting our strength and creation with the pure." The insinuation sat clear across the room.

Ainlin made a struck, disgusted huff.

Naralin remained on his nest. He held more power from there and would only budge against a physical challenge. "You insult my family deeply. My daughter will mate with a respectable dire until they produce their first. It will not be some young, upstart inbreed with a keen thirst." He let that sit for a moment, glancing to Ainlin as she shifted her wings uncomfortably. He turned his full attention back to Caslir. "My pride is my life, and they serve me loyally. My rule carries strong, because I rule it to its greatest potential. Not to the potential of it serving me."

"They serve you as a leader, not a direlord."

"And yours to you as a brainwashed tyrant. Take your weak, struggling pride and return to the Edges where you belong. I cannot believe you dare to call yourself 'of the God's Tear.' Dire Kristel owns those lands, not you."

A harsh, single noted laugh cracked from Caslir's beak. "The God's Tear remains ours. We were the first dires, and we will be the last. Regardless of where Kristel claims her borders."

"Your claims mean nothing. Your words and our reality are two very different things." Naralin was losing his composure. Venom seeped out in his words as Caslir dared to press further against him.

"Consider your words returned to you, Kinsbane," Caslir said. "You speak of loyalty, when you sit in blood."

A loud roar echoed through the chamber walls, deafening those present. In a flash of white feathers, Naralin dismounted his throne and rounded Caslir. His tail thrashed behind him. "You dare speak of that within my chambers!" Naralin growled heavily as stricken anger appeared in every visible form.

Caslir stood firm, allowing Naralin to circle him. He followed the white dire as he crossed him. Now, Caslir remained calm, showing Naralin's ferocity for the room to see. "I speak the truth."

Naralin stopped in front of Caslir and growled a very strong and stern warning. The four guards moved forward and stood on either side of their direlord as the two massive gryphons stared each other down. Naralin's ferocity stood against Caslir's composure. A shock of adrenaline coursed through Eural's body as he stood beside Naralin, poised to attack the moment Caslir made a move forwards. He would not survive against a beast almost thrice his size, but his direlord would manage to end it.

"Leave my borders. Do not return," Naralin said darkly.

To Eural's surprise, Caslir mantled slow and contemptuously before taking a few steps back. His feathers and wings returning to a neutral position. "As you wish, Dire. But I should warn you: the rule is failing. An undired pride is a weak pride. Rada's clan is an example of that detriment."

"Out," Naralin snapped. "Out!"

Caslir turned confidently and left the chambers, his head held high. The gryph that had arrived with him, followed behind. Eural had forgotten he was there. Naralin's growling continued, his feathers still raised. He turned sharply to his family. "See to it that all ties are cut with the Edges. I want strikers in his borders. I want to know everything he does."

Ainlin stood stiffly next to her mother. They were cautious about approaching Naralin in such a fiery, dangerous state. "Father, this is what I was concerned about. He is desperate."

Silence sat for an eternity. It was unusual for Naralin to lose control in his court sessions, particularly against another direlord. Naralin's intense glare followed from one gryph to the other as they held their breaths, waiting for his response. Ainlin was surely correct, but her timing was disastrously poor. He looked as if he were about to attack any one of them.

Eural couldn't believe Caslir's gall. He had heard that the old world gryphs were dreamers, clinging to the rule they once had, but he had never seen it directly. Whatever thoughts were crawling through Naralin's head, none of them would be good. He knew Naralin. He knew what Naralin would do to preserve his dominance. When Naralin had been this riled before, it nearly ended in Dire Haynil's death for almost the same reason. Naralin hated the name that followed him. He never denied the stories, and never allowed them to be spoken. To speak of Kinsbane to Naralin's face was to test fate itself.

Eventually, Naralin turned away from the group with a frustrated but conceding grunt. He stalked out of the chamber, his hackles visibly raised. The tension in the air flowed out the hallway with him. "See to it my orders are completed by changemark. My rule will not be challenged by some fledgling from the Edges."

EURAL RETURNED TO HIS NEST. HIS LEGS THREATENED TO GIVE out. Organising the strikers with Tayrin hadn't been easy, especially when his mind kept returning to the events of the throne room. He groaned and lay down, trying to clear his head. He was relieved he wasn't assigned to Caslir's borders. He didn't want to leave Euraiya behind.

He could smell her scent among his nesting materials, and it eased him. He had missed her. Now, after their reunion, his priorities had shifted. Once, his duty to the pride had been his identity. It filled his entire being. He would stand for Naralin at every given opportunity without fail. Now, he wanted to be with Euraiya, the only family he'd had in fractures. He sighed, conflicted between duty to his pride and to his family. He wanted nothing more than to work for his direlord, but if he did, he would rarely see Euraiya.

He would request she join him on assignments, should she survive the trials. The thought excited him until another crossed his mind. If Naralin was setting his sights on Caslir, the assignments would be dangerous. The Edges were almost exclusively filled with dires who despised the outside world, and while Naralin's warriors, dired and undired alike, were trained with strategies to take down a dire, many of them would fall. More concerning was the leadership that governed them. Caslir's grasp on his pride was even stronger than Rada's, fuelled by centuries-old grudges. It was the last dregs of an eroding lineage.

Despite his arrogance, Caslir was an interesting

direlord, Eural mused. He was young, confident, prepared. Comparatively young, to be more correct. Caslir was older than Eural, perhaps by ten or fifteen fractures. This was still young compared Naralin, who had seen at least two generations of gryphs in his lifetime. Regardless, Caslir's words had been rehearsed, as if he'd expected them to fail. He would have known Naralin's disposition when he arrived and should have known he wouldn't succeed. Why had he even tried?

Ainlin had been correct in her observation. Caslir was desperate with very little land to claim and an ever-shrinking border, he was backed into a corner. No dire wanted anything to do with the old world gryphons. At least, that's what Eural hoped.

"Eural?" A familiar voice sounded from the entrance, cutting through his thoughts. Eural shot up and mantled to the huge figure that stood there.

"Lady Ainlin, I'm honoured to welcome you here," he said, following the well-rehearsed script of an undired subject to a Lady.

Ainlin ducked her head, making her way into the cave. She looked around at Eural's displays. She had never visited him personally before, and had never truly seen the presentations and dedications to his career and family. His first armour and weapons, the gifts of silver and gems, they meant almost as much to him as the pride itself, and it filled him with an insurmountable honour for Ainlin to see them.

"Lovely," she commented, seeing the four feathers of his family. His dedication to it. She bowed her head in respect to it, as was Naralin's custom. Her voice was soft, unlike her father's. "You have a lovely lineage, a strong one. Your sister will be impressive, in time."

"I know," Eural said. "She'll realise it one day, too." He

relaxed, then forced himself straight, remembering to whom he was speaking to. "You have business with me, Lady?"

"This is not an official visit. I've come for your counsel." She stood in front of one of Eural's animal pelts, waiting for his invitation. He gestured for her to lay down, and she did. Once seated, he joined her opposite her on the stone floor. Her white feathers made his greys seem dull and dirty.

Eural's eyes widened. "Mine? Lady Ainlin, I'm not remotely trained for that."

"Which is why I desire it," she said. "You are valued within my father's cohort, and I would value your opinion on certain matters." Her eyes regarded him with a hint of concern.

"I can try." Eural shifted. It was not his place to offer his opinion on pride matters nor did he want to. However, if Ainlin desired it, he would abide by her. It was his duty, after all.

She nodded. "Thank you. It's about Caslir. My father refutes me at every turn. I need another perspective."

Eural thought for a moment. Ainlin had already been concerned about the other direlord, and she was right to feel as such. Naralin was likely forcing her to second-guess herself.

Eural considered his words. "I think he's presenting all of his feathers. If he doesn't put everything in, he will lose whatever remaining land he has to Kristel, Haynil, and the wyverns."

Ainlin watched him pensively. "What does he hope to gain?"

Eural shrugged. "Exactly what he asked for, I'd say."

"It's ridiculous. Any gryph who knows what happened at the God's Tear will stand against it," Ainlin said.

Eural nodded. The story of the Blackbeak Rebellion was

inspiring. After the rebellion, the new dires changed the world's order and established their modern system, but not without consequence. While the undired flourished, the dired dwindled. The separation of dires throughout the lands had reduced the number of dired mating pairs and removed the taboo of partnering with the undired. It was difficult enough for a kit to be blessed with dirism between two dires, let alone with diluted genetics.

A question rose to Eural's beak. He held it, thought about it, and worded it carefully. "If I may ask, what do dires think of their lowering numbers?"

Ainlin stared at him as if deciding whether to grant him an answer or not. It was the same look a mother would give when her kit asked a question they may not be ready to learn the answer to. "They are unhappy. This is why we prefer dires to mate other dires. It's why my father has arranged a mateship between myself and another." Her words cut into him. He knew that gryphons and opinici were forbidden to mate and that a Lady of the pride would never mate below herself. But some deep part of him wished for it.

"If our dires wish to be with undired, we will not prevent it. However..." Ainlin paused, her feathers sleeked. "Caslir's belief is not a new one. His family holds pure dire blood above all else." She breathed. Her crest puffed slightly as she looked down at him. "Thank you, Eural. This was what I hoped to hear." Her words ignited within his chest.

Eural didn't know if he had truly helped or not nor had he realised the complexity of the dire's situation. They seemed to have a more privileged life than the undired, particularly those within the upper tier, but perhaps it wasn't as easy as he realised.

Ainlin regarded him and inhaled. The tenseness in her

features eased. "Now, one further question: how is your sister?"

"She's adjusting. She's having trouble, and rightly so," Eural said, a twinge of guilt sparking within him. He could have done more for her. "A day with Tayrin should have been good for her."

The dire laughed lightly. "My sister has a poor grasp on emotions, and her advice may not help Euraiya mourn, but she means well. She may try to fly her into the ground in a misguided attempt to help."

"Exactly." He echoed Ainlin's laugh. "An introduction to the workings of the pride might help keep her from focussing on her emotions. I asked Tayrin to keep an eye on her. In truth, I don't know what else I could have done. I don't fully understand what she's going through."

"You are wiser than you think you are, Eural," Ainlin said. "She's lucky to have you."

Eural shook his head. "I owe her a lot. I wouldn't be here, if it wasn't for her."

"Not many of us would be anywhere, without support. Euraiya will find her own way through this, though she will appreciate the assistance."

Ainlin went quiet. She seemed to contemplate her thoughts before voicing them. "Do you believe your sister, about the wyverns coming?"

Eural nodded. "I do. But Dire Naralin is ordering her to be quiet."

"I know," Ainlin said. "I'm trying to convince him to heed the warning. He needs to listen to her, prideless or not." She stood and arched her back in a long stretch. Eural joined her. "I will apologise to her in person, at the earliest convenience. She will not receive one from my father, but she will from me. I suspect a good time will be during the territory divide."

Eural puffed his crest. If Ainlin was willing to extend a branch between Naralin and Euraiya, he hoped Euraiya would take it. They made their way to the cave's entrance. "She'll be here."

"Then I will see her. You'll be joining my father, I assume?" She turned at the cliff's edge. Her eyes reflected the moonlight. Eural nodded, captured by them.

"Dire Naralin asked for my attendance." 'Asked' was not the word he intended to use. "We're hoping it'll be smooth."

"Let the spirits make it so," Ainlin said, pulling her wings to their full length. "Be well, Eural. We'll see each other again." She spread her wings, leaned forwards and off the cliff. She pulled up and glided away.

"Let the spirits make it so," Eural echoed.

14

SPREADING ROOTS

E uraiya stumbled backwards, tired. She wasn't prepared for Tilear's speed. With each swipe of his claws, she dodged again and again until they had made multiple circles around the arena. Then they stopped. The opinicus puffed his crest, pleased.

"You're getting better," he panted.

She took a moment to catch her breath, unable to talk until her body calmed itself. "It's getting easier." The movements themselves were, but as far as her fitness was concerned, she would soon collapse.

She had been training alone for days, but today, Fiir and Tilear had offered to teach her some basic techniques. Their approach was unexpected, but she wasn't going to turn down such an offer. She had spent the previous week watching guards train and tried to emulate their moves, but without anyone to advise her, her progress was dismal. Now, Fiir sat to the sidelines and watched while Tilear tested her. He was a tough opponent even whilst holding back.

Fighting was harder and more exhausting than she had expected, and she had found a new appreciation for the warriors. They taught her basics, extensions of what she'd developed when play-fighting. Simple slashes and kicks wouldn't suffice. Instead, they would need to be well-placed and considered, a skillset that she hoped would become second nature. She needed to understand where to attack and what would leave her open to a counter. She had trouble grasping the concept initially, but slowly, she understood it. Watching oneself as much as one's opponent was an acquired skill.

"Now, let's combine a couple of things," Fiir said. "When Tilear attacks, either move into him or back away. Remember to consider his direction."

She measured herself against Eural. He had shouldered into each of her attacks from the same direction as her strikes. The moment she had gotten past his defence, he had changed and moved with her. It was all so much to remember. She stood as they had taught her, wide and grounded. "Shoulder towards or back away."

Tilear moved beside her, pushing her limbs and twisting her body, adjusting her stance. "Stand your ground, but be ready to move. Work from your dominant side." He moved in front of her. "Basic defence, remember? Keep steady. When they come for you..." he leaned forwards with his right side and pushed her forcefully. Grounded, she stayed in place. "Push."

At his slow, controlled swipe, she followed the same movement into him and shouldered his chest. His foreleg rested against her neck; his paw glanced away from her body. This allowed her to understand where they would likely end up during a real move.

"You're doing good," Tilear commented, placing a paw on her shoulder. It was soft, friendly. Something welled inside her at the touch.

"Thank you," she said. The feathers on her cheeks prickled. She appreciated their help. She hadn't seen Eural for most of the week due to his schedule. These two had been the only gryphs to spend time with her. Granted, she assumed that neither knew how poor her skills were. They hadn't been present when Eural had beaten her.

"Take a quick breath, and we'll do it properly." Fiir said, leaving them to drink from the well beside the arena.

Tilear smiled to Euraiya. "Enjoying the pride? Naralin can be a little harsh, but as long as you keep away from the upper tiers, we're usually good gryphs here."

Euraiya shifted her wings in a heavy, laboured movement, trying to release tension. "Eural likes to say so."

"He's mostly right," Fiir said, rejoining them.

"I need to ask you," Tilear started, looking her over. "Rumours around the pride are that you're a remnant. What's that about?"

"She's from Rada's clan," Fiir padded between them, prodding Tilear with his shoulder as he passed.

"Oh." He paused. Whatever he was about to say fell away as he gave her a sympathetic look.

She was getting used to these comments, whether they were innocent or otherwise. "Yeah," she breathed. "A lot of things are...different."

"Must be tough," Tilear said.

She swallowed as her body recovered. She was fatigued, but she could continue. "A little."

"Alright. That's enough. Let's do this again," Fiir interrupted. He nudged them both, and they distanced themselves a few paces.

They went through the drills a second time. She was becoming more familiar with them. Tilear increased his speed, assuring he would remain a challenge. Each lump was a testament to each failure, and each time she stood back up, she returned with renewed vigour. She owed that to herself. She had to try. It was paying off. As her confidence increased, her movements became fluid and instinctual. When a paw came, she moved towards it or away as instructed.

She was naturally inclined to avoiding the attacks. An innate part of her mind told her to move, and she did. Then, without thinking and without warning, she struck Tilear across the beak. He paused, surprised.

Fiir made a curious hum.

He came back for another, and she pulled to the side and tapped his wing. If she'd used her claws, he would have bled. He twisted his body and kicked her in the side of the neck. She moved into it. A spike of pain lanced through her. She fell to the side, paralysed and winded. Her world blurred, and her neck throbbed. The shock of the attack amplified the pain of the blow.

After a moment she inhaled sharply and the pain subsided. She got back to her feet.

Tilear stood back, allowing her to regain her bearings. He opened his wing, bending it to see if Euraiya had drawn blood. "Good try," he murmured. She offered him a weak puff of her cheek feathers, unable to provide much more. "Don't block that. Ever. Only if you can hit their body do you shoulder them."

Once recovered, they continued. Similar motions and results followed with each additional round. She was getting better, and Tilear's compliments came in the form of pushing her harder. Each failure was followed by a lesson that she took to heart. She did not make the same mistake twice. Anything they offered, she heard. Without their guidance, she would not have improved. Fiir praised her from the sidelines, followed by further advice on how to effectively retaliate. As the day continued, she realised they weren't teaching her to fight like Eural.

"Strikers," Fiir eventually explained, "don't fight like guards do. Guards defend, we don't." He moved in and took her place in the arena. She sat on her haunches in the sidelines.

"And I think you might be naturally inclined to it," Fiir said. "Fighting like your brother is going to kill you."

Fiir and Tilear squared off. They circled each other, waiting.

"What we lack in strength, we make up for in speed," Tilear added.

Then, with a speed Euraiya had only seen from the wilders, they fought. Their dexterous and calculated moves surprised her. She watched in awe as they dodged and swiped, rolled and kicked. Where fighting Eural was like attacking a mountain, Tilear and Fiir fought like they hunted each other. It was as if they followed a complex choreography to the rhythm of beating drums. Euraiya was stricken.

She tried to glean something from their movements. She recognised some of what they had taught her, but most were too advanced. Fluid twists and turns met swipes and kicks. It all seemed impossible. Tilear slipped under Fiir, swiped his stomach, and pulled out the other side. Fiir kicked but missed. Their dance continued with mesmerising technique and control. She wanted to fight like that, if only for the impressiveness of their skills. She wanted to learn to fight, to show Eural that she could improve.

If the pride accepted her. The nagging thought caught her off guard.

No words had been spoken on the progress of her place

within the pride. Tayrin rebuffed her during hunting, and Lenrin ignored her entirely. It was still possible that all of this was a waste of time. She couldn't let that happen.

"When you're done digging to the spirits, we'll reconvene." Fiir's voice ripped her from her thoughts. She looked down to see the hole before her.

"You okay?" Tilear asked. They both stood over her. They were tired but otherwise unscathed. It was to no surprise. She wouldn't have lasted a second at their intensity.

She nodded and stood. "Let's keep going." The thought of exile spurred her. Perhaps, if she were lucky, she could prove to Tayrin that she was worth keeping in the pride. "We've got a lot to do."

FIIR'S AND TILEAR'S TRAINING HAD TURNED INTENSE AS THE week went on, their movements faster and more realistic. Tilear's speed and strength caught Euraiya off guard and consistently sent her sprawling. Eural's attacks may have been forceful, but they were identifiable in the midst of battle. Tilear gave her no such luxury, and she paid for thinking otherwise. This was what she wanted, and she refused to stop, despite their offers.

They admitted she impressed them, and her chest filled with pride, but what ego that built was quickly tempered by their next spar. She had a lot to learn and was not prepared for a real fight, but she would get there in time.

Today, the drills warmed their bodies against the cold that had rolled in overnight. The seasons were changing, and the sun was beginning to see its life behind a wall of clouds. Soon, the mountain gryphons would have use for their long, feathery manes. Euraiya dreaded it. She hated the cold and was assured that the snow and rain would batter them for many moons.

A loud, sharp voice cut through the air, ending their session. Euraiya froze. It was not the chill of the air but the two gryphons who approached them.

She had anticipated this day.

There was little pleasure in either Tayrin's or Lenrin's faces, neither betraying what they were about to pass down. A thousand scenarios coursed through Euraiya's head, each more damning than the last. They melded together into an incoherent mess of thoughts and exile.

"What's this?" Lenrin demanded. Tayrin followed behind him.

"Euraiya needed some basic training. We've been helping her out," Tilear offered. He met Lenrin with a bow of his head.

"It was by my organisation," Fiir added. "Just because she's Prideless doesn't mean we can't—"

"Quiet," Lenrin snapped. He shot a look at Euraiya. Her stomach sank as he held his silence. This was her executioner, the one who would pass down her exile and kill her.

"What brings you here?" Tilear asked. He moved beside Euraiya with a comforting flick of his tail against Euraiya's leg.

The two siblings looked between each other, silently deciding who would speak. With a huff, Tayrin passed the task to Lenrin. The lack of fanfare concerned Euraiya. Every one of Rada's inductions was partnered with celebration. But not here. The only ones who would see her fate were her friends and her murderers. If there were no fanfare, there was no good news.

"Euraiya," Lenrin started with the distaste she had come

to expect. "Your performance has been far from exemplary. In fact, I dare say, it was dismal." The ground opened beneath her. "Your first trial was a disgusting display of weakness and lack of training. You were a kit, nothing more."

Euraiya glanced to Tilear, then to Fiir. Both were quiet. She didn't know what she expected them to do, nor herself. Tilear's tail brushed her again, his eyes remained on Lenrin. Tilear supported her, filling that hole as best he could.

"Your fishing was no better," Tayrin added. "Be glad that you're teachable."

Lenrin nodded. "Teachable." He looked over the other opinici. There was a knowing glint in his eye. "Don't, for a moment, think that we don't know what you've been doing."

Fiir marched forwards, the curve of his wings blocking Euraiya's path to Lenrin. "We haven't done anything wrong. Until she's deemed otherwise, Euraiya is considered a part of the pride."

Lenrin shot a glare to the white opinicus. He took a step and shoved Fiir with the full weight of his body, throwing him to the dirt. "I don't need the likes of you telling me how my father's pride works. If there's anything else you have to say, consider Euraiya's fate before you say it."

Fiir picked himself up, eyeing the grey gryphon.

He turned back to Euraiya. A quick glance to Tilear prevented the stony grey from trying something, as well. "We've been watching you train. Don't think that hasn't gone unnoticed. And I will admit, I am impressed."

"You *are* your brother's sister, that much is clear," Tayrin said.

"After much discussion, and I mean *much*," he glanced back to Tayrin, who gave a long, coy shrug of her wings. "We have come to a decision."

Euraiya didn't know what to think. She hadn't seen them watching her. She'd been too focussed on her training to notice anything that wasn't Tilear. She reminded herself that it was her training, not Tilear. Thoughts coiled around her throat and strangled her. Lenrin's and Tayrin's expressions remained flat. Not a single puff or flattening of their feathers indicated where her life would end. Would she have a chance to say goodbye to Eural? Surely he already knew. If he didn't, he would find out eventually. She knew he hated the wilders, and perhaps he would grow to hate her as well.

She regretted not reconciling with him. His warm personality had been absent since their fight. Life had mostly passed them by, and she'd failed to apologise. They were on friendly terms, but that encounter and her words still hung over their heads. She had avoided crossing the awkwardness between them. She should have said something earlier.

Lenrin continued. "You are welcome in this pride, for as long as you see fit to stay here."

The hole sealed, failing to drag her into it. "I'm not exiled."

Tayrin chuckled. "No. Not for now."

She turned to Tilear, repeating herself. Each word ripped the thoughts from her mind, and disappeared into the ether. Thick layers of tension evaporated from her muscles. She was safe.

Tilear pulled her close with his wing and preened her. "I knew it."

Fiir, on her other side, did the same. "You can relax now."

Lenrin cleared his throat. "Your assignment. While we were considering assigning you as a hunter, after what we've witnessed, we'll be training you as a striker. You will be trained properly, and then we will see about assigning you to missions. Outside of this, like other strikers, you will be expected to hunt. You have met your hunting team."

A striker. A warrior. It was where she wanted to be. Something nagged in the back of her mind. Fiir and Tilear's offer for help, Lenrin and Tayrin's watching from afar. It wasn't a coincidence. She looked at the group around her as the question rose to her throat.

"Who told you?" she asked.

The sudden silence that filled the air confirmed her suspicions. She repeated herself, eyeing each of the gryphs around her.

Lenrin turned with a huff. "Talk to your brother." He walked away from them without another word.

Euraiya trotted after him. "What did he say?"

"Talk to your brother." His pace increased, turning to a trot. Euraiya stopped and turned as Tayrin approached from behind with a soft chuckle.

"I agree. But before I head off, Lenrin forgot to mention a couple of extra things," she said.

"More?" Euraiya queried.

"All gryphs within the pride are expected to have minimal education. We'll provide you with such. Reading, writing, and the rest. And if you desire, we'll house you on your own." She flicked her talon from side to side to punctuate each point. "Be proud, Euraiya. You made it."

Elation filled her, and air of pride surrounded her. Weeks ago, she would never have pledged herself to another pride. She had admitted that. The idea had been absurd. One pledged themselves to a direlord for life. Now, she realised that Rada's control over the clan had been twisted and sick. She couldn't understand why she hadn't fled when she had the chance. He had prevented her from growing, from learning and experiencing the world. His entire clan had been subdued by his paranoia and encased within itself. Part of her hated him for it. It was a far cry from the Euraiya she knew before. An opportunity to change that presented itself, and she had taken it. She took a breath and prepared her speech. "Thank you. Please pass my thanks to Dire Naralin, for letting me be here. I will shed my past an—"

"Hold on a moment," Tayrin said quickly. Her eyes were wide. "What do you mean?"

"It's expected that I pledge myself entirely to the pride," Euraiya said. Her ears lowered.

"No, not at all," Tilear said, coming up to them. Fiir was behind him. "No gryph is expected to do that."

Tayrin nodded. "Remember where you came from, even if you never go back." She gave a puff of her crest, urging Euraiya to continue.

Euraiya held her breath. Rada's claws had been wrapped around her syrinx for too long. They released her. "I will serve Dire Naralin as loyally as I did Dire Rada. I will serve better."

She might finally be able to cast away the thoughts that had plagued her. She had held herself accountable for too long. Now, there was an opportunity to try again, a fresh chance to prove that she could do it. Not only to her new home, but to herself. "I may have failed Dire Rada, but I won't fail you." She may have failed Rada's clan, but she would defend Naralin's pride with her life. She would not fail twice.

With that said, she lifted into the air. There was one last thing she needed to accomplish.

EURAL HADN'T BEEN IN HIS CAVE WHEN EURAIYA HAD ARRIVED. Instead, she opted to search the pridelands for him. She flew over the most obvious places still unable to find him. She wasn't familiar with his hiding spots, and anywhere they'd visited previously was empty. It wasn't unusual that Eural couldn't be found. He was always working. Her visit to the direlord's chamber was unsuccessful. The guards on the plateau told her that he wasn't rostered to work. Now, she scoured the pridelands for him, checking every bit of land.

The cool air whipped against her face as she flew over the river, downstream out of the mountains. This was the same river, she remembered, that had led her to the pride during the Fracture. In the daylight, nothing was familiar. Forks were oriented differently; outcroppings weren't where they were supposed to be. She only recognised one a bend along the riverbank and the cave adjacent to it. Barely a single landmark looked as it had in the light of the world's blood.

In truth, it was a comfort. It didn't remind her of her previous clan or evoke the pain of the memories. Either that or she had begun to come to terms with it. She hadn't realised the progress she had made until it hit her in the face. She considered herself lucky there was nothing to remind her of her old life, following her around like a shadow.

She found Eural at the edge of the water, walking with a red opinicus. She had seen the opinicus before but only fleetingly. Whenever she approached, the opinicus would leave. She had an idea of who it might be. The interactions she had seen had been intimate. Why he hadn't been introduced to him, she didn't know. She lighted beside Eural, watching as the other opinicus fled. She gave Eural an expectant look as she walked beside him.

"He had somewhere to go," Eural said. "How are you?"

That same awkwardness permeated the air as it had around them for the past weeks. He, like her, wasn't certain how to approach it.

Euraiya didn't answer. She let the sound of the river fill her mind, calming her. "It was you, wasn't it?"

"What do you mean?" Eural said, his feathers bristling.

Euraiya looked at him curiously. Surely he knew. "You spoke to Tilear and Fiir and the coordinators, didn't you?"

His feathers lowered, and he exhaled. "Oh, that. I may have had a few words."

"Sounds like it was more than just a few." Euraiya wanted to hug him, and scratch him. Part of her was relieved that Eural had helped her, but the other part felt robbed of the opportunity to prove herself. Although, considering what she had accomplished in the last week, he had given her that chance. She bumped him gently, careful not to push him into the water. "Thank you."

"I had to do something after the arena." He looked to her, worry and sorrow in his eyes. "I knew it wasn't fair. So I did what I could."

"It's fine," she lied. The pain of being humiliated in front of the guard still lingered. It would until she could prove otherwise. She would have that chance. "They decided to train me with the strikers."

"Really?" Eural stopped for a second, then caught up. "That's surprising."

"Wasn't that your intention?" Euraiya asked.

"My intention was to give you an extra chance," he said. "Let them see you could learn, in case your time with Tayrin bent your feathers. I hoped Tayrin might reconsider, at the very least."

"It wasn't straight forward." She had gotten better since then. "Seems like I impressed them." She went quiet, working the courage to say the words she had almost forbidden herself to say. The words lodged in her throat, something within her smothered them.

As if sensing her struggle, Eural nipped at her ear. "It's good to have you back." His feathers opened ever so slightly on his face, and he preened her again.

"Yeah," she said.

They walked for a mark and finally talked, letting the air clear between them. It was refreshing, another weight off Euraiya's shoulders and another reason for Euraiya to rebuild her life. She tried to broach the subject of the mysterious opinicus, but Eural's deflection ceased it.

She dropped it for the moment. She wanted to know why the other opinicus was being avoidant, and why Eural didn't want to introduce him. If she tried hard enough, she would find out eventually, whether he wanted her to or not.

"To the new pride!" Eural shouted, raising a piece of meat to the air, and three opinici joined him.

The same excitement and pride that coursed through Euraiya manifested itself in the flame in front of them. The din, drowned by their elation. After their walk, Eural had herded Tilear and Fiir to join them and celebrate their new pridemember.

She sat between him and Tilear as they ate and shared stories of their own success of being accepted into the pride. The meat tasted juicier and fresher than it had any previous night. The realisation that she was safe had finally struck her, and everything was brighter. The drums sounded louder, the colours more vibrant, and the scents of meat and cooking more pronounced. She was home.

"It may surprise you to learn, but Tilear is the only one among us who was born into the pride," Fiir said after swallowing a large chunk of meat in his paws, having forgone cooking it over the fire. "I'm originally from Haynil's pride. Gryphs left in droves after the food stocks dried up. They mostly went between Naralin's and Kristel's prides. Heard that some dires went to Caranel's pride."

"What, no one went to The Edges?" Eural said with a cheeky puff of his feathers.

"You leave a pride for a better life, not a death sentence," Fiir said.

The group laughed. Euraiya looked between them. They were the closest thing to friends she'd had since Rada's clan. Even then, Lillia, while a friend, wasn't immune to the stigma of being associated with a fringe-walker. Euraiya remembered the feeling when Aurok had gripped her foreleg, the flush of heat. Now, friendships were forming. These were closer and warmer than the one she had experienced with Lillia. For the first time since Rada's clan, she felt safe and wanted.

"Eural almost ended up as a hunter," Tilear said. "I remember the look on his face. Then, we didn't see him for two weeks. He came back, ready for his trial, and barely passed." He leaned over to Eural, his body brushing against Euraiya's paw. Euraiya breathed. "You never told us what you did in that time."

"I trained. Hard. I had no idea what I was doing, but figured if I tried anything, it was better than nothing." Eural dropped his bone into the pit and crossed his paws in front of him. "That's partly why I was named Fireheart."

"Ah, yes!" Tilear looked to Euraiya. "You thought of a name yet?"

"My name?" she asked.

Fiir's beak hung open, and he let out an incredulous chuckle. "That's a joke, right?"

Euraiya furrowed her brow and looked at each of them. Tilear and Fiir were confused, and Eural apologetic.

"Second names are common," Eural said. "It's a sign of status and acceptance within a pride. It could be a parent's name, for achievements, or chosen by the gryph. Here, we either choose one for ourselves, or have it chosen for us based on achievements." He tapped his chest twice with the side of his fist, "Tayrin called me Fireheart, for my determination and change."

"Quickstriker, for me," Tilear added. She should have expected that.

"S'Erril," Fiir said. That sounded similar to how Aurok's second name.

Euraiya thought about it and drew a blank. Aurok had brought the subject up with her as well, and she had dismissed it. That conversation suddenly sparked in her mind, and she felt a tinge of sadness.

A second name meant nothing to her. Rada's focus on calling gryphs by their titles seemed natural. Just as he was Dire Rada, she was Hunter Euraiya. Before Aurok, she'd never heard of second names. "I'll think about it."

"You should!" Tilear said. "The upper tiers will take you more seriously. To them, the status of a second name is a big deal." Tilear offered a shrug. Over time, she had learned that not many held respect for the upper tiers. "The middle and lower tiers don't really care, as long as you're not Prideless."

Euraiya nodded. "That was insulting, at best." The title still stung. She wondered how long it would be before the pride saw her as one of its own. She may have been officially inducted, but how long would that name last? She could see gryphs around them glancing in her direction and muttering amongst themselves.

"It'll be shed soon enough," Eural said.

Tilear leaned over and patted the nape of Euraiya's neck. "You'll figure it out. In the meantime, you can figure out your place in the pride." Euraiya's feathers lifted at his touch. She looked at him, her cheeks flushing. Whether he noticed or not, she couldn't tell. The warmth of the fire was nothing compared to the elation and relief within her.

After a moment, she realised she was staring at him and glanced away.

The group spent a fair time in the mess chamber, discussing the differences between the prides. It was so long into the night that even the drummers had retired, leaving the mess hall to the din of conversation and crackling of fire. Eural had forgotten much of Rada's clangrounds. The shelter assignments and the regimented hierarchy of gryphons over opinici had fled his mind. It had been so long since he had thought of it that it had lost significance. She wondered if she'd forget it, too. If Rada's memory would fade into obscurity, replaced by better and happier memories. The thought disturbed her. She couldn't imagine losing that part of her as her brother had. Yet, once, she couldn't imagine living within a different pride.

Eural was clearly happy here. This was made clear multiple times as he regaled them with a tale of his transition from Prideless to Fireheart. How, from barely avoiding exile, he had been installed as part of Naralin's regular retinue. His friends, having either heard the story before or experienced it themselves, were quickly bored. Euraiya, however, listened intently.

Deep into the night, the group broke and retired to their homes. It had been a long and exciting day for all of them. Tonight, Euraiya hoped, she would sleep better than she had since her arrival.

Silence.

Fire burned. Wooden shelters collapsed around Euraiya. A large, hided beast flew overhead, spewing flame across the already-blackened ground. Gryphs ran past her as she walked slowly through the burning clangrounds. She was cold. A wyvern landed beside her, plucking a gryphon from the ground with its jaws. Another torrent of fire followed from its mouth towards the escaping gryphs.

She ran. An opinicus fell to the ground in front of her. It clasped its claws together, begging and pleading. The wyvern turned and snatched it. Euraiya focussed ahead of her. Through the heavy black smoke stood the remains of the Dire's Den, destroyed by a torrent of fire twisting and writhing towards the sky. A beastly, black dire fought a hided behemoth in front of it. Beak met neck, fire engulfed feather, talons scratched eyes.

The closer she came, the further away they were. They fought, blind to the chaos that surrounded them. Gryphs burned around her. The smell of ash and fire filled her nose. A quiet rumbling filled the background. Yet, she kept walking. They didn't matter. It was too late. The dire was still alive. He needed to know.

The dire's feathers burned, their black colour crackling away into white. Naralin. The wyvern's hide tore, exposing the bone underneath. Neither saw the carnage around them. The ground crumbled under her. She continued to run, her feet failing to touch ground yet still propelled her forwards. She ignored the gryphs as they died around her. She had to. She had to tell her direlord what happened. The rumbling grew louder.

The fire rose higher. Still, the dire fought. Her movements were slow. Something constrained her, as if claws, talons, and jaws held her back.

She was almost there. The dire and the wyvern turned to her. The wyvern screamed, its form melting away to reveal the feathers and beak of her brother. Eural and Naralin shouted. Their words, drowned by the loud rumbling. It thumped in her ears. The two creatures were smaller than she remembered. They looked like rodents. She stood over them and roared.

Her jaws cracked as she opened them wide, her chill replaced by scorching heat.

Fire spewed from her mouth, engulfing her brother and her direlord.

Everything went black. Silent.

She killed them.

15

EXILES AND WILDERS

"I'm going to kill them before they starve," Aurok complained.

He cast a look around at the camp. Shelters stood half-erected as wilders worked around them. The din of construction work filled the air, drowning out conversations and other noises. Aurok had managed to convince some of his gryphs to work. Some hunted, fewer built shelters, and only one volunteered to stand vigil for threats. Detaloning himself was easier than motivating his camp, but at least he'd found minor success. These days, the clan looked more like a wilder camp, with muddied gryphs and the smell of grass underpinned by unpreened feathers and rotting meat. They had been too morose to bath or clean, much to the chagrin of Aurok's nares.

The past few days had been spent on re-establishing the camp and organising roles for any gryph that would listen. They had travelled for a day before deciding to move further within Naralin's borders with Kristel's in view. This area was much more sustainable. Both food and water had been scouted within a half-mark of their location. Before them stood Naralin's mountains, and in the distance, with a squint, they could make out the shapes of gryphs who lived in aeries, communities of gryphs who didn't live within inner-pridelands but still wanted to the security of a direlord.

About one mark's flight behind them were Kristel's mountains. A ground-based aerie sat deeper within, and if Aurok was lucky, they would remain as such. Kristel had no power within Naralin's borders and would be unable to harass them. Word, however, might still reach Naralin's ears. The camp would need to keep to themselves and hope that their new neighbours were empathic enough to let them stay.

The materials strewn across the camp spoke volumes to how successful Aurok had been in convincing his gryphs to set up and served as a constant reminder of how much work there was left to complete. The only thing they had started to do was hunt, and it was mostly for themselves. This was in contrast to Trein's camp, who were nearing completion. Aurok had fought with too many of his gryphs, and Trein was growing tired of subduing both him and his camp.

Leading gryphs was cutting through Aurok's patience. They were infuriating. With fewer gryphs than there were tasks, it was sheer laziness that kept them from being completed. In the end, he had given up on trying to convince them to help and had started construction on his own shelter with the help of Lillia and Fenri. He shared it with them during their nights, despite the dissenting cries of his camp outside. If they wanted shelter they would need to construct it themselves.

A glint of light caught his eye in the distance, and he whipped to face it, hackles raised. His stomach lurched with dread as he prepared to call the camp's retreat from a wyvern attack. Ever since they had moved, Aurok stood alert, jumping at the slightest noise or movement both day and night.

What Aurok saw now wasn't much better. It was the reflection of light on metal. The metal of Naralin's guards. A white gryphon and greyish brown opinicus approached after lighting fifty metres from the campsite. A yellow gryphon and a grey opinicus, neither wearing armour, walked between them, their heads and wings hung low. Aurok called to Trein and met the guards at the edge of the camp.

"Wilders," the grey guard said. Something familiar about him caught Aurok's attention. He had seen that face before, he was sure of it.

"What's this?" Trein cut in before Aurok could say a word. He gestured at the two middle gryphs. The guard glared at him.

"It should be obvious. Exiles from Dire Naralin's pride, and *your* newest additions," the white gryphon said. He was a mountain gryphon, proudly displaying his feathered mane over his armour. "Our responsibility ends here." They made an abortive turn as Aurok spoke.

"Wait," he said quickly. "We barely have enough food for our own camp, let alone the addition of others." He gestured behind him, favouring his own gryphs over Trein's. There was no doubt they would join their kin.

"That's not our problem," the opinicus guard said, motioning for the two exiles to move in. They trundled forwards, dragging their feet as they passed their new leaders. Aurok didn't have the heart to turn them away.

"We haven't even set up!" Trein snapped.

The opinicus sighed gruffly. He glanced at his partner, who rolled his eyes. "Fine, then. Names."

"Aurok and Trein," Aurok said, gesturing to each. "We know what Narali—"

"*Dire* Naralin," the gryphon interrupted.

"Dire Naralin," Aurok said flatly. "We've kept our heads low in hopes we'd avoid this. We're just asking for a chance to set up. We'll be happy to take—"

"Wilders don't get to choose who they take," the opinicus said. "They're either given exiles, or they're removed as per his agreement with the upper tier. You should count yourselves lucky that you have allies within the pride at all. Dire Naralin is being considerate." His curtness was a trait all on-duty guards seemed to share. He looked Aurok up and down, likely sizing him up for a fight. He looked strong, moreso than the other guard. If they came to blows, Aurok would be careful.

"We don't need your bravado," Trein snapped. "You can tell Naralin where he can stick his 'consideration.'"

"Trein," Aurok warned. As much as he shared the hippogryph's disdain for prides, it was unwise to cross them. Not enough anger in the world could protect them from a direlord's coordinated attack.

"I'll be happy to stick you." The grey guard pulled up to Trein and stared him down, his hackles raised and stance wide. The edge of his armour brushed against Trein's blue feathers. Trein met his glare, he was too old and stubborn to fall for physical threats. Aurok was not.

He pushed Trein to the side, taking his place and standing between the two. He craned his neck and leered at the guard who was at eye-level to his chest. He looked him over, measuring his plan of attack. If he were lucky, he might be able to take one down before the other joined in. He needed to defend his camp. "We're taking them. You can leave."

"Good," the grey said, looking up to Aurok and taking a step back. "Wilders would do well to learn from you." A wry chuckle escaped his beak. "You might even do well in a pride."

Aurok's expression hardened, and he held his tongue. His feathers rose and fell as he considered his actions. The guard was only trying to get under his feathers just as Ter had. A shiver of anger ran through him. He'd taught that little rat a lesson and would do the same to this one if he needed to. If this meeting went on any longer, he may be the one to instigate the fight.

The two stared down, refusing to move. Their raised wings and squared stances mirrored each other. Anger and adrenaline flared inside Aurok. This guard was a manifestation of everything he hated about direlords. If it wasn't for their lust for power, it was the hierarchy they forced on everyone below them.

The white cleared his throat, and the grey relented. He brought his wings to resting and straightened himself. "Listen, Aurok. You seem like the most intelligent one in the camp, so I'll put this to you simply: You take our exiles, we leave you be. This will happen every quarter-fracture or so. Be pleasant, and Dire Naralin won't have any reason to be rid of you. He's a good dire to good gryphs." He spoke as smugly as the expression he held. Aurok's hackles riled further.

He growled under his breath. "Understood." He had repeated himself enough. He would take the gryphs. He would find them a place in his camp, and perhaps they'll be more useful than Rada's gryphs. Naralin's pride wasn't shy about their duties.

"Then we'll be off," the white guard motioned dismissively. "At least we have a new wilder camp to dump the rejects in. And this one is closer!" The two guards laughed.

"If you've finished showing off, then leave. We've got gryphs to feed," Trein said, still behind Aurok. His words came with far less impact behind his shield.

The grey guard gave a conceited puff of his feathers. "Expect to see us again, wilders." He eyed Aurok. "Stay out of trouble." With a commanding flick of his head, he and the other guard flapped hard and took off, coating Aurok and Trein in dust and dirt.

Trein's insults followed after them. Some of which Aurok had never heard before.

With Naralin's eyes on them, Aurok needed to figure out what to do and fast. He wondered how the other wilder camps dealt with this. Did they manage to survive, or did they become bloated and collapse?

The latter seemed likely. Wilders had no experience with prided gryphs. They didn't know how to handle them, nor could they. Direlords made sure the two were worlds apart. They degryphed wilders, turned them into thieves and murderers. When exiles arrived in their camps they were lost within their new environment, and the prided gryphs never assisted them.

Aurok, however, had experience with prides before becoming a wilder with both Kristel and Rada. It had been a mistake to try to find security in Rada's clan, but his time there solidified why direlords were no better than they had been hundreds of fractures ago. Aurok could use his combined experience to teach these gryphs how to be wilders, or perhaps find a way to change their minds about their pride. If he didn't, his camp would collapse or starve. Splintered wilders were dangerous. He didn't need the camp killing each other over food.

Trein was still cursing. Aurok's thoughts were too far elsewhere to register them and asked, "how are we going to survive?"

Trein stopped his onslaught. They looked around their camp. The exiles had found a spot behind the tents to mourn their lives.

"We'll have to do whatever we did before," Trein said.

"We're already starving. Can we afford to feed more beaks?" Aurok started walking, looking for a solution to manifest from the spirits under the earth. Trein joined him, his smaller legs carrying him eight steps for Aurok's every four.

"Just keep trying. You're getting there." Trein cautiously stepped over discarded materials as they came through Aurok's gryphs. It was a stark contrast to the fluid workings of Trein's wilders, as if someone had split them down the middle and declared who belonged to which side.

"It'd be easier if these lazy bastards pulled their weight." He received glares from a few gryphs, as intended. Out of the corner of his eye, a couple of gryphs shuffled away towards the construction.

Trein chuckled. "Prided gryphs aren't wilder material. Treat them the way they need to be treated," he said, skirting to Aurok's other side to give his working gryphs some room. "Firmly. Change your approach depending on who you're dealing with. Remember when you first came to my camp?"

A moment of clarity clicked in Aurok's head. "You ripped through me. Called me out in front of the whole camp. I thought you were driving me out. But you were—"

"Doing what I needed to get you moving." Hopping on three feet, he gestured to the hippogryphs around them, "They all get it." He continued to trot properly beside Aurok.

"But only do it when you need to. If you do it to that one girl...Fenri...you'll push her off and kill her."

Fenri was a concern. She was trying hard, but her fortitude was minimal. Talking to her was like walking through the crystalline perimeter of the God's Tear. Any disapproval or dissenting opinion flattened her feathers and ego. What worked for him would not work for her.

He needed to try something. He was learning about his gryphs and how they responded to him. There were a few that a hard push would be all that was needed to get them moving, while others needed a gentler nudge. His gryphs had motivated themselves to hunt when they were hungry. He just needed to get them to do anything else.

Trein stumbled as Aurok suddenly stopped in front of two gryphons. He looked them over as they stared up at him.

"It's time to stop lazing around. What did you two do before you were displaced?" Aurok asked, mimicking Trein's air of authority.

"Hunters," one replied.

"Good. Get up and get hunting." He flicked his head towards a gryphon as he landed at the edge of the camp, the current huntsmaster. "Learn the hunting grounds."

One gryphon stood, aborting a move towards the gryphon. The other opened his beak to protest.

Aurok leaned down, squatting his front legs to meet him. A memory flashed in Aurok's mind of Trein doing the same thing. "Or starve. Your choice."

16

CONNECTIONS

In the coming days, Lenrin trained Euraiya as intensely as he had Eural. Any thought that this would be easy was quickly swiped out with another strike of Lenrin's talons. He had the strength of a guard and the speed of a striker. Against him, Euraiya was nothing, and that seemed to drive him.

In between their bouts, as Euraiya lay exhausted on the ground, he explained the use of strikers. They were hidden fighters, trained to surprise their enemies and strike quick and dexterously. Guards, however, were their defenders, strong and armoured, ready to deflect enemy advancements. In a fair fight, a guard would always win, but strikers never fought fair.

Their skills, he explained, were utilised in other assignments. They were often tasked with gathering information or assisting envoys. Every striker needed to possess the skills necessary in order to conduct each assignment flawlessly, and while Euraiya was a decent hunter, she had a lot to learn.

"Get up!" Lenrin snapped, picking Euraiya up by the

scruff of the neck and placing her back on her paws. Euraiya's legs shook under her, threatening to give. "I don't have time for snivelling."

"And I don't have time to recover," Euraiya said bitterly. The more exhausted she was, the less control she had over her beak. Lenrin smacked her across the brow, adding to the others she had earned.

"If you picked things up quicker, we wouldn't be having to go over this for a *fifth* time," Lenrin said.

Euraiya's chest heaved as she breathed through an open beak. She forced her slow, heavy limbs into a defensive stance and waited. Lenrin came in quickly with a feigned movement. A left swipe quickly became a right. Euraiya pulled back, correctly this time. She ducked, launched upwards and swiped Lenrin in the face. She tried to push back and failed, falling into the hard dirt.

Lenrin stood over her. "Nice try, but don't try something that stupid." He loomed over her and pressed a talon under her stomach. The same place Eural had hit her. "I pierce you, and you're dead."

Euraiya's body was like stone. A tingle emanated from under her stomach, coursing through to the tips of her extremities. She grew hot, her body refusing to move, despite the uncomfortable position of her wings trapped under her. Her wings throbbed, like a thousand claws digging into her. It was a friendly reminder not to over-exert herself.

Lenrin's feathers flattened, his eyes widened. "You...don't know what that is, do you? Spirits, did Rada teach you nothing?" He sighed. "Don't answer that. This is your stirin. It's where your spirit essence is stored. It's what allows us to live, acting almost as a second heart." He lifted his talon and strutted around her. "If that's pierced your essence leaks, like blood, and you die. Every sapient creature has this, and every sapient creature can die from it. Keep it guarded, and always wear your armour."

It clicked. Eural had used it against her in order to gain the advantage. No one in the clan had ever mentioned the existence of a stirin, and she wondered just how many had died because of it. A phantom pain throbbed where Lenrin had pressed on her.

Lenrin scanned her and clicked his beak. "Take a breather. We can't have you dying on me. Let's see..." he paced around her. "Next is understanding what makes you a striker. Striking is like hunting. You get your opponent before they have a chance to get to you. It's simple. Remember, though: you're not a guard. Unless you can control the situation, you get in, kill, and get out."

"How...how is that different from a guard?" Euraiya asked.

"They're stronger than you, and are trained to control a fight for longer. You should know that from your brother," Lenrin said.

Euraiya blew air from her nares. The sting still sat under her feathers. "Okay, fine."

Lenrin let out a chuckle. A rare sound. "But that's why we teach you the basics. If you find yourself in a situation where you can't escape, or you don't have your team, then you need to know how to fight."

"Right." She rolled onto her stomach. A flash of pain burst through every vein. She gritted her beak and stood up, thankful she had regained enough strength to move.

The gryphon gave Euraiya a sidelong glance and stopped for a brief moment. "That reminds me: you've met your hunting team. You will fight with at least one of them in your assignments. Which is why you have five per team."

"So Tayrin wasn't there just for show?" Euraiya asked.

Lenrin shook his head. He rounded Euraiya and knocked her with the back of his talon, forcing her to stand. "You might even fight with her one day. Up."

Her limbs were still heavy, but the feeling had returned. While the break helped, she still wanted to sleep for days. Unfortunately, that wasn't going to be an option. Neither Lenrin nor his sister would allow it.

Lenrin forced her into another drill of ducking and weaving. She was forbidden from retaliating or blocking. Each swipe, kick, and charge came at different angles, speeds and strengths. He mixed attacks to throw her off-guard and succeeded on many occasions. It dawned on her just how far behind she was and how far Eural had really come.

In their final round, Lenrin dropped all pretence of training. He charged at Euraiya with full force. In her surprise, Euraiya dipped to the side. Her paws were dragging along the ground, but she managed to escape the coordinator's attack. Lenrin turned, and Euraiya ducked. Instinct took over, and she forced herself into the Lenrin's chest. Lenrin rose to his hind legs. Euraiya forced her weight and drove him backwards. Lenrin snapped his beak, grabbed the back of her skull with his talons and squeezed. Euraiya screamed as each tip drove into her head. Lenrin tossed her to the ground and stood on her.

He brushed his feathers with a talon. "I told you not to do something stupid. Get up and go find Tayrin. We're done here."

THE FROZEN WIND CHILLED EURAIYA TO THE BONE. THIS CLOSE

to the snowy mountains, her feathers did little to assist her. She could appreciate why the mountain gryphons, like Tayrin, had manes to keep them warm. It was in this part of Naralin's borders that they resided, living high on the crests of the Inilrin Mountains that made the majority of the direlord's lands. The distant landmarks Euraiya had grown up with were not simply 'Naralin's Mountains' but held their own history and significance to those that lived within them.

The long, prickly, cone-shaped trees covered the grounds leading to a lake that extended far into the horizon. Euraiya marvelled at the different landscape before them. Her world grew larger and larger with every mark outside of the pridelands. Unrecognised animals and birds skittered around the group as they landed.

The group followed Tayrin deeper into the trees. Euraiya was briefly and formally introduced to the team, and they inducted her quickly. They promised Euraiya that as long as she watched out for them, they would do the same for her. Their group consisted of three opinici: Rinli, Hintala, and Pyrin, and their leader, Tayrin. It were a refreshing change after being surrounded by males every day.

Pyrin took great interest in Rada's clan and questioned the way Euraiya had been trained to hunt. Euraiya explained her trapping methods and how useful they had been when hunting alone. The group chuckled but indulged her. Trapping wasn't a common practice within their assignment, due to their preference of hunting larger prey. None of them had trapped an animal since they were kits. As a celebration for their newest member and the novelty of a different hunting style, they followed Euraiya's lead.

The group stopped at Tayrin's expectant look. Euraiya passed her and picked up a nut. She placed her bait, finding an open area free of obstruction, and joined the others in hiding. She listened carefully, the chatters of small animals and birds filling her ears. It would be easy to claim a prize.

The smell of mould and water wafted over her, overpowering the piny scent of the trees. It reminded her of her weekly visits to Rada's local lake. She wondered if gryphs had drowned in this one, as well. Her focus returned from the brief lapse, and she chided herself. Now was the time for focus, and she wanted to impress her new peers with her skill. A small tree-rat of various browns descended towards the bait. It was disappointing but it was something.

Without warning, Tayrin pounced from her hiding spot, a loud snap replaced the chittering din. Warning cries sounded across the area and silence remained for a time.

The opinici joined her as she dropped the bleeding carcass to the ground. She looked at Euraiya, letting out an approving chirrup. "I haven't done that since I was a kit."

"It was an effective way to—"

"No," Tayrin interrupted, waving her talon dismissively. "I haven't hunted alone in fractures. It's refreshing." She puffed her cheeks, her crest rising ever so slightly. Euraiya had to admit she was a little disappointed and felt robbed. She hoped to show off her trapping skills, and now Tayrin had stolen that opportunity.

"Same 'ere," Hintala said. "S'easy to bog down on routine, and not end up doing something different, eh?" She ribbed Rinli with her elbow, Rinli shot her a filthy look.

With Euraiya's gift of leading the first kill out of the way, Tayrin brought the group deeper into the taiga. She halted them and pointed forwards, towards a herd of deer grazing a little ways ahead. The five hunters moved in. Each were designated a cry to indicate their readiness.

After they called out, Tayrin pounced from within the

trees and downed a deer, catching the herd off guard. The other deer charged deeper, and the gryphs followed.

Rinli and Hintala downed their prey in seconds. Euraiya bolted past them, following her target. Sticks and stones crunched and kicked as she chased. The deer cut left, and she followed. Adrenaline filled her veins, and she pushed harder. She jumped, latched onto the deer's rear, and pulled it down. They scuffled until Euraiya's beak clamped down on her prey's neck. She held strong as the deer writhed and screamed. Its frantic movements grew slower, its yells quieter, and its struggles weaker. It laid its head on the ground, silent and dead.

She stood up and stared down at the corpse, surprised at how short the chase had been.

She'd always hunted covertly, as if she had something to lose. She'd relied on her skill rather than her natural strength and speed to take down prey that had no chance. She'd forgotten how much faster she was than those creatures. Pride flashed through her again. She turned to the others as they approached. They each dragged their kill with them.

Tayrin chuckled, dropping her carcass in front of her. "That's one of the reasons why we don't trap. We don't need to."

Euraiya nodded. As proud as she was, a small bit of disappointment crawled into the back of her mind, stinging her like a spider. She enjoyed trapping animals and assignments would cut into her time for it. She would need to make the time, and perhaps she would. She considered the different animals that Naralin's borders contained and what foods they would eat, what would entice them. These were the skills she knew that would transfer to her life as a striker. If gryphs weren't taught to hide and trap, it would be her advantage against them. The thought simultaneously excited and frightened her. She had never killed another sapient creature before, and deep down, she wasn't sure she wanted to.

"Wake up, Euraiya," Pyrin trilled. "We're not carrying your deer for you."

Euraiya pulled out of another daze. The last week had certainly gotten to her, and she realised just how tired she was. She grasped the deer in her claws and dragged it to a clearing before flying off back to the pridelands. Her thoughts drifted again. She would kill, one day. Not some dumb beast, but a creature capable of thought and under-standing. She visualised her reaction to killing something, visions of her proudly standing over a wyvern carcass filled her mind, one of the wyverns that had attacked Rada's clan. She was fearless. Every action was rehearsed and fluid. She steeled that thought, holding it. That was how it would work. When she eventually had to kill, she would be strong.

She would be victorious.

THE NEXT MORNING, EURAIYA WOKE TO FIND EURAL READYING for his assignment. He was donning the metal plate he wore around his neck and back. Another small plate clipped under him, resting under his stomach. A phantom pain flashed through her, her veins on fire, her entire body like a boulder. She shook her head, scolding herself for still holding that against him.

"What's your assignment today?" she asked, forcing herself away from the thought.

"Dire Naralin is meeting with Caranel and Kristel to

divide Rada's land," he stated. At her reflexive expression, he paused and offered an apologetic tilt of his head.

The shock passed, and she nodded. She knew it would have to be done eventually. She eyed his armour again. "You're expecting trouble?"

"We're being careful," he said. "Caranel is...unpredictable, at best."

She let out a wry grumble. "I've heard that."

Eural made a thoughtful noise. He picked up a metallic object and looked it over. Multiple loops, large enough to fit his digits through, were connected to claw-shaped extensions that were clearly sharp even to the naked eye. He slipped it over his paw and scratched the ground, testing it. He inspected the scratch marks and then the points. He did this with a second one, too. These were the weapons that Euraiya would be trained with. Most guards preferred these claw extensions as it gave them an edge in battle. Eural had explained that while it wasn't a requirement to wear them, it was heavily implied.

"I expect to be back some time this afternoon. Should things go well, we might be able to hunt in the old forest again." He turned to her and inclined his head. "Me and you. It'll be fun."

"Sure." The thought wasn't pleasing. She didn't want to return there and relive the memories. She wanted to stay as far from Rada's clangrounds as possible for the rest of her life. While she had mostly come to terms with the destruction of the clan, she couldn't stop those memories returning. The fire still burned her, and the screams still filled her ears. She could never forget them, even if she tried.

"Ainlin will be visiting you while I'm gone," Eural said. The look on his face suggested he had forgotten. Euraiya tilted her head, and he elaborated. "She's Dire Naralin's

daughter. She's wanted to talk to you since your meeting
with Dire Naralin."

Euraiya rolled and stretched her back, slowly waking
from her doze. She would need to be completely awake if
she was to meet the heir to Naralin's pride. She had slept the
moment she returned from the mess, and despite the aches
in her body, she was ready. She yawned.

Bird squawks and calls caught her attention, and she
turned. A flock flew through the expanse over the pridelands, playing in the air. They weren't so different from
gryphs in some regards.

"I'll keep my eyes open for her. After yesterday, I don't
think I'll be going anywhere." She spread her limbs out
across the nest.

Eural laughed. He came over and pulled her close with
his wing, nearly dragging her onto her paws. He preened
the top of her head. "Lenrin will drive you to death. Even
more so if you challenge him." He removed his wing and
tapped his beak with the sharp metal claw. "Come to think
of it, you can't win with him. He'll keep pushing you regardless of what you do." He shrugged.

Euraiya rolled her eyes. "Why am I not surprised?"

"Naralin's children are raised like that," he said. "I've
heard stories of Inilrin, too. Her wrath is partly what keeps
the tenders going."

Euraiya blinked. She tried to imagine small, caring
Inilrin acting as controlling and domineering as her father.
The thought was comical at best.

Eural nudged her side with his wing and made for the
edge of the cliff. "See you soon."

"Come back safe," Euraiya muttered. The words were
unintentional, but she meant them just the same.

He paused and turned. There was a look in his eye she hadn't seen since they were kits. A promise. "I will."

For half the day, she did as intended. She lounged around the cave or at its edge, watching life go by. Everything ached, right down to her tail. She was lucky Tayrin and Lenrin were busy for the day and had no time to teach her. Otherwise, she might be digging her own grave before the next moon.

As she stared out over the pridelands, she realised she still had trouble comprehending how different and vast Naralin's lands were. Soon, perhaps, they would be even larger. The mountainous landscapes were still foreign and exciting, as were the different types of forests she now hunted, and even the aeries atop the cold peaks. She wanted to explore. She wanted to see the chambers inside the mountains, visit the rivers and plains, the crags and caves that Naralin claimed. There was a new world for her to experience, and she now lay in the middle of it.

She vowed to herself that she would explore it. To hell with Rada, that would never be her world again. It seemed, too, that neither would Naralin. Perhaps one day, she'd be assigned to the Edges or the God's Tear. Thoughts of visiting places she had only ever heard of rushed through her mind. Her feathers raised as excitement her excitement flushed.

A dire left Naralin's chamber and made its way towards her, closing the distance twice as fast as any undired. It was as white as Naralin himself. Were it not for his known absence, she would have thought it was him. As it approached, she noticed that it certainly wasn't. This one was female, her feathers well-kept and her features softer. The dire lighted on the edge of the plateau beside Euraiya with a certain dignified grace. Euraiya stood and mantled respectfully. A faint smell of lilies filled the air around her. There was no doubt who this was.

"Dir—... Madda—..." she stuttered. She tried to correct herself, stumbling over as many titles as she could think of before the dire raised her claw.

"The term you're looking for is 'Lady,' which is used to denote me as the female heir to the pride." She lowered herself to Euraiya's level. Her feathers puffed contentedly. "You may call me Ainlin."

Euraiya looked at Ainlin, taking in the view before her. Ainlin held herself softly and open. Her blue eyes were comforting rather than full of anger. The spikiness that most dires possessed was masked by careful grooming. She didn't loom over or try to assert her dominance, as most other dires did.

Ainlin sat on her haunches, as regal as if she already ruled the pride. Euraiya sat as well, lowly by comparison. She wondered if Ainlin had been groomed to act as she had or if it was her nature.

"I trust Eural told you I was coming?" Ainlin's voice was gentle and measured.

"Yes," Euraiya said. "He said you've wanted to talk to me since I met your f— Dire Naralin."

Ainlin nodded, ignoring the slip. "I wanted to extend my apologies for my father's conduct. It was uncalled for, and I have had words with him. I know he will not apologise, so I will do so in his stead."

Euraiya stared up into Ainlin's eyes. She tried to temper herself. She was captivated. With such an aura about her, Ainlin would prove to be a dangerous direlord. "I-I appreciate it, Lady Ainlin."

The dire looked over the land, her land, and sighed. "My

father lets his temper get the best of him. An unfortunate trait of dirism."

Euraiya's ears flattened. She didn't know how to respond. She knew dires were prone to anger and that it was a leading cause of death within their subspecies. No dire had ever confided information to her about their kind, and part of her wondered if it was taboo. "Rada was the same."

"They were far from friends," Ainlin said.

"We were well aware of that," Euraiya replied flatly.

Ainlin gave a soft laugh and raised a talon to cover her beak. "I think most are. It was difficult to keep them in a chamber together, let alone to discuss pride matters." She turned back to the opinicus. "What else have you heard of my father?"

"Not much. Dire Rada," that habit again. He was not her direlord, and she owed him no such respect, "compared him to Caranel. Called him a 'brutish ruler with illegitimate power.' He never explained why."

Ainlin made a thoughtful hum. "'Illegitimate power.' I warn you not to speak about that around here. My father's pride don't believe it."

Euraiya's ear twitched and turned towards Ainlin. Euraiya regarded the dire, considering whether to act on the question in her throat. She did. "Do you?"

Ainlin paused. "I'm not sure. He is called the Kinsbane for a reason. But it's said the pride has prospered since his leadership."

Rada had used that term before. Kinsbane.

"But whether he deserves the power he craves is another thing entirely," Ainlin said. "We will never know how my uncle would have ruled." She turned to Euraiya, inclining her head and winking. "Consider that thought a means of reparation for his treatment of you."

Euraiya flushed. She knew she should keep that to herself. "Thank you, Lady Ainlin."

"A pleasure," Ainlin said. "You should ask someone for the story of the Kinsbane some time. It's an interesting tale. I would suggest doing so deep in your chamber, however."

A distant sound cut Euraiya off, sending a chill through her. It carried through the mountains, echoing across the rocks, rumbling through every chamber in the pridelands. Her stomach seized. Her heart pounded. Ainlin stood quickly, hackles raised. It sounded again.

A fierce, guttural roar.

17

DIVIDE AND CONQUER

Grass stirred in the wind until crushed under the talons and paws of the white direlord Naralin and his escort. The smell of rain permeated the air, threatening to drench them all. They had arrived early, allowing enough time for the strikers to be in place. The hills and tall grass behind them provided enough coverage that a small number would remain hidden until they were needed. Eural looked around, pleased. The trees concealed their warriors watching carefully from hiding posts at the edge of Naralin's territory. The darkening sky would allow them the benefit of lower light, but it would also prove to be a disadvantage.

They stood between the two connecting borders of Kristel and Naralin. The two more successful direlords had chosen the meeting grounds, allowing them to safely remain in their borders. The third direlord to join this meeting was neither flourishing nor welcome. Ahead of them was the very end of the wreckage of Rada's clangrounds. The fire had spread far and had threatened to claim parts of other territories, were it not for the luck of rain after the Fracture. A sigh escaped Eural's beak. He still had fond memories of his past, and it pained him to see its destruction.

Naralin stood pensively, shifting his weight from one side to the other. He had barely spoken on their journey, only offering curt orders and responses. Eural knew why. Caranel was worse than Rada in almost every facet of his existence. He was a constant thorn in Naralin's side and seemed to make it his duty to rile Naralin at any opportunity. This, and the stress of civilly dividing up land, was likely stabbing at Naralin's mind like a gryphon's beak. The only saving grace would be Kristel's presence among the two brutes. Should this go smoothly, the strikers would remain stationed, and blood wouldn't stain the ground.

One further issue, Eural thought, was Caslir. Naralin didn't speak openly, but the change in his demeanour since the meeting spoke volumes. The old world gryphon concerned him more than he would ever admit.

The sound of wings caught their attention, and their gaze fell to the west. The shape of a dire broke through the clouds the distance.

"Thank the spirits," Naralin breathed. "I would not have lasted alone with that whelp."

Yellow feathers stood out with an iridescent sheen despite the overcast sky. The gryphon glided towards the ground, pitched with a single flap of her wings and landed. She looked over the group with innate condescension. A golden wire crown sat neatly on her head, contoured perfectly around her skull. Little hooks wrapped around her ears and the base of her upper mandible to hold it in place. Small rubies studded along the top of its structure between the intricate designs of the wire. A red cover sat loosely over her front and connected around the back of her neck. These were the markings of the one who owned the

God's Tear, the only other gryphon that other direlords would defer to.

She acknowledged Naralin with an incline of her head.

"Kristel," Naralin responded, dipping his head in return.

"Naralin, a pleasure as always." Kristel raised herself to full height, her slim neck rising like a snake. Her hazel eyes looked through her beak at Eural and Ilir as they flanked their direlord. "Your guards stand ready."

"And you come alone," Naralin said.

Eural followed the landscape behind the yellow dire. Despite its undisturbed setting, it certainly was not.

One of her cheeks pulled in a wry sneer. Unlike Naralin, Kristel could afford such a look. She was here only for appearances. Rada's lands were too far from her pridelands and would prove a constant battle between her and Caranel. He was the only dire in the land stupid enough to provoke her.

Naralin turned his gaze south. "The runt has yet to arrive."

"Indeed. And are we surprised?" Kristel said.

Naralin scoffed. "Not in the slightest."

As if on cue, the shape of the third direlord appeared in the sky and began his descent towards them. Even at a distance, it was noticeable that he was not as large as the other two, or at least, not as tall. Covered in blue feathers, leading to an unkempt lionesque body, the beast landed with a loud thud, grasping the grass with his clawed paws to cease his momentum. Caranel glared.

"There you are, runt." The words fell from Naralin's beak like venom. Caranel stood half a head shorter than the dire gryphons but that much wider. Where Naralin, Rada, and Kristel held themselves tall and proud, Caranel was low as if ready to pounce. He stalked towards the group.

"Have you come to insult me or divide the land as promised?" His voice lacked the resonance of the other direlords. In its place was an irascible quality, a scraping tone that cut Eural's ears like gravel. He was always happy to see a dire opinicus as long as it wasn't Caranel. Eural stood firm, eyes trained on the direlord. Caranel had a reputation for swiping before talking.

"We were waiting for late arrivals. As it appears that he has arrived, we can begin," Kristel said. "We would normally speak of respect for our fallen brethren, but I have no such thing for the likes of Rada. The fool was intolerable at the best of times."

Naralin scoffed. "I believe any words I have for him have been said to his face. His spirit does not need to hear it again."

Caranel made a circular motion with his paw. "Let's just get on with this." He tapped his back foot and whipped his tail.

Kristel clicked her beak. "I have no interest in this death-ridden land. It serves no purpose, aside from providing me with territory to rival our dear Naralin." She gave the white dire a sidelong glance.

"And we can't have that," Caranel responded wryly. "I expect the land in its entirety. Rada was one of my closest allies."

"Rada had no close allies," Naralin said, his wings shifting slightly. "Least of them you. I expect his forests. My pride require food."

"The forests...no, I don't think so." Caranel said.

"You do not think much, runt," Naralin snapped. "Half of this territory has yet to have a rightful claim. If Kristel does not make any, the forests are rightfully mine."

Kristel made a noncommittal noise and continued to

watch the two male direlords. Eural expected that she knew what would flare between them. He held his vigil. This was an expected turn, but the potential for a fight was always present.

"My gryphs need more food and space. There's barely enough fish to keep them from killing each other!" Caranel snapped. "I have greater need for land than one who claims a third of the continent."

"You deserve nothing if not to lose your land entirely," Naralin said. "I have fought Rada for these forests for more fractures than you can even comprehend. The forests are mine, and you get the rest."

"That's barely enough room for an aerie!" Caranel stamped his foot, storming towards Naralin with half-splayed wings.

"And it's more than I should allow you." Naralin held his ground and tone, looking at Caranel through his beak.

Eural watched them cautiously. He glanced around, trying to locate other hidden guards. He knew Kristel's were behind her, but Caranel's seemed invisible, as if there weren't any at all. Eural leaned in and whispered to Ilir, "Where are his guards?"

"No idea," Ilir answered, a curious look crossing his face.

"I don't like this," Eural said.

It was unsettling but not surprising. Caranel often acted alone, unless an alliance provided him with a much greater benefit. He'd had a minor relationship with Haynil at one point, which lasted less than a fracture when Haynil learned that Caranel's pride was stealing most of his food.

Caranel and Naralin displayed differently, but each was as power-hungry as the other. Where Naralin was cold, his pride flourished. Caranel was fiery, and his pride fought amongst themselves as their food ran low. However, they had both claimed their power by another's blood.

"You can't claim every piece of land, Naralin." Caranel narrowed his eyes. "Others here have needs, and they *will* fight you for it."

Naralin stepped forwards, his patience clearly thinning. "I will claim what is mine, little clawfoot. Whether that is accomplished with your territory as well will be another consideration entirely."

Cold air brushed Eural as the wind changed direction. A chill ran through him. The clouds darkened further, threatening to unleash upon them all. Still, Caranel and Naralin bickered. Kristel waited, feathers flat and eyes glazed. Eural stood vigilant and careful, waiting for any direlord to call an attack. But it never came. Only the hard voices of the dires filled the air.

"*There* he is!" Caranel shouted, looking Naralin up and down. "There's the Kinsbane we all know. Let's see where that takes us."

Naralin's wings shot out, and he held himself to full height. Eural and Ilir closed in, halted by a stomp of Naralin's foot. "A challenge will not end in split land. Consider this," the words froze the air around him, "if you dare to call me by that name."

Every eye fell upon Caranel, who raised his head. Slow and considered, he matched Naralin's stance, meeting his eyes in a confident leer. "I dare."

The moment held for a lifetime as the two stared down. Naralin brought his wings to his sides and Caranel did the same, each giving the other one last chance to reconsider. Eural and Ilir grounded themselves, preparing for their call. Eural didn't want to come between the two, but it was his duty. Trying to fight against two dires was a death sentence.

He caught the muttering of strikers and warriors, all of them on edge.

Eural held his breath. He begged the spirits to let this settle without bloodshed.

"Dire," Ilir said quickly. "We shoul—"

Naralin was the first to move. He charged Caranel, each talon and paw pounding loudly against the ground. The two clawed and bit. Blood-covered feathers fell to the ground around them.

Eural's chest constricted. He wanted to defend his direlord, but his order had been clear. He glanced to Ilir, mirroring the look of worry.

Naralin caught Caranel's head in his talons, squeezed, and pushed him to the ground. A sharp crack filled the air as bone collided with hard earth. Caranel twisted and pulled back, blood pouring from an open gash above his eye. Naralin closed in with such ferocity that Eural was concerned Naralin would soon turn on them.

Blood-thirst filled their pinned eyes. Eural had seen this before and had experienced it himself. Naralin's eyes were wild with the hunter's gaze. Eural knew the world his direlord had fallen to. Naralin saw nothing but the prey before him.

Naralin's look held Eural in place. He hadn't felt fear in a long time, but seeing his direlord fall to his anger struck him. Behind him, the mutterings continued. Some readied themselves, preparing to charge. Eural hissed and silenced them. They had their orders.

Kristel watched, seemingly unfazed. She only waited.

The space Naralin and Caranel occupied increased as their fight intensified. Powerful swipes narrowly missed bystanders, their force threatening to cut as sharp as their claws and talons.

Caranel drove Naralin to his hind legs and towards his guard. A slash caught Naralin under his eye and another across his chest. Caranel gripped Naralin's feathers, lifted and threw. Naralin's wings collided with the ground, and he shrieked.

Eural and Ilir backed off, calling to their direlord, unable to reach him.

Caranel took to the air. Naralin twisted and jumped up, opened his wings to their full span, and leaped.

The two dires collided. Naralin dug his claws into Caranel's body and climbed him. Caranel yelled and tried to shake the larger dire off as he dragged him down. Caranel finally looked worried as Naralin's claws dug into his skin, reaching his throat. Naralin took his opportunity. White skull met silver beak and another crunch filled the air. Naralin's bodyweight shifted and drove the dire down. They slammed into the ground, cracking the dirt under them. Naralin's talons squeezed into Caranel's neck, Naralin's other limbs firmly pinning the dire to the ground. It was a finishing move that all of Naralin's chosen knew.

Eural and Ilir bounded towards them. Naralin lifted his wings, halting them. Under Naralin's weight, Caranel choked and squirmed, thrashing his legs under the white direlord.

Naralin's gaze fixed on the struggling opinicus, his talons covered in Caranel's blood. "I will kill you here and now if you dare to challenge me further. I tire of your provocations and you."

"No, stop!" Caranel managed a strangled screech. His words came stilted and slurred by the cracks in his beak.

Naralin's grip tightened, his sides heaving with every breath. Blood dripped from his face onto Caranel's. The opinicus' struggles weakened under Naralin's strength.

"Dire Naralin, stop!" Eural stomped his foot, trying to draw Naralin's attention. If Naralin turned on him, he wouldn't stand a chance.

"Either finish him or let him go. I do not have all day, Naralin," Kristel said with a disinterested snap in her voice. "This land is yours."

The fire in Naralin's eyes lifted, and he released Caranel. The blue dire coughed and gasped and struggled to stand. The metallic scent of blood filled the air, splashes of it mixed with the missing feathers that littered the ground. Naralin's chest was dyed red, bare skin visible where chunks of feathers had been ripped from his body.

Eural inwardly shuddered. If this were what two dires were capable of doing to each other, an undired wouldn't stand a chance.

Naralin bestrode Caranel. "Should I see you or yours hunting in my land, I will personally finish what was started."

Caranel coughed through a chuckle. He stood shakily, meeting Naralin's eyes. "If it remains your land."

Kristel and Naralin shared a look, then eyed him.

"Speak," Naralin ordered.

One eye closed as blood pooled over it. Caranel skulked between them and away, creating distance for an easy escape. "Things are changing. An undired pride is a weak pride."

Eural gritted his beak. He knew those words. He caught a sharp breath, holding himself steady.

"You have spoken with Caslir." Naralin struggled to hold himself with a straight back. He winced and faltered.

"Do not tell us that you have heeded that fool-dire's words." Kristel shifted from her spot, a look of unease broke through her dignified stance. The first that Eural had seen.

Caranel shrugged, limping away from the two. "You were offered a chance to stand with him, and declined. What happens next is on you."

"You are an idiot! Joining with that fledgling will be your death," Naralin snapped.

"My dires will thrive. The undired will serve us," Caranel said with a look to Eural and Ilir. He sounded desperate. "Not *with* us. Caslir has a heritage to reclaim and has offered me large borders and strong dires." He turned his gaze between Kristel and Naralin, watching them as if they were food. "Your borders. Your dires."

Before Naralin could respond, Kristel stomped a foot. Her wings rose in her own unexpected challenge. Her feathers glistened in opulence even under the clouds. She stepped towards Caranel, her voice rising as she spoke, "You are a fool. You will be ended before any of that comes to pass, and I will take great pleasure in splitting whatever borders remain. Or perhaps you would dare to tussle with me like some barbaric primitive?"

Caranel stood low, wavering and unable to find the gall to challenge the direlord of the God's Tear. His tail swished behind him, every so often pulling between his legs. There was a slight bend in his stance, his head lowered to his shoulders as Kristel stood over him. She feinted, provoking him to attack. He didn't.

"It won't be me who challenges you." Caranel's words were subdued and measured, unlike when they had been directed at Naralin. Yet, even beaten, he remained malapert.

The concealed threat didn't appear to register with Kristel, or she chose to ignore it. "See to it that you do not. Now be gone with you. For as long as you align yourself with such archaic ideas, you are unwelcome in our lands." Eural couldn't see her expression but imagined it matched the iciness in her words.

Caranel looked to Kristel and then Naralin who stood multiple paces away. "Let it be so, then." Something in his tone made Eural and Ilir tense. Eural couldn't pick why.

Caranel turned from Kristel, his demeanour broken by his tense back and limping walk. He opened his wings, revealing broken primaries. His flight home would be long and painful. "Spirits watch you. You'll need them." He lifted and flew away. Each beat of his wings was careful as he tried to maintain balance. As he left into the distance, not a single guard came out of hiding to follow him. He had come alone.

"He is hiding something," Naralin said.

Kristel turned, keeping her distance. Eural noticed the ragged look Naralin had gained from the fight. Compared to Kristel, he was a lowly arena fighter, unworthy of being called a direlord. Despite being separated only a few paces, the distance between them was enormous. She had remained calm while Naralin bickered and fought. Even now, not a feather was out of place. "Bluster. Let us return and...clean ourselves." She looked him up and down, her ears pinning to her head in disgust. "I would suggest you look into securing these borders. If Caranel and Caslir are truly working together, they will be troublesome. Whether your warriors behind the hills can handle them or not, is not the question. It is whether *you* can."

Naralin appeared unfazed by the comment. He attempted to smooth his feathers out to little success. "They will be a blight, but I will handle them. I will not stand for them attacking my pridemembers, if that is their goal."

"Good. Spirits make it so." Kristel let out a quick, sharp squawk, and her guard appear from the their hiding spots.

Together, they lifted and flew. Kristel bared no further word or look in Naralin's direction.

"Spirits make it so," Naralin said.

Eural echoed the words under his breath.

A breeze blew past them, carrying a familiar, acrid scent.

Naralin whipped around. His wide-eyed gaze passed his guard and over to the mountains. He swore, flapped his wings, and shot away like lightning. His guards rose and chased after him. Eural's stomach tightened as the mountains spewed black smoke above the pridelands and its aeries. A distant roar echoed around them, the sound of wyverns. It was clear. Caranel hadn't had any intention of dividing Rada's land—he had intended to divide Naralin's forces.

Eural needed to defend his home. Another thought crossed his mind, something that hadn't been there for fractures. Something more important he needed to protect.

Euraiya.

18

THE STRIKER AND THE WARLORD

Euraiya's stomach twisted and gripped. She stared towards the western mountains. Large, leathery wings appeared over their tips carrying brown-hided bodies. A torrent of flame followed, spreading down the mountainside with explosive force. Gryphs fled smoke and debris as rock shattered around them. Behind it, others followed. A swarm of wyverns swept over the pridelands, each following its own direction. War drums filled the air. Gryphs raced out of their nests and chambers to mount their own unorganised defence. Dired and undired fought as one under a banner of chaos.

Ainlin picked Euraiya up to her feet with her beak. "We have to go," she urged. "I'll find Lenrin and organise a counter."

Familiar screams and suffocating smoke filled Euraiya's mind, memories of fire wrapped around her limbs. Ainlin's talon tapped her back.

"Do what you can. Do something." She jumped off the cliff and flew into the mess of wyverns and gryphs, shifting left and right as she cried orders on her descent.

Memories strangled Euraiya and held her in place: the smoke, the roars of wyverns, and the screeches of gryphs mixed into a cacophony of noise. She tried to move. Nothing responded. A wyvern bit through an opinicus. *Through* him. The wyverns sizes were vastly different to each other, but many were the size of a dired gryphon.

She saw Tayrin engaging a wyvern about the size of an undired gryph. Lenrin joined her. There was no hesitation in their actions, they just fought.

A high-pitched scream rang out, and a brown mass slammed into Euraiya, sending her sprawling to the back of the cave. She scrambled up, tendrils of fear snapping from her limbs. Her heart pounded, and every part of her body quivered with it. A wyvern roared at her. It was barely her size but every bit as dangerous as its larger counterparts. It snapped its jaws and stomped a three-clawed foot. Guttural and glottal noises raked from its mouth like claws scraping on stone. It was speaking to her. She didn't understand a word.

"What're you doing here?" she asked, and by the look on its face, the lack of understanding was mutual.

A familiar sensation built inside her, drowning her fears. It focussed her mind and filled her with strength. She saw it in other gryphs and in the wyvern in front of her. She knew this state, hunting animals that dared to fight back. Adrenaline coursed through her body, but it wouldn't be much help. Unlike wyverns, the animals she hunted couldn't roast her. She had to be careful.

She raised her wings in challenge, whipping her tail. The creature responded with its own display. Its lack of forelimbs made it look as if it were crying to the sky and celebrating. She would have believed it were it not for the hunter's gaze in its slitted, raptorial eyes.

The wyvern pounced, its rear claws scraping the air between them. She moved to the side, turned, and bit at its wing. It pulled away, dragging Euraiya off her feet. She clambered back. The wyvern pounced and snapped its teeth. It caught her shoulder, digging in deep. She screeched, the sound echoing off the walls and back to her. She pushed the creature backwards. Flesh tore away. Blood dripped down her foreleg. The wound pulsed.

She charged the wyvern into the wall. It slipped backwards on one of Eural's displays. She was on top of it, biting at its neck. Its claws dug into Euraiya's body, scratching her ribs. The two scrapped along the ground, biting and clawing until Euraiya stumbled away. The wyvern stood, its blood slickening the ground beneath it. Its chest heaved, and its eyes slitted to lines as thin as her feathers. Its gaze hadn't wavered, even bloodied and hurt.

A shriek filled the air outside. A wyvern fell past the cave opening. The ground shook as it collided with the cliff. Fire followed the gryphs that flew after it. She considered herself lucky that her opponent hadn't tried to burn her. It was chaotic outside, and she was stuck, unable to fight alongside her pride.

The wyvern opened its mouth. Flames flowed and flickered between its teeth. Its throat pulsed orange and yellow. She'd asked for that. She darted away and to the side. A plume of fire shot from the small wyvern's mouth, following her and singeing the tuft of her tail and exploding against the wall. Another jet. This one missed her completely. The third caught her leg.

Unimaginable pain lanced through her. She shook the leg frantically, rolling to smother it. The wyvern took its opportunity and pounced, biting at her neck. She gripped its face, trying to force it away. It bit her claw, snapping it as if through wood. She struggled. Claws stabbed her side and she yelled, her grip weakened.

Before it could bite, the cave rumbled. The corpse of a dire gryphon landed beside them and slid off the edge followed by a rain of rock and dust. The wyvern was distracted. She kicked wherever she could connect and forced it away. Her claws dug in below its stomach, piercing it. She stood and eyed the wyvern. Its wings drooped and it looked weak. A mix of blood and clear liquid spilled from the new wound, mixing with the dust on the floor. She saw light rapidly drain from the creature's eyes, its focus turning vacant. Horror crossed its face. Empathy crossed hers for the briefest moments as that same spot throbbed in her body.

She tackled the wyvern, driving it off the cliff. The wyvern collided with the mountainside, Euraiya on top as her claws dug into its neck. It hit an outcropping, and they tumbled. Rocks pierced and grazed her body. She mounted the wyvern again and glided down further. Hide and bone scraped against rock and branch. She focussed forwards, opened her wings, and pulled backwards, letting go. The wyvern fell, hitting a large stony outcrop with a sickening crunch. Its limp body fell to the ground below. She watched, heaving, and after a moment, followed.

Euraiya landed next to the small wyvern, confident the creature was dead. The fire masked the smell of blood and flesh, replacing it with ash and smoke. Cries of defeat, victory, and pain sounded around her. She prepared herself, imagining the scene of her victory in her head once more. Until she looked down at the body and registered what was in front of her. The din of the fighting drowned away. The rising heat cooled to frost.

The wyverns back was mangled, blood stained the ground underneath it. It was likely dead before they had hit the mountainside. The sight pulled her from hunt as she realised her actions. She had killed a sapient creature. She knew, staring down at it, that it wasn't the same as hunting for food. The creature was dead, and its body would waste. A sickly feeling wormed through her stomach and up her throat. Food that wasn't there threatened to come up.

This wasn't what she'd pictured in her mind. She hadn't imagined the pain in her body or the empty feelings following her kill. She wasn't proud and gloating; she was repulsed. She knew she had fought in defence, not only for herself but for her pride. But this was not the glamour she had expected. The thought of its family flashed in her mind, and she squashed it. She couldn't afford it. It was likely, she hoped, that its relatives was fighting as well. She had fought to defend her own family, and in turn, she had destroyed another.

She looked over the corpse, forced herself to see it. To see what she had done in the name of her pride. Conflict twisted and writhed within her as different emotions fought for dominance: accomplishment, disgust, relief. None of them were right.

She tried to rationalise them. Defending the pride meant that she would kill. If she didn't, others would die. She had pledged to protect the pride, and right now, she had little choice as to how she would do that.

This was how she would fix the destruction of her last clan.

A feathery wing draped over her and pulled her close. She flinched, startled. Her world returned in a flash. A blast of noise, heat and light crashed through her. Beside her, a stone-grey opinicus looked at the corpse, his grey eyes reflected the same emotions as her own. Confusion, sadness, anger. There was a gash along his chest where feathers matted with congealed blood.

"It's awful, I know." Tilear said. His crest puffed, trying to console her. "Not to be rude, but we don't have time to walk you through this."

She stared at him, unable to speak as everything inside her fought for dominance.

He lifted his wing and moved in front of her, wings slightly raised and blocking her view of the wyvern. "Look around you. We need to move. Lenrin needs help. We need to do what we can until Dire Naralin returns."

Her eyes widened as it dawned. This attack was planned.

"Euraiya!" He pointed towards a group of gryphs. She followed the direction and saw Lenrin fighting off a larger wyvern with one of her hunting partners, Pyrin, and a few other gryphs. "If we don't act now, more will die. Let's go."

In the reflected light of the flames and his stern but understanding expression, Tilear looked strong and fearless. There was a flicker in her chest. He saw her staring.

Before she could respond, Tilear flew off, leaving her with the corpse. She glanced at it once more. The creature, once ferocious and capable of killing her, now barely seemed more than a deer carcass. The thought surprised her. It was a terrible thing, but it was true. If she wasn't careful, she would be one as well.

Fire exploded near her, throwing her away. Embers rained down, joining the already suffocating smoke.

She picked herself up and flew to Lenrin.

THE MOUNTAINS WERE UNRECOGNISABLE IN THE BATTLE. FIRE and debris terraformed caves into hills of rubble. Corpses littered the mountainside. The heat was incredible. Euraiya joined Lenrin's battle and latched herself onto the nearest dire gryphon-sized wyvern. She bit the base of a wing. It flapped hard and threw her off. She righted herself a few feet under it. A shard of a beak fell beside her as its clubbed tail met with a gryphon's face. The gryphon descended, dizzy and disorientated. Euraiya took his spot.

Pyrin's metallic claws dug deep into the wyvern, and it roared loudly. Fire burst from its jaws, and she was moved away. Lenrin barked an order and Euraiya acknowledged. She flew behind the creature and grabbed it under the jaw, wrenching herself backwards and exposing the creature's neck. Lenrin sidled and slashed through the hide with ease. The weapon made his claws as sharp as a dire's. The wyvern went limp, and Euraiya let go, watching it fall to the fire below.

Other gryphs fought around them. Euraiya moved to help, biting and cutting where an opening presented itself. They outnumbered the wyverns and used this to their advantage. It was their only chance at winning. Two or three gryphs piled on one wyvern, regardless of size. Another wyvern tried to flee, only to be caught by a charging dire.

Lenrin snapped at her. "About time you grew some talons." He whirled around to Euraiya and thrust his own talon at her. "Don't think I didn't see you down there. Get the wind under your feathers." He looked her over, disapproving and fierce. "You're with me and Pyrin. *Stay* awake. I will throw you to the wyvern if I have to."

He probably would.

Euraiya nodded. At Lenrin's order an injured opinicus pulled up beside her and passed her a pair of metal claws.

Impatiently, Lenrin held Euraiya's paws and forced her digits through the loops. They were too large and she had to clamp her paw closed in order for them to stay put. It wasn't preferable, but she would have to use what she could. The injured gryph left, and Lenrin led his group away.

Gryphs who were unable to fight busied themselves with quelling the burning ground. They flew back and forth between the closest source of water, before racing back again with full buckets. A wyvern crashed down, gripping a small gryphon in its claws. Euraiya, Lenrin and Pyrin dove in, slicing at the wyvern. It released the gryph, who scurried away. Lenrin made it quick. He dove, turned his body, and slashed through the hide. Pyrin followed with a similar motion. Euraiya attempted the same. She flew close and turned, clipping the wyvern's huge mass. Her claws dragged across the wyvern's neck as it turned orange. Flame exploded from the puncture, throwing Euraiya several metres. The wyvern fell.

Pyrin checked Euraiya for burns. By some miracle, she had managed to avoid it. Lenrin laughed, impressed. He allowed Euraiya a moment to regain herself, then led them once again.

They followed a line of gryphons before trailing the river. Lenrin didn't tell her where they were going or why they were leaving the main battle. She assumed they were clearing another area while the main force protected the nexus. Burned foliage mixed with rubble and bodies, washing into the river below. Debris from nests and displays similar to Eural's littered the ground, dented, crushed, and destroyed. She looked around, seeing neat rows of small caves at the base of the mountains. It was easier to breathe here, since the wyverns had moved further towards the nexus, leaving the smoke to rise. But through the haze, there was only destruction. What may have once been compact and neat was now a mess of rubble and wreckage. Large holes replaced where multiple caves had met. Gryphs dug frantically through the rubble screaming for their kin. Euraiya wanted to help them, but Lenrin pushed her forwards.

The memories of Rada's clan endured in Euraiya's mind. She tried to force them away. She couldn't afford to let them swallow her now. The fire, the noise and the heat was too familiar. It battled the adrenaline pulsing through her, threatening to turn her hunter's state into mewling flight. The pride needed her. She couldn't falter now.

Lenrin let out a sharp squawk. He rushed ahead of them towards two wyverns fighting a dire opinicus. The dire struggled to keep them at a distance but wouldn't do so for long. Lenrin, Euraiya and Pyrin swooped in. Lenrin assisted the dire gryph while Pyrin and Euraiya took the other wyvern. Pyrin called orders for Euraiya.

The wyvern's throat glowed orange as flame built inside it. Pyrin shouted, and the gryphs dove away. The fiery jet spewed over the wyvern's partner, engulfing it in flame. It screeched loudly, flailing to smother the fire. Their hide wasn't immune to it.

One wyvern snapped at the gryphs. The other shouldered and pushed the first away, yelling and snapping. Taking their chance, the gryphs resumed their attack. One wyvern crashed to the ground. The other lost its balance and slammed Euraiya with its tail. She landed with a thud. Her head pounded, and her world spun.

"Get it!" Lenrin shouted, followed by a commotion of noise and a crash.

Splashes and thuds sounded from the river. Someone

was drowning. She sprang up. Pyrin was safe. She looked for Lenrin. Her eyes widened and she gasped.

Lenrin held himself firmly on the wyvern's neck as the dire opinicus pinned its body. Lenrin forced its head under, laughing. The wyvern thrashed. It gripped the bank and tried to push out of their hold.

"He thinks he deserves mercy!" Lenrin shouted in the wyvern's ear hole.

Euraiya stared in horror. She had been forced to kill out of defence, but this was beyond that. Lenrin's look of glee sent a shiver through Euraiya's body. Lenrin's eyes were pinned, his feathers rigid. He enjoyed this.

The wyvern jerked its head out of the water and screeched, its voice gurgling through the water in its throat. Lenrin forced it under again. The wyvern struggled and flailed. As its movements slowed, Lenrin pulled its head up again.

"This is what you deserve," Lenrin said. "If I could do this to each and every one of you, I would."

He submerged the wyvern again.

This was excessive. Foul. In an instant, Euraiya found a line she didn't know was there. A border she couldn't cross. This wasn't defence of the pride, or even the hunting of prey. It was torture. It was murder.

Words caught in her throat. Her breaths quickened as the wyvern's writhing weakened. Its claws slipped into the water.

A wing spread in front of her, stopping her from moving forward. Pyrin glanced over it and shook her head. "Don't."

"This is...it's too far!" Euraiya hissed.

"I know," Pyrin said.

The wyvern's body sagged as the final bubbles of air reached the surface. Lenrin huffed and dismounted from its neck. The dire nodded to him, then looked over to the undired opinici, an expectant look on his face.

"We do what we have to," Lenrin said.

"You could have killed it quickly," Euraiya snapped.

Lenrin rounded on her, closing the distance in a second and forcing Pyrin to the side. With those hunter's eyes he looked as large as his father, and they scared her. "I will do what is necessary in order to protect my pride. By oblivion, it's a damned lot more than you did for yours."

Lenrin's words stung her deeper than any of the wyvern's claws. His sudden change struck her. Naralin wouldn't reprimand him for torturing their enemy nor his enjoyment of it. She couldn't believe it. Euraiya looked to Pyrin, who lowered her head and looked away. It spoke more than she needed: this was normal, expected.

Euraiya couldn't find a response. Instead, she wrapped her tail around her leg and inclined her head.

Lenrin huffed, turning from her. "If you expect to be of any use to the pride, you'd best get over it." His hackles stood rigid, and his tail thrashed.

The dire opinicus took this as an opportunity to leave. He didn't offer a word to either side, instead casting a disapproving glance to the other opinici.

Pyrin came beside her and whispered, "Don't speak of this to anyone. He'll punish you if he finds out."

Euraiya sighed and nodded. She remembered Tilear's words and tried to calm herself. She faltered. They weren't comforting or reassuring. They were fact. Doing the right thing didn't mean she would enjoy it or even approve of it. But she could defend her pride with more honour than the direlord's child in front of her. She didn't kill for pleasure. They were not rodents or deer for hunting. They deserved the same respect as any gryph.

Lenrin turned to them. "We're going to continue down the river until we reach the end of the residential chambers. Once we do that, we'll round out towards the nexus and then back towards the throne chambers. If we're lucky, my father and his guard will be there." His gaze fell squarely on Euraiya, and he held it for a moment, an unspoken threat hanging in the air. "Any questions?"

Euraiya eyed him. Contempt rose, tempered only by her sense. "No questions."

19

DUTY AND FRITH

Battles boomed through the mountains, echoing across the rocks. Gryphons screeched, and wyverns roared. It was difficult to place where the battles were, for the closer they came, the further away they sounded. Eural's mind raced anew with each pump of his wings, lost within his own mind, afraid for the safety of everything he held dear. He wasn't alone. Not a single word was spoken between the guards as they chased their direlord towards the pridelands. They barely kept pace with him.

The sky was hazy, and the smell of smoke overpowered the usually floral air. They could see it billowing into the sky ahead. Eural's wings burned. He hadn't exerted himself this hard for a long time, and never had he felt such fear. He had to keep pace with Naralin if he were going to defend the pride. He knew that the remaining coordinators would mount a defence, but whether they could manage with only a quarter of their fighting force would be a challenge.

His thoughts turned to Euraiya. More than returning to defend his home, he needed to protect her. It was a new thought, one that he hadn't struggled with. Euraiya now meant more to him than his pride. Something bit him inside. Euraiya was one gryph, but he had a duty to the entire pride above all else. He had made that oath before he had something else worth fighting for.

A plume of fire cut through the ranks of guards and strikers. Eural's world slowed. Gryphs screeched and fell, blackened and burning. Others disappeared entirely. There was no warning, no cry or roar to announce the wyverns' presence. They were there, and tearing into his warriors. He forced himself to focus, his world returning to the din of fighting and fire. There was no time to mourn.

Wyverns circled like vultures. Naralin was already upon one of them, tearing into its neck. Eural and Ilir each called a team of gryphons and turned against each foe. Eural's orders pierced the clamour of battle, calling his gryphs to attack in formation. Each swooped in, slicing with their claws, followed by the next gryph behind them. It was a basic manoeuvre but an effective one.

The wyvern flapped hard, breaking the pattern of swoops and dives. It caught a gryph in its jaws, crunching through the metal armour protecting his stirin. The clear liquid of his spirit spurted out of him. The gryph would be dead before he hit the ground. His name was Rhag. His spirit now joined all others.

Eural, lost to the phantom pain, almost joined him. The wyvern surged in front of him, jaws open and throat glowing. He dropped and flattened as the flame burst over him, catching his underside. He pumped his wings, fanning the flames before they could damage more than just his skin. He lashed his claws and caught the wyvern's foot. The metal talons caught bone, and jolted, forcing his paw to slip.

Before it could retaliate, his warriors were upon it. Eural caught his breath. The creature fell to the ground. Part of him was relieved. It deserved its fate.

His underbelly throbbed, a familiar pain. He looked down, quickly examining the wounds. Skin mixed with the fur and feathers of his chest and stomach. He inhaled, focusing away from the pain. He screamed inwardly. He was disciplined and would not give the wyverns the pleasure of his agony.

An opinicus conflagrated before him. Her screams cut through him. His stomach gripped and turned. The large, bloodied form of Naralin caught the wyvern's head, twisted, and snapped its neck. The sheer strength was incredible. Eural knew dires were strong, but he hadn't known to what extent. Naralin's hunter's gaze had returned. Except there was an underlying fear behind it, the same state for a different reason. Naralin's eyes reflected the fire below.

"We must move," Naralin said. "The wounded will clean this mess. The rest will return with me."

Eural surveyed the damage. Corpses burned, and wounded writhed on the ground. Some had been crushed underneath the dead wyverns. The ambush had led to most of their casualties. This was the damage done to trained warriors. Dread gripped him as he imagined the destruction that awaited them in the pridelands. Eural picked out his wounded and ordered them to bring the bodies back when it was safe. With his orders complete, he and the rest of the guard fell in behind their dire and charged home.

THE PRIDELANDS BURNED. GAPING HOLES REPLACED THE

structured homes that once decorated the mountains. Flames and ash covered the grounds below them, blackening the foliage and stone. Embers rained down as fires erupted around the lands. The concentration of battles was closest to the nexus. If the wyverns managed to breach those halls, the gryphs hiding within them would perish. The remaining forces of gryphs fought tirelessly against their attackers. For each wyvern they downed, they had taken twice as many casualties. Hopefully, now that Naralin's force had arrived, the tide would turn.

Naralin's roar rang through the sky. He seethed with a fury Eural had never seen before. He looked ready to lash out at the nearest thing and kill it. The dire's body heaved with each breath. He growled with each exhale as he surveyed the area around them.

Eural pulled up beside Naralin. "Dire, we can still drive them off. What are your orders?" He tried to remain calm and keep his voice measured. By Naralin's look, he hadn't succeeded.

"We *will* drive them off. You and Ilir will join me with two others. I expect your best. The rest..." He looked over his lands and tensed. "Kill them. Kill them all. Do not let a single oblivion-spawned creature get out of here alive."

Behind them, Ilir began barking orders. The remaining force broke immediately and filed down into the battle. By sheer numbers, they might win.

Eural squinted, trying to locate Euraiya in the chaos. He couldn't see her. Every gryph merged into another in the mess of wings and claws. His stomach sank. She was neither in the air nor on the ground. She had to be somewhere that wasn't burning or dead. He saw Tilear, Ainlin, and Tayrin. She wasn't there. He followed the horizon and saw Fiir fighting a smaller wyvern. Something clamped his heart. She wasn't there.

"Ilir. Do you see Euraiya?"

"There's more important things to be doing, Eural. Your sister can wait."

"I need to know!"

Ilir gave him a concerned look before turning and surveying the battle. He pointed towards the river. "There. Now get your head back."

Three gryphs flew above the nexus. Lenrin, an opinicus, and...Euraiya! She was in poor condition, but she was alive. She was alive, and that was all that mattered. He swallowed hard. Fighting with Lenrin meant Euraiya would have seen him go beyond acceptable measures. It was well known within the pride yet as taboo as speaking of Kinsbane. Lenrin punished anyone who dared to challenge him. Eural had seen it. He made a note to speak to Euraiya and warn her.

"Dire, perhaps we can assist Lenrin." As soon as he said those words, he regretted them. His intentions were transparent. Naralin knew what his sister meant and had likely expected this.

Naralin gave him a sidelong glance and a short, gruff grunt. "Your sister will learn to fight without you, or she will die trying."

Eural stopped, struck. His look tore between Naralin and Euraiya. He had always obeyed his direlord. He knew he should remain as such. Tension grew inside him as he fought for a solution. He couldn't bring Euraiya with them, nor could he bring them to her. He was left with a choice: abide by duty, or abide by family.

Naralin turned, his tone darkened, "Speak."

Eural searched for words, but none came. There was no

reasonable or convincing answer to give. "Dire, she's my sister."

"My children are fighting. I trust them to fulfill their role in the pride. I expect your sister to do the same. Now, you will follow me. Do I make myself clear?"

Eural hesitated. He couldn't both save Euraiya and follow his Dire's orders. He knew his duty to the pride and had embraced it thoroughly. It was his world. But that had been before Euraiya had arrived, and he had someone to watch over. He had promised himself she wouldn't come to harm. Now, he was stuck.

A low growl came from Naralin's throat. A warning that spoke volumes. If he left now, he would be punished, and severely. His choice was made as the blood-stained direlord hulked before him. Eural breathed. He would protect his pride, and then return for his sister. "Yes, Dire."

Naralin held his gaze. He ordered Ilir and his chosen warriors to follow. Eural, with a final look cast towards his sister, fell in behind them.

They charged for the nexus. Naralin cut through a group of small wyverns as though killing deer. They followed around the mountain towards the western side. Small, high-pitched shrieks filled the air. Eural's stomach turned. He knew where they were going. Female gryphs fought on a plateau in front of a cave entrance. Each gryph wore a blue covering across their chest, indicating them as kitcarers. The entrance that was once embroidered in a similar patterned material burned with the rest of the entrance.

Bones crunched as a wyvern came down on top of one of the gryphs. Flame followed. Naralin charged and redirected the wyvern's head away. Flicks of flame travelled down the hall, scorching the ground below it. Naralin snapped its neck. Eural pushed in with Ilir and cut at a wyvern's chest. Naralin's large form took it down, scraping its face against the rocks.

Kits squealed deep within the halls.

A wyvern cut through Ilir's side. He screeched and pulled away, and looked at his wounds. Two long cuts formed from his back down to his stomach. He faltered and fell. Eural tensed and hesitated. He wanted to save him. Eural's distraction was enough, and he was buffeted across the plateau. He dug his claws into the rock, scratching the stone and saving himself. His digits burned. He strained and pulled himself up with a flap of his wings. A wyvern's foot slammed down. He rolled, grazed by its claws. Blood dripped down his side.

The squealing turned to terror. Eural shot into the cave. The other guards would handle the last wyvern. He skidded and careened into a wall as he banked a corner. He jumped between two wyverns and a series of nests. Little kits cried and screamed, huddling together. A kitcarer guarded them. She hissed and stamped with the ferocity of a parent protecting their own. Eural's anger boiled. That these primitives would kill kits was abhorrent. He eyed them both, seething.

A voice from the past echoed in the back of his mind.

"He's just a kit. Leave him alone!" Euraiya stood in front of him. Ahead of them, Ter stood with his cronies, laughing at him.

"You're defending that?" Ter laughed.

"If I don't, who will?"

Eural swallowed as the memory faded. Euraiya's examples had resonated and guided him through his training and assignments. She was the reason he was here. Even fighting her own battles, she was still beside him.

"If I don't, who will?" he muttered under his breath. His

anger rose and boiled manifesting in a loud, resounding roar.

The wyverns' throats glowed in unison. Eural moved in and frantically cut at them. Their heat subsided, and the wyverns stepped back. He focussed on them, warning them off again with a pump of his wings and a scrape of his claws on the stone ground.

Loud, heavy thumping and tapping claws echoed through the cave. Naralin burst through the hall and charged a wyvern and slammed into it. The kitcarers and guards took the other. Eural turned back to the kits and their defender.

"Are you hurt?" he asked.

The kitcarer shook her head. "No. They're relentless. I don't know how much longer we can stay here."

"That's the last of them, I hope." He looked over the huddled kits. None had yet fledged. They still retained their fluffy, white hatchling plumage. They stuck so close together, there was no difference visible between them.

Naralin's furious roar caught his attention.

The direlord held the last wyvern against the wall, a talon pressed against its throat, every feather standing upright in a display of anger. Eural almost pitied the wyvern. The sight before it must have been horrifying, and it would be the last it saw.

Naralin spat words at the wyvern in the common language. Its musical quality destroyed by the venom that delivered it. He slammed its hided head against the wall. Its horns snapped and hung from the remains. The wyvern screeched. It stammered in its ugly language but was cut off by the dire once again.

"Speak!" Naralin said, switching to his native gryph tongue. "Tell me who led you here!" His words were terrify-

ing, filled with an anger and fear that was not the direlord
Eural knew.

The wyvern spoke again. Not a single, recognisable word
registered in Eural's ears.

With a loud snap, the wyvern slumped to the floor, its
neck twisted.

Naralin shoved the body away. "Bastards!"

He turned. There were holes in his plumage, and clotted
blood covered half of his face. His eyes were pinned and
wild and every feather stood rigid. Eural had never feared
his direlord before, but now it gripped him like talons
around his throat. Everyone was silent. Naralin glared at
each of them, looking for an answer. They didn't offer any
and he stormed out of the cave. His warriors fell in behind
him. Eural cast an apologetic look towards the kitcarers and
followed.

They halted on the plateau. Ilir waited for them, shakily
regaining himself. Eural knew he wouldn't give up until he
was dead. He seemed halfway there as it were.

Naralin's ears twitched in different directions. Before
Eural could question him, the noise reached his own. Loud,
pumping winds filled the air, deeper and louder than the
wyverns around them. He knew the difference. He had
heard it thousands of times. A chill ran through him. It was
a dire.

"Good," Naralin said. "Now let us finish this."

"Dire?" Eural said.

Naralin didn't answer immediately. He dropped off the
side of the cliff and glided towards the main battlefield. His
guards followed. He tempered his speed, waiting for them to
form around him.

"Dire wyverns are a dying species, as they deserve to be."
They banked around the mountain, and over a series of

cliffs. "They would not send a dire unless it was absolutely necessary." Naralin's feathers relaxed, but the bloodlust in his eyes remained.

"If they're sending a dire—" Ilir started.

Naralin's eyes focussed ahead of them. "Then they are desperate."

20

DIRE

Euraiya stopped. A roar filled the air, carrying further than any undired wyvern was capable of. By a glimpse of its wings through the smoke, she knew what it was. Lenrin and Pyrin hovered beside her, both silent as the gigantic form of the dire wyvern crossed over the mountains. Its hide was a pale blue instead of the browns and reds that had swarmed the pridelands. Scales crawled along the ridges of its head and spine and tapered into spikes, much like a dire gryph's feathers. Its huge head was framed by curved horns and spikes along its jaw. It was immense, twice the difference in size between an opinicus and a dire gryphon. On flat ground, a single claw would stand at Euraiya's chest and rip through a gryph without a second thought.

Its hide reflected the light of the fire below as it surveyed the pridelands. Around them, surviving wyverns continued their attack, and wounded gryphs fled for their homes. The remaining gryphs, dired and undired, fought to defend them. The dire wyvern's roar coursed through Euraiya's body as it echoed through the lands, and what bravery she had left went with it. She shivered, the same fear gripping her as it had when she found the wyverns outside of Rada's borders. This thing could kill a dire gryph with as much effort as she could a deer or a rat. A familiar thumping rose in her head.

Ainlin flew towards it, banked and hovered near the gigantic beast. Her smooth feathers were now marred by blood and burns. Still, she held herself calmly and even regally in the face of this new threat. She called for its attention with a shriek and then spoke. Unknown words came from her beak. The opaque language was indecipherable, but its sound was incredible. Each word flowed into the next like a bird's song.

There was a long silence as the creature eyed her. It didn't attack but instead considered her words. It spoke in the same tongue. Even a wyvern, with its rough, disgusting sovereign language, made the words beautiful and melodic. As it hovered in front of her, the power from its wings pushed Ainlin backwards, forcing her to right herself against it.

"He wants to see my father," Lenrin cut in. He could understand them.

Euraiya scoffed. "It's a bit late for talking, isn't it?"

"Ainlin would disagree. Come." Lenrin flew closer.

Euraiya hesitated, then followed. She considered fleeing and rejoining the Euraiya who had led to the destruction of Rada's clan. She couldn't. She had changed.

Even from this distance, the wind from the wyvern's wings brushed against her. Lenrin's eyes pinned as the two continued to talk. The near emotionless coordinator tensed and his hackles rose. Whatever they spoke about disturbed him, and in turn, chilled Euraiya further.

A cry came across the way. Naralin and four others flew

and hovered beside Ainlin. To her relief, Eural followed. From his expression, he had been just as concerned for her. She wanted to join him, but neither her body nor mind would let her venture closer to the beast.

Naralin spoke in the same tongue as Ainlin. His words were filled with an anger that destroyed their quality, turning it into a forced screeching sound. The wyvern responded, seemingly ambivalent to his emotion. All three spoke between each other.

"What are they speaking?" Euraiya asked.

"We call it Common. It's a language designed for leaders," Lenrin explained. "My father wants to know why they're attacking." Naralin snapped something and Lenrin sucked in a breath. "That's impossible."

"It's not going to tell him." Euraiya furrowed her brows.

"No. He's offering to halt his attack if we surrender," Lenrin said.

"That's stupid." A part of Euraiya's mind refuted her. That one dire could destroy half the clan with its fire. It could kill Ainlin and Naralin with ease. They were lucky that it hadn't led the attack, or the pridelands would have burned.

"Perhaps not," Lenrin said.

Whatever was on Lenrin's mind was cut short when Naralin raised his voice. The wyvern responded in kind, snapping its long, sharp teeth. Even without the language, the rising tension was clear. Peaceful talks were failing, if they had tried to be diplomatic at all. Naralin's feathers were raised, just as Ainlin's. Their bodies squared. Both were ready to attack. Yet, Euraiya wondered what they could do against it. The two were big, but compared to the wyvern, they were only gryphons.

The wyvern spoke. Lenrin swallowed hard.

Naralin growled deeply. His language switched to their own, starting from a mutter, "Attack." Anger rose in his voice, exploding like fire. Ainlin grasped at him, trying to cut him off, but he pushed her away. He faced the wyvern. He shouted, his voice carrying across clearly and fiercely in one simple and clear order.

"Attack!"

THE WYVERN ROARED. SOME OF THE CHARGING GRYPHS turned and fled. The braver few, Eural included, continued their assault. Euraiya, gripped by terror, hovered in place. Gryphs brushed past her, following their direlord's order. She couldn't move. Her body refused to die to this behemoth.

Claws raked the air and cut through a couple of unarmoured strikers, confirming her fears. The wyvern swooped through the group, buffeting gryphs with its body and wings and catching one in its jaws. Euraiya was thrown. She caught herself and stared, beak open. The wyvern's throat glowed brighter and brighter. The solid blue flame that followed burned hotter than anything she had ever experienced. The burn on her leg throbbed in beat with the pulse in her ears. The flame cut the earth and spread across the grass like water, turning everything into ash. His line crossed the black ground beneath them and across the closest cliff.

The wyvern banked towards the nests, gryphs chased after it. The talon of its wing clipped the trees below, scraping one from its roots. Something shoved Euraiya, breaking her gaze. She turned. Lenrin shoved again, his talons digging into her chest. "Where's your spine? Go!"

At one final, aggressive shove, she flew, cutting through the wyvern's arc and straight towards it. Lenrin followed behind her. Sound drained around her, replaced only by the thumping in her ears. The fire, the roars and screeches, drowned out by constant drumming. She had to keep going. The wyvern turned again and faced the gryphs. It clawed at a few, cutting them down. Naralin and Ainlin swooped in, attacking at its throat and chest. It turned, and they bounced off its hide. It twisted until it faced them again, its wings throwing gryphs around as if it were playing with rocks.

Undired wyverns flew in and caught gryphs in separate combat, Tayrin included, pulling them away from the dire. Only a few were left to chase it.

Lenrin, still beside her, shouted across the din of fire and wind, his voice breaking through the beat in her ears. "We go after the dire. Leave the others to those who are already fighting them. If they need help, they'll get it."

She watched him for a second, her mind still lagging behind her, then nodded. He looked over her, likely seeing the panic in her face.

"Die for the pride, or die alone. Those are your choices." He watched her, then flicked his head towards the fight. "Let's go."

They cut through the undired fights, avoiding claws and flames. Lenrin flew over Euraiya, directing her. He dove, forcing Euraiya with him. They broke free, finding a clear path towards the dire. It came down on the cliffs, its gigantic feet breaking through a cave entrance. Gryphs screamed, crushed under the rock. The remaining warriors pushed forwards, forcing it off its perch and towards the ground.

It stomped and roared, scraping at the warriors who fought it. Lenrin and Euraiya joined Naralin and Ainlin. Eural and Ilir, were with them, though the latter looked half dead. Each heaved and nursed some form of injury. The two dires tensed, an aura of anger surrounding them. Euraiya backed away, putting Lenrin between them.

"What's the plan?" Lenrin asked.

"This oblivion-spawned cur..." Naralin rasped, "is tougher than I believed."

"Can we pierce it?" Eural asked.

"No. We can barely approach it," Ainlin said.

"We have to distract it," Eural said. "There's enough of us."

Naralin grunted. "I do not care what we do. I want him dead."

"Dire, we-"

The wyvern took to the air and turned to the group, its throat burning brightly. They scattered as flame rushed between them. Euraiya rushed to a safe spot and scanned the area. Each took a position around the wyvern. She followed suit, circling the beast until she found an open spot to its left. She swallowed hard, trying to ignore the pulsing in her head. She adjusted her grip on the ill-fitting claw weapon before it slipped from her paws. The wyvern pumped its wings with immense force, throwing wind like a heavy storm. The rocky crags around them would prove deadly if they weren't careful.

Up close, the creature's age was evident in its pale eyes and cracked hide. The armoured scales along its head were scratched but otherwise unscathed. Each muscle in its body was as large as her. A single tooth would easily kill her, if its gigantic claws didn't get to her first.

She could flee now to safety. The others would kill the wyvern, and she would keep her head down. They would eventually forget she had run.

"No," she spat.

This was her chance for redemption. Rada's clan had been destroyed for her lack of action, and she would not let it happen again. She wasn't a coward, not anymore. Fear threatened her, ready to hold her. She forced it down, internalised it. The thumping in her head dulled until it was indistinguishable from the shouts around her. She would control it.

She had to defend her pride.

Dire and undired fought in tandem, each following the cue of the next. Eural attacked one flank; Ainlin followed with another. Each kept out of the wyvern's grasp, keeping him distracted and flailing between them. Euraiya flew in, ducking under its wing and slashing at its hide. The metallic claw grazed its leg, dragging scratch marks across it. She flew around to its back and caught its side. The base of its wing clipped her ears.

As she came out from behind it, a loud screech rang through the air. Her heart sunk, and she whipped around. Ilir's side opened up in a gush of blood. He all but fell, hitting the ground with a crash. Eural's roar filled the sky, and he charged. She followed, charging at the back of the beast's head. The wyvern reared as Eural scratched at its neck and she collided with its horn. The horn cracked under her weight. The wyvern roared and slammed its head backwards at her.

She held out her claws, reflexively trying to soften the blow. Everything went white as its skull collided with her. The metal claws gripped the hide, dragging her with them. Her world spun as heavy pounding returned to her head. She was dizzy, disoriented. She flattened herself, waiting for her senses to return.

The wyvern roared and flapped backwards, pushing the attackers away. With a powerful push of its wings, it shot up.

The sheer force of its flight flattened Euraiya against its hide. Her head pounded, and her stomach twisted. The wind whipped in her ears, harsher than ever before. The force was unbearable.

The wyvern slowed, turning its head to see its pursuers.

"Euraiya!" Eural's voice was distant.

Her senses returned. She looked around. Gryphs raced towards them. She could see nothing but the wyvern. She was in a prime position. She could hurt it somehow. She racked her brain. The skull would be impenetrable, and the wyvern would surely be rid of her before she broke its hide. The wyvern pivoted and faced the group. Sudden heat exploded around her as the wyvern's throat glowed.

The flame burst out, catching Naralin's side. He roared and rushed ahead of the group.

Fire burned in the wyvern's throat again as Naralin charged its chest. The wyvern's flame fizzled and it threw its head backwards. Euraiya scurried towards its snout and clung to the ridge of its brow. The wyvern's large eyes crossed and stared straight at her. It brought its head back and snarled. It spoke grating words, its pupils pinning and dilating as it emphasised them.

"What are you saying?" she snapped. "Why are you here?!"

It spoke again and followed with a deep laugh. It was unmistakable. The same laugh she'd heard when Ter warned opinici of a future beating. It was a laugh with no falsity. The wyvern knew something, and it had just told her what it was.

Ainlin tore through its wing with an enraged shriek. The wyvern roared, whipping around to face her. It pumped its wings harder but began to fall. It twisted around, throwing

Euraiya upwards. Its throat glowed bright as it faced towards the group in the sky.

Euraiya's mind flashed, and she found her opportunity. She tucked her wings and dove. Her world slowed. Flame licked around the wyvern's maw. She held her claws out, aiming the sharp, metallic points towards her target. The flame burst from the wyvern's mouth as she collided with its neck. Her claws dug in deep, the sheer force of her fall pushing them deep into its flesh. Hot, boiling blood seeped out of the wounds followed by flame.

Unimaginable heat rushed around her, surrounded her. The force of the exploding fire flung her. Her weapon flew from her paw. She spun in the air, glimpses of the mountains ready to receive her. She panicked, failing to open her wings. The gigantic, heavy body of the wyvern fell past her. It crashed down the mountain. Her heart skipped. She flailed, trying anything to break the fall. A voice trailed behind her.

She shut her eyes.

A FAMILIAR SCENT FILLED EURAIYA'S NARES, REPLACING THE fire and blood. The warm and earthy smell of feathers mixed with cold metal. She looked up. Blue eyes returned her gaze. He pulled her close.

"Are you okay?" Eural asked.

"Y-yeah," she responded.

He let her go, and they descended together, joining the dires at the corpse. Her heart pulsed in her chest, her brain pounded against her skull, but she was safe.

The Common language spat from Naralin's beak, turning its beautiful music into a series of horrible sounds.

The language was not designed for such use or perhaps his words. He clawed its muzzle, as if trying to reach its spirit for answers. With a defeated yell, he turned back to Ainlin. "Bastards. Curs. Edge-dwellers!" he snapped.

Ainlin kept her eyes closed, forcing herself to breath. She shivered and opened them. "Father. We must tend to the pride. This can wait."

"*I* will decide what is worth waiting for!" Each breath was forced through his nares. His red eyes were pinned and frightening. He stomped the ground, looking for another fight.

"I understand." Ainlin stood firm, raising herself to her father's posture. "But you must calm yourself, before you're no longer here to lead."

"You speak—"

"A dead ruler is no ruler at all. Is that not what you say? You cannot just fly off and chase a thought." Ainlin's eyes returned to the strong yet captivating look that Euraiya knew. Ainlin's anger had yet to be quelled, but she tempered it better than her father, her hackles the only sign she was not as calm she appeared to be.

Naralin stared down at his daughter and huffed. His feathers softened slightly. "It is correct."

"Then listen to it," she said. "Let's return, organise healers, and then work on what we've learned."

Naralin was quiet. His feathers moved in rhythm with his frantic, heaving breaths. Eventually, he relented and stood down from his daughter. He turned from the group and lifted, flying away from them back to his chamber. The group watched him. This side of Naralin was difficult to see. He had presented himself as a powerful, controlled gryphon, and seeing him frantic, furious, and even afraid was unsettling.

Ainlin waited for Naralin to depart before speaking, addressing all except for Lenrin. "My father expects this part of your stories will be left unspoken. And I would appreciate it, should you keep it as such."

Euraiya nodded instinctively. Rada had a similar expectation. Outbursts were kept quiet under penalty of exile even though his clan heard them often. Euraiya expected that a leader like Naralin would have a similar policy. Direlords had an image of control to maintain for both their pride's admiration and the opinion of other direlords. It was important to appear faultless. Regardless, she wouldn't breathe a word. Her loyalty now lay with him, and she would obey whatever orders were placed on her.

The gigantic carcass shifted as its bones and muscles settled and stiffened. The events pieced together around her and struck deep. She had defended the pride. She was no longer the opinicus who had spent her days lazing about the clangrounds and hunting alone, and a far cry from the one who had arrived in these mountains, expecting the world to care for her. She had earned her place within the pride and proved to them and herself that she was capable of protecting it.

She puffed her feathers, feeling pride course through her. It was a feeling that, she figured, Eural knew well. It was intoxicating and driving, pushing her for more, compelling her to go further.

Eural chuckled and nuzzle her cheek. "You did well."

She held her breath, savouring the moment, allowing herself to fully take it in. "I did."

21

SURVIVAL

The smell of smoke wafted over the camp, mixing with the scent of rain. A light haze covered the air, saturating the colours around them. Aurok's gryphs murmured. Some demanded to help Naralin's pride, while others declared no business with them, especially after Naralin's guards' theatrics.

Aurok watched the mountains from the edge of the camp, turning those back who dared to put themselves in danger for the likes of a direlord. If Naralin was intent on intimidating them, he could survive without their help. Aurok's jaw tensed as frustration and anger filled him. He couldn't help but see the attack as justified, a comeuppance designed by the spirits. They didn't often intervene in the affairs of the living, but when they did, souls were claimed to join them.

The camp returned to their work. Over the past few days, they had begun to coordinate better. Aurok rallied a few to join the hunting shifts and others to begin construction of their camp, despite their refusal to cooperate with the hippogryphs. While the fighting had eased, tension still remained. It was an improvement, at least.

Lillia padded over and sat beside him. "The new gryphs want to help, so I've sent them with the hunting group. I'm not sure where else they would be best suited."

Despite their exile, the two additions to the camp had been productive, offering their assistance where possible while trying to keep out of the way of more established members. Aurok had yet to remember their names but made a note to talk to them. He needed to make sure they found a place within the camp before the underlying bitterness of Rada's clan overtook them as it had everyone else. His gryphs, for all their claims of being a successful clan, had been sullen and lost without their bullish leader. They were overcoming it as they recognised their situation, but some remained entrenched in their petulance.

Aurok's eyes remained on the smoke. "We'll find them a space."

Lillia watched the smoke with him. "What's going on?"

Aurok grunted. "Wyverns. I saw them fly over, likely due to Naralin's antagonising."

"I'd hope he's smarter than that," Lillia said.

"Direlords don't understand the world further than their own beaks." Aurok let out a gruff sigh and looked down to the green opinicus. "I hope you'll understand the world better outside of a pride. We take care of our own."

"I know, it's just—" she stopped, perhaps deciding better than to dissent.

Aurok's feathers flattened. He wanted his gryphs to speak freely.

He looked back to the mountains. A deep part of him wanted to help, to save the gryphs that didn't deserve to be caught up in this. Those in the aeries throughout Naralin's lands would have had no defence against the wyverns while the guards defended the nexus. Another, more prominent voice, refused. Those who followed direlords needed to learn the truth. They were not protected or valued. They were only a means to their leader's end. Casualties would be notable, and if they were lucky, Naralin would be among them. The pride would survive. But whether it was under the rule of a tyrant would be the question.

Aurok hoped gryphs would abandon the pride to live a better life and perhaps even join his camp. But they had to do it on their own volition. Those who didn't want to become wilders would turn the camp against itself.

The thought prodded his mind. One of the largest issues he faced were gryphs who refused to embrace the new camp: involuntary wilders. Gryphs had been brainwashed into thinking that serving a direlord was the only way to survive, and when they were thrown out of a pride, they were lost. They didn't know how to exist outside. The gryphs in Trein's camp, however, adapted to their new situation. No wilder would ever admit it was an unglamorous lifestyle, but it was free. In their freedom, Trein's camp worked cooperatively to survive. In the end, they were a stronger community than any pride.

Aurok's attempts at forcing his camp to become wilders was doomed to fail. That was evident. If he were going to keep his gryphs alive and cohesive, he needed to change his approach. One that would benefit not only his current members, but those that would eventually join them.

"When the smoke clears," he said. "I'm going to visit the aeries."

Scenarios and dialogues echoed in his mind, each another plan to pursue. After this attack, some of Naralin's gryphs would need a place to flee, somewhere that their direlord would never find them, and they could live their lives freer than they had ever known. He could provide a safe haven while providing them everything they needed in their prides. Prided gryphs rarely desired to be wilders, and it was impossible to force them to it. They needed to be given what a pride offered: safety, security, and community. It was here that Aurok knew what he needed to do.

If he wanted his gryphs to survive, he couldn't lead a wilder camp. He had to lead a pride.

22

EURAIYA THE PRIDEFUL

E uraiya and Eural sat on the plateau outside Naralin's
throne chamber, listening to Naralin's orders from
within. A large chunk had been carved out of the
entrance, destroying part of the decorative hallway.
Medical gryphs tended to their wounds as they waited.
Euraiya marvelled at the bandages that now covered a
good portion of her body. Made from a stiff cloth, it was
more comfortable than the mud and leaves she was
familiar with. The ointments under them appeared to be
the same sticky and sweet substance that Rada's medical
gryphs used.

Down below, many warriors, exhausted and bleeding,
sat in makeshift medical camps while those who were able
tended to the lands. There was much repairing to do.
Naralin and his children organised gryphs to their temporary assignments, coordinating efforts to efficiently revive
the pride. Blackened ground and trees were cleared and
replanted, caves were cleaned of debris, and the dead were
buried for the spirits to claim them.

Gryphs cried out for the maimed and dead alike.

Euraiya had made those same screams and understood their pain. She didn't want to hear them now or ever again.

Beside her, Eural looked like a rat wrapped in a wolfskin bag. He was quiet about his injuries, but the medicine gryphs warned him against exerting himself for the next few moons. Despite this, he was alive. That was all that she needed.

"What a disaster," Eural sighed, watching the efforts below.

"At least they're alive," Euraiya said.

He nodded. "We were lucky that Dire Naralin wasn't too far away."

Euraiya made a noise in agreement. The turning point had been their arrival. Had they arrived later, the pride may not have survived. "Why did they attack?"

Ainlin rounded the entrance and onto the plateau. She sported the same stiff bandages and had taken time to smooth and preen her feathers. "We can answer that question, if you'll both join us."

They followed the dire into the main chamber. Euraiya limped. The ill-fitting weapon had tore the pads of her foot when it flew off. Naralin stood at the edge of the platform to his throne, tended by three medical gryphs who provided far more attention to him than any gryph in the pride. At each particular limb, they requested permission to touch and move it. A strong, eye-watering smell of ointment filled the air as if they bathed him in it.

He had visibly calmed since they had last seen him. The intensity of his eyes had dimmed and returned to the cold stare that was a permanent fixture on his face. Whether that was his own doing or Ainlin's remained a mystery. His feathers had yet to rest.

Around them, gryphs worked to restore the throne

chamber to its former glory. While the damage was mini-mal, a fight had clearly broken out here during the attack. Fixtures had been knocked and destroyed, littering the floor, and a portion of one of the audience plateaus was missing. Some of the gryphs who worked hung their heads low, their feathers flat. Euraiya wondered if they had yet to find their kin.

"The losses to the pride are disappointing," Naralin said after a moment. He was pensive, distracted. "We will cele-brate their memories."

Ainlin presented the two opinici with a formal, wide gesture of her talon. "Father, Eural Fireheart and Euraiya are free for counsel."

Naralin looked over them both. His eyes set on Euraiya for an eternity. A familiar weight grew on her, forcing her head low. "Your performances were admirable. You should be proud to have assisted in the death of the wyvern's direlord. It is an honour most gryphs will never experience."

Her kills sat like a rock in her stomach. She tried to take Naralin's praise, engage with this apparent honour. She had defended herself as much as she had the pride. The thought of being one of those bodies that littered the grounds reminded her to keep fighting, to not leave Eural behind. It was survival that Naralin praised her for. She was proud of her achievement; that elation still filled her. Yet, something didn't feel right.

"It was my duty to the clan, Dire." Eural spoke with a stiff and disciplined air, brushing Naralin's words away. Ainlin let out a short chuckle.

Naralin watched Euraiya. She swallowed. "I failed before, and it cost my clan. I will not make that mistake again."

One of the medical gryphs lifted Naralin's talons and

applied the sticky ointment to a gash on his foreleg. He kept his gaze on her. "It is likely your warning would have fallen on deaf ears." He huffed. "The space between his ears was likely larger than his ego."

Tension loosened from her. She stared up at him, shocked. The empty chasm between them closed slightly. She had proven herself to him. Or perhaps, it was an apology. It didn't matter. An unknown desire to impress him cleared from her mind. She stood silent for a moment, letting his words sit in her mind.

"Thank you, Dire," she said, surprise escaping in her tone.

"Indeed. Now," he staccatoed, "tell me what happened while I was not present."

She told him of the attack and where Lenrin had taken her. She forewent Lenrin's conduct and his drowning the wyvern. Ainlin followed, filling in Euraiya's gaps with stories of her own efforts to defend against the wyverns. She had tried to defend the kitcarers but was unable to get there.

Naralin gave Ainlin a stern look. "I expect better of you in the future, Ainlin. We are lucky that Tayrin, Lenrin and even Inilrin, are capable of organising defences without you." Ainlin winced. "Tell me of the other kitcare chamber."

It was an abhorrent thought that wyverns would attack defenceless kits and their carers. A brief memory of Lenrin's torture of the wyvern flashed in her mind.

"It was too deep within the nexus. They did not get there," Ainlin responded curtly. She cowed.

Naralin's eyes flashed. He held his leer on Ainlin.

"Why did they attack?" Euraiya interrupted, trying to prevent an outburst.

Naralin rumbled. He ordered the medical gryphs away with a stroke of his foreleg. "Xhililm," the name was cumbersome in his beak, "was one of the few remaining wyvern dires. He was trying to re-establish his dominance."

"That sounds familiar," Eural muttered.

Naralin's demeanour soured. His hackles raised higher.

There was another question that bothered Euraiya. "He spoke to you. What was it?"

Ainlin's feathers puffed, impressed. "An undired pride is a weak pride. They're common words, recently." The two dires shared a concerned look. Eural shifted beside her.

"What does that mean? There are plenty of dires in the pride," Euraiya said.

Eural nudged Euraiya, pulling her away from the boundaries she was about to cross. She held her tongue, despite the deep, instinctual desire to continue. These were things she should know.

"We will discuss it amongst ourselves," Naralin said, a hint of warning in his voice. He regarded Euraiya, observant as ever. "Speak."

Euraiya thought for the right words. "It was no coincidence that you weren't present. How did they know? They had an army. They knew."

Naralin nodded. "Rada's clangrounds were no more larger than a combination of wilder camps. You were unaware of the size of prides outside of his self-imposed cultural pit." The words hurt, but they were true. "Four wyverns could have easily destroyed it. The size of my grounds, and my pride, require much more effort."

Ainlin made a thoughtful noise. She drew Naralin's attention. "We should make sure that the aeries are safe. Most of our fighting force is located here."

"Indeed," Naralin said. "We will send representatives to get reports. Eural, you will be among the first. You will visit the northern aeries with your partner."

Eural stood tall and disciplined. He hesitated. "As you wish."

Euraiya watched him. She hadn't known Ilir, but she knew his position and the importance he held to her brother. Even though the mistake was clear, Eural didn't dare speak against his direlord. The wound was raw and clear in Eural's eyes. A silence hung in the air.

Ainlin opened her beak, "Father, I—"

"I'll go," Euraiya said. The abruptness of her words shocked her. Their reflexivity carried the confidence of a veteran, not the gutless kit she knew. She deferred herself, "if you'll let me."

Clumsily, she tried to replicate her brother's posture, appearing like a kit mimicking her father.

Naralin clicked his beak. Ainlin stifled a giggle.

"So be it," Naralin said. "For now."

Euraiya puffed her chest out. Pride filled her once more, for a different reason.

Eural glanced at her, his crest rising. Euraiya couldn't replace Ilir, and she didn't want to. She wanted to give back to the pride that accepted her and the brother that helped and housed her.

"Tomorrow, though. Rest now," Ainlin added.

Naralin agreed.

"I expect to see you two in the mess chamber tonight. You, and every other warrior, deserve their meal," Ainlin said.

The two opinici nodded.

"You are dismissed. Spirits watch over you," Naralin said.

The two siblings bowed and made their way from the throne chamber. Behind them, Ainlin and Naralin spoke that opaque language. The words were not discernible, but the tone was clear. They would see conflict again. Euraiya focussed forwards. The wyverns would not attack again for now. Naralin's pride would have time to recover.

Back on the plateau, the siblings surveyed the remains of the pridegrounds.

Euraiya looked to Eural, his gaze stuck firmly on the mass of gryph bodies ready for burial. "Are you okay?"

He nodded. "I need to go. I'll see you at the mess, tonight." He leaned over, nuzzled under her beak. She returned it.

They broke, and Eural pushed off the edge.

She turned her gaze, following the mountains to the north, seeing the silhouette of an aerie in the distance. Excitement filled her. She didn't know what aeries looked like or how they operated. They were another mysterious part of this new world that had opened to her.

She dropped from the plateau and lifted to the sky.

So much had changed. The lazy Hunter Euraiya was a shadow of the past, forgotten and replaced. She was finding her place in a larger world.

Perhaps, though, she had already found it.

ACKNOWLEDGMENTS

It's a weird feeling, being able to finally accomplish something you've dreamed of since you were thirteen, passing each chapter of your novel through your English and P.E. teacher (the latter of which threw my paper at me when I killed off her favourite character). But here I am with an arguably better story to tell.

Incidentally, Aurok's name is a carryover from that first novel, and I still have that novel sealed in a yellow envelope in my wardrobe fifteen years later.

But, we're not here for an unedited draft from the early 2000s are we? If you are, you're in the wrong place. We're here to talk about *Dire* and what made it possible! *Dire* is the culmination of the desire to write something and having both the inspiration and support to create it. Its inception came shortly after starting The Summer King Chronicles by Jess E. Owen—a recent and highly-recommended gryphon series—and deciding it was about time for me to follow that one dream.

However, it wasn't inspiration alone that completed the book. I've been blessed with the help of some very special people. If it weren't for them, I'm not sure this would have been possible. While I can't realistically list everyone I'd like to, there are a few people who I would disservice if I didn't.

First and foremost, the endless help, mentoring, and sheer patience of K. Vale Nagle who edited and copyedited *Dire and* offered as much advice and knowledge as he possibly could to help make the story as engaging as it could be. Alongside the first editing pass, he wrote up over twenty pages of additional material to bring my writing skills up to par, as well as thousands of suggestions and edits (literally thousands!) for me to wade through. I owe him more than I could ever provide. Don't ask him if I do, though. He's likely to deny it. If you enjoyed this book, then I would highly recommend his own series, starting with *Eyrie*.

Following this was the beta reading pass by Glenn Birmingham. He provided just as much, if not more, suggestions and edits during his beta-read. His feedback brought the story to the next level, particularly with some important considerations. Glenn is an excellent craftsman, and I cannot thank him enough for his feedback. Another author whom I recommend for his upcoming Reunification series.

Incredibly, as well as being an inspiration, Jess E. Owen also provided feedback on a few scenes. In particular some of the bigger ones in the book. Jess has offered expansions to actions, ideas, and character interactions and reactions. She's been an exceptional help throughout the creation of the book.

Next up is Melissa Downey, the one responsible for the amazing cover art. The idea I had been tossing around has been rendered better than I could have imagined, and the extras that you have made for *Dire* are incredible. I cannot thank you enough.

The Gryphon King himself, Larry Dixon, for his

support, advice, and conversations about the intricacies of gryphon anatomy, world-building, and writing themes. You have been an incredible help and influence.

Jennifer Miller for some eye-opening advice and thoughts during betareading. Thank you for your contributions and opening up an extra avenue for gryph culture.

The beta readers were invaluable. I cannot recommend beta readers enough as part of the story-writing process. They provided amazing and fresh feedback that, as an author, I was unlikely to spot easily. To each of those who contributed, I thank you, and I hope to see you again when the second book is ready.

And finally, the unending support of my family and friends. My mother and grandmother have been supportive of my writing endeavours since I wrote my first novel. Their support means the absolute world to me. Also, the friends who have provided feedback, support, and bounced ideas have been more helpful than they know.

But that's exactly what this is: the first journey. *Dire* has more to tell, and it will be told. The next story will be larger and deadlier. We know that Caslir and the wyverns are encroaching the lands around Euraiya and co. Soon, they'll be ready to strike. But the question is: who will own the lands once it's over?

I'll see you, dear reader, in the next book, where we will discover this together.

AFTERWORD

Thank you for reading *Dire*! If you enjoyed it, please consider leaving a review at your online retailer. Reviews help not only other readers find books they like, but also the authors who write them. If you know people who are interested in fantasy creatures, let them know about this book. I assure you, you will make both of us happy.

If you want to know when new books come out, or hear about some unreleased information about the world, cultures and characters in Feathers & Flames or just gryphons in general, you can support me or sign up for my newsletter at patreon.com/AngryOpinicus. My Patreon is public, and there is no expectation to pledge, but it would be appreciated!

Want to contact me? You can do so below:

Email: authorjohnbailey@gmail.com

 twitter.com/AngryOpinicus

Made in United States
Orlando, FL
02 February 2023

29328166R00168